"Pasta line is moving," Ralp̣ "I didn't hear anythi and started to get up.

Then his face contorted witḥ ___ ____ for ward and into the table, screaming incoherently as the table slid away under him. Ralph and Sheryl were on the floor and next to him as soon as they noticed he collapsed.

"Why is he screaming like that?" Meredith shouted.

Carlos rolled onto his back and his screams went silent while his face continued to twist. He gripped at the side of his head as if he was trying to stop something from exploding out of it.

Whether in answer to Meredith or to describe what he was feeling, Carlos shouted an answer.

"Our world is cracking apart!"

As if his words had summoned something, half of the students in the Union vanished. Two of the walls, specifically the one near the exit and the wall touching it, also disappeared. In their place was a vast field of swaying blue grass and a pink sky.

In the field, and moving at incredible speed, a herd of … something … ran at them.

The things in the field ran on two legs with brown, meatball-shaped bodies. Instead of mouths, or perhaps covering them, tentacles writhed as they caught the scents of food.

Throughout the cafeteria, students and staff screamed in terror and confusion. They scrambled to get out through the service doors or over the food counters. The only people who didn't run or scream were the five friends.

MISKATONIC UNIVERSITY
ELDER GODS 101

BY MATTHEW DAVENPORT &
MICHAEL DAVENPORT

MACABRE
Ink

INTRODUCTION

The briefest moment provided a glimpse of the moon. The singular darkness surrounding it was empty of stars and if not for the unfamiliarity it would have been quite beautiful. The lonely moon was framed by the cedar wood surrounding the window and cast an uncomfortable beam on Dean Ward's desk. The moment ended as the seams in reality tore open and propelled all of Miskatonic University into the nameless madness of the universe.

Moving through the vast emptiness of space by means of a tear in reality's construction was akin to being birthed through fire. Every person still on the campus, mostly consisting of the custodial and managerial staff during those sweltering summer months, screamed as every cell of their bodies was removed from one geometrical place in the cosmos, funneled through an abstract reality of more than three dimensions, and then reassembled in a new three-dimensional space in an entirely different reality, similar to their original yet wholly different.

Dean Ward picked himself up from where he had collapsed on the floor. Before he could get his bearings, he was greeted by the first unpleasantness of this loathsome place.

The air was permeated with the stench of rotten meat. It filtered through the walls and closed windows and was still wretched to his senses.

The man, of lengthier years than his chiseled jaw and dark hair would have implied, returned to the window to determine what other circumstances threatened their continued existence in this new place.

The landscape had become a vastly foreign experience. Where previously the city of Arkham had been a bustle of activity, now was only a vast plane of dried plant matter. Above the expanse of orange plateau hung a mauve sky with a shattered moon. Within the moon, or perhaps not a moon but an egg, something terrible writhed as if in anticipation.

The door to Dean Ward's office burst open and the wiry administrative assistant to the dean, Carol Berg, lurched forth clutching a weathered book.

"Reality has shifted," she stated. Sweat beaded on her brow and Dean Ward sympathized with her, recalling the pain from the shift.

He forced himself away from the window and gestured at the view before releasing an exhausted sigh. "Obviously."

"Do I need to remind you that without the university, Earth is in danger?" Carol's frustration masked her fear and that made the dean nervous. There wasn't much that Carol Berg feared.

"No," he responded slowly. "I don't need to be reminded. What does his journal say about it?"

Carol set the decades-old tome down on the dean's desk. The book's only power was in the knowledge it bestowed upon the staff of the university, but the history of the book carried its own weight and the dean wished not to be anywhere near it.

"It calls this," she waved her hand past the dean and toward the vista outside, "an unmooring. It is unlikely that this was an accident. Someone is attempting to remove the university from our reality."

"They appear to have succeeded," Dean Ward countered.

Carol shook her head. "It takes a considerable amount of effort to remove the school and a sustained effort to stop it from returning." She folded her arms across her chest. "This might just be a test before the actual effort."

"To what end?"

"Anything is possible without the university acting as an anchor to our home reality." Carol's eyes glazed over as she began to remember some of the terrors she'd seen in her years working for the school. "Our reality has always been protected. Without the school, it is under a constant threat of collapse."

The dean hadn't taken his eyes from where his secretary had placed the book. "How large of a threat?"

Carol's voice came out in a whisper as she spoke the forbidden names.

"All threats. Nyarlathotep, Icthosthau, Yog-Sothoth …" she only mouthed the last name, "Azathoth."

"The wards are solid and unbreakable," the dean's voice seemed to reverberate across this new planet. "How can we begin to discover our attacker?"

"That is tomorrow's problem." Carol picked the book back up and hugged it to her chest, almost motherly.

Dean Ward dragged his hands slowly down his face. "Yes, I agree. We cannot address the disease while the symptom persists." He waved at the book. "How does he say we reverse this unmooring?"

"You know what it says," Carol's face filled with disgust. "We can't do that, though. It's inhumane."

"Are you referencing the Scion Cycle?"

Carol's words were laced with venom. A torrent of emotions flooded her mind at the thought of what they were considering. "Of course, but the cost is too high. It isn't right."

The dean's eyes implored understanding from Carol. The activation of the Scion Cycle was the only thing that could anchor Miskatonic University to its home reality, but it would take years to fully take effect and in that time anything could happen to derail it. "The children don't deserve it." Her voice got quieter. "Arkham does not deserve that."

"He was your friend," Dean Ward said coldly. "If there was another way, would he have only provided this dark path?"

Carol shook her head. "No. If this is the path before us, then it is the only path that he found available."

"Then the cold truth of the matter is that we do not have a choice," he said with finality. "Again, it does not solve the current situation." Ward waved his hand to indicate the foreign landscape outside.

Carol joined the dean at the window and stared out across the alien landscape. Something, at the edge of the horizon, shifted and sent a chill down her spine.

"It might just correct itself," she hoped. "The best course of action may be to wait it out."

Dean Ward grunted as he answered, "Even if we could just 'wait it out,' it wouldn't suffice to let this happen again during the semester. How many students would be lost, driven insane, or devoured when we reached the next random destination? No, we need to slow the unmooring until we can fix it."

"There is a method in the book to force us back," Carol sighed, "but we will need to activate the armory."

Miskatonic University's armory was a large collection of ancient and powerful devices both of scientific and magical nature. They were too dangerous for the public and locked away for use only during the direst of circumstances. To 'activate the armory' meant to channel all that magic into a single purpose. To do so would slowly exhaust the magic and machinery of the armory. They could buy time from the unmooring of the school, but it wouldn't last forever and their weapons against the darkness would be unavailable to them.

"Then let us get started," the dean said.

To Carol's surprise, Dean Ward must have taken the time to familiarize himself with the procedures and methods of the tome, as he began to unbutton his shirt. She had always assumed that his disgust with it would have pushed him from ever cracking the spine. The truth could not be further from the reality.

He was disgusted with the book because he had taken the time to memorize it and its pages were filled with horrors only marginally less mind-shattering than the alternatives.

Waving at a drawer in the bookshelf across from his desk, he mumbled, "Could you get the dagger, please?"

For reasons beyond the understanding or even the curiosity of most of the staff, Carol Berg had been at Miskatonic University longer than any of them and was fully aware of everything from the mundane to the esoteric. The history of the school, the occult practices that were too prevalent in Arkham, Massachusetts, and the spells and witchcraft that made up the secret history of the surrounding New England countryside were not history to her, so much as memory. She had witnessed much of it over her years and upon occasion had been forced to practice it as well.

She knew the exact dagger that the Dean referenced. The bone handle, worked into shape by insects and the stone blade, carved from a moon of Venus. How it had arrived in the possession of humans in Arkham she was surprised that she didn't know.

The dean had laid on the floor and his shirt was open. Kneeling down, the surprisingly-aged secretary took the ancient blade and began to drag it across his chest.

Reality shook.

CHAPTER 1

The bus pulled to a stop and the door opened.

Ralph Allen was the only one on the bus and had been since he was picked up over an hour ago. The ride had been one of dread and hope. Hope that the past was behind him and dread that it wasn't.

A duffle bag and his high school jacket were all he needed. The jacket was in the dull brown and green of the Innsmouth Chompers. On the back was the school mascot, "Chompy," who was a smiling fish head with razor-sharp teeth. On the front was his school letter, the 'I' sewn to the front.

Ralph was tall and broad with a pale skin tone and a huge forehead only accentuated by his receding dark hair. Racists in the area like to refer to his large eyes and broad lips as the "Innsmouth Look." One look at Ralph made most people decide against saying it in his presence.

He stomped toward the front of the bus and was almost free of the dread of his past when the bus driver grabbed his arm.

"This is stupid, boy," the man said.

Ralph turned and stared him directly in the eyes.

The driver wore a faded coat and smelled of body odor and what Ralph decided to call regrets but knew to be the constant smell of his hometown, fish. His jacket had faded lettering where a name had been sewn on. If the lettering was still legible, the driver's first name could be seen.

"Get your hand off me, Joe," Ralph growled.

Joe's large eyes never moved from Ralph's. He released Ralph's arm, but his gaze held Ralph's.

"I won't lie to your mother," he said. There was no tone other than whatever was accompanying his look of disappointment.

Ralph made it down the stairs and onto the sidewalk before answering Joe.

"I wouldn't want you to. She knows where I am, even if she doesn't want to admit it." He shrugged and started to walk away.

"I'll be back to pick you up for the Solstice," Joe called after him.

"Don't waste the gas," was all Ralph had to say as he did his best to put even more distance between himself and his past.

Arkham, Massachussets had nothing to offer a graduate of Innsmouth High School except for the prestigious university that offered a decent football program. Ralph hadn't been the best on his team, but his actions had somehow warranted the first ray of hopeful freedom to shine down on what he considered a miserable existence.

Miskatonic University had offered him a football scholarship.

The bus stop had been a block from the main campus. Ralph was invited to a campus tour but couldn't convince anyone back home to bring him. He was worried that finding his dorm room, getting his assigned classes, and finding anything else he might need was going to be a struggle.

He was pleasantly surprised to discover that this wasn't the case.

"Freshman meat," someone called out to him as he approached the large collection of tables and students near the front of what looked to be the main administrative building.

Turning toward the voice, Ralph saw a guy about his size holding a clipboard and waving him over.

"Innsmouth, huh?" the guy was older than Ralph by a year or two and seemed almost too excited to be there. He wore a bright orange polo. "Don't get too many of you guys here." He looked at the clipboard and then back at Ralph. "I thought you guys mostly became fishermen or something."

"Not all of us," Ralph said quietly.

"Big and silent," orange polo said. "What's your name?"

"Ralph Allen."

Orange polo stuck out his hand, "Glad to meet you. I'm Arnie. Arnie Collins."

Ralph shook Arnie's hand quickly and let his duffle fall to the ground. "Do you know where I need to go?"

Arnie looked over the clipboard. "You're in luck," he pointed to a confused looking boy about half a head shorter than Ralph standing off to the side. He was staring intently at his smartphone. "That's your roommate. Carlos, come here."

Carlos wore a tucked-in black shirt and khaki pants. Behind Carlos were two suitcases on wheels. He was thin to a degree that made Ralph suddenly want to find him a sandwich. He was also bald and had the faint wisps of a mustache on his upper lip.

At the sound of his name, Carlos turned and walked over to where Arnie and Ralph were standing.

"Ralph Allen, this is Carlos Davies. Carlos, this is Ralph," Arnie introduced them and then handed each of them a map that looked like someone had made it in a basic word program. Leaning over he pulled a marker from seemingly nowhere and circled a building on both of their maps. "You are at the star at the bottom. The circled building is Peasley Hall. Your room is 207."

Turning back toward the table, he rummaged through a bucket until he came up with a keychain that read '207' and had two keys on it. "Here's your keys. My room number and email are on the paper in case you need any help. Just swing on by and give me a shout. The door is always open," he winked at them, "unless it isn't, if you know what I mean."

Carlos smirked and then turned to Ralph. "Hi," he stuck out his hand, which Ralph shook quickly and scooped up his bag. "Did Arnie say you were from Innsmouth?"

Ralph nodded, desperately wanting to not talk about himself. "And where are you from?" He glanced down at his map and started walking in the direction he figured Peasley Hall had to be in.

Carlos wasn't even looking at his map. The closer Ralph looked at his new roommate, he found himself wondering where Carlos's attention was, because it wasn't here.

Through his drifting look, Carlos answered, "Born and raised in Arkham." His eyes came back to the now and he pointed back toward where the bus from Innsmouth had dropped off Ralph. "About that way a mile."

"What are you doing getting a dorm room then?" Ralph asked. "Home cooking and your own room has got to be better than roommate farts."

Carlos's look became intense. He came to a halt, focusing entirely on his new roommate. "Do you fart a lot, Ralph?"

"What?" Ralph had to spin to meet Carlos's gaze. "I don't think so. As much as anybody, I guess."

Carlos suddenly burst out laughing and resumed walking in the direction of their future dorm room.

"I'm just screwing with you," he said. "Relax. No one here will give you anywhere near the level of judgment that you received at home."

It was Ralph's turn to stop walking as the statement hit him hard. He grabbed Carlos by the shoulder and spun him around, getting in his face as Ralph's duffle hit the ground.

"What's that supposed to mean? Who have you been talking to?" he said through gritted teeth.

Carlos's eyes went wide. "No one, I swear." He raised his hand and slowly took Ralph's off his shoulder. "I can … read people. Sometimes." He shrugged. "You carry a lot of baggage." He stepped back, putting a comfortable amount of space between them. "You can let go of some of that fear. Like I said, we are all free of our trappings now."

"Innsmouth never leaves you," Ralph grabbed the handle of his duffle and started again on his trek. "Sooner or later we all hear the call."

"Then let's plan on it calling later," Carlos was smiling again. "And let's also plan on not answering it."

"Why a dorm?" Ralph asked again. Guilt flooded him from his reaction. He chose to pivot the conversation again. Avoiding everything would make it feel even further behind him than the bus trip did.

He hoped.

"You're not the only one who wants to not be judged," Carlos's cheery demeanor didn't shift as he spoke. "You're also not the first person that my perceptive skills have bothered. I think my parents are exhausted by me." He let go of his suitcases and spun in place with his hands in the air. "This is as much a break for them as it is an adventure for me."

They walked past large pillars, each with an odd symbol in it. In the center of that was the Welcome Pole, that was shown in each of the school's advertisements on television. The pole itself was just a multicolored post in the ground with the word "Hello," carved into it in about thirty different languages.

Ralph hadn't said anything at Carlos's statement and Carlos wasn't oblivious to it.

"For entirely different reasons, I'm sure, we both don't want to dwell on yesterday. Let's not worry too much about our pasts," Carlos added, grabbing his suitcase handles again and marching forward. "The future awaits."

Peasley Hall was an open-ended box with the opening to the courtyard facing the front of the university. It took them a minute to orient themselves. Their room had a normal key but another row of tables, much smaller than the first, was handing out student identification cards that could be used. They both approached and gave their names.

"I heard there was a Chomper on campus," a short jock with blond hair and clothes that were way too tight said to his friend. "And there he is." He let out a ridiculous laugh. "They really do have a 'look,' don't they?"

The person next to him was a woman with pink hair and dark clothes. Carlos couldn't help but assume she was trying to bring back the goth look.

"Don't be a dick, Levi," she flipped off the jock.

Ralph hadn't even heard her. His short temper flared again, and he began stepping forward until a hand touched his arm.

Carlos stepped in front of Ralph before his new companion could release his rage on this new target and instead leaned in.

"Levi?" Carlos asked. "Were you named after your great-grandmother?"

Levi's face blanched. "What did you just say?"

"I said," Carlos shoved his hands in his pockets, "your great-grandmother wouldn't appreciate your racist remarks."

Levi mumbled something and then turned and walked away at a hurried pace.

The woman who had told Levi to shut up smirked. "What just happened?"

Carlos shrugged. "No idea, really. He's from Dunwich. They're a little touchy."

He turned back to Ralph who was standing there as unmoving as a statue. "A lot of people are here to escape who they were. You are not alone."

"Thanks," Ralph said, but it wasn't for the way Carlos had handled Levi. As the usual rage had built up inside of Ralph, stemming from his home, his heritage, and the memories he associated with what both of those demanded he become, he knew he was about to hurt Levi. Then Carlos had touched his arm. It was done to stop him from stepping forward, but somehow Carlos had removed all that rage in a single touch. It was like a valve had been pushed in his mind and the pressure just vanished.

He had no idea how Carlos had done it, but perhaps his new roommate could help him stay in check.

"Names?" the woman asked. She had a clipboard, but she didn't look older than Ralph or Carlos.

They gave them their names and Carlos immediately followed up with, "Isn't this supposed to be handled by sophomores or something?"

"You saw what happened when a sophomore was handling it," she cast a quick look in the direction that Levi had dashed toward. "I'm Sheryl." She pointed at the clipboard. "Sheryl Mason. You guys are in the room directly above mine."

She dug around in a carboard box and found their identification badges. Most schools made you wait in line for a photograph to affix to your ID. Miskatonic University let you email one to show that they were a modern and up-to-date school. That and the Wi-Fi were the major things it used to boast that very small fact. Everything else reflected the age and traditional ways of the practically ancient school.

Ralph was still a little fixated on his instant cooldown. "How do you know Levi, then?"

Sheryl shrugged. "I don't. He was hitting on me when I asked for my card." She pointed at a stack of suitcases sitting off to the side. Then she held up the clipboard. "I needed help with my bags and putting up with him looked like my only course of action until you two," she smacked Ralph on the arm, "strapping young men showed up."

"We're the same age as—" Ralph started.

Carlos also smacked Ralph on the arm.

"Why is everyone hitting me?" Ralph mumbled.

"Let's get her bags," Carlos was beaming. "Look at that," he added. "We just made a friend."

Ralph looked to Carlos's hands and how they each carried one of his own bags. Then he looked to his one duffle and sighed.

"Sure," he said. "I can grab one or two." He pocketed his ID card and stepped over to the stack of luggage. He scooped up one with a strap and wrapped it around his chest before fitting another under his arm and grabbing a third by the handles. All this luggage looked like it should have overwhelmed him, but Ralph wasn't even straining.

"Lead the way," he flashed a quick smile to show that he was happy to help.

"Innsmouth sounds fun," Sheryl said and other than the flash of a reminder of the earlier confrontation, Ralph wasn't bothered this time. "I like the ocean." She eyed Ralph to gauge his reaction to her words and then continued. "Innsmouth has a lot of rumors, but they all stem from family." She paused again. "My family isn't the best either."

The statement was strangely comforting. Perhaps Carlos wasn't wrong. Perhaps Sheryl was a friend. He wished that he could open up about … everything. Instead, he chose more small talk.

"And where are you from?" Ralph decided to ask before Carlos could just tell them and derail their conversational momentum. He wasn't sure what this Holmesian skill was that Carlos kept showing off, but he couldn't be the only person who was weirded out by it.

Sheryl picked up a few of her own bags and started walking toward the outer edge of the Peasley Hall building.

"Providence," she answered. "My family was originally from Arkham and we still have family here, so if you guys want to know any of the good pizza places, I'm the girl to know."

"Carlos is a local, too," Ralph said. Carlos was holding open the door once they all checked that their keycards worked. Ralph walked through after Sheryl lead the way.

"I don't know anything about the pizza shops, though," Carlos added. "My family didn't like going out."

Ralph nodded toward Carlos and smiled. "He's weird."

Carlos laughed. "It's true. I am." His voice got a little quieter. "I didn't get out much because of it."

"A Chomper and a hermit?" She dropped her bags outside of room 107 and bowed. "Then I shall be your guide to the world." She pointed at the bag under Ralph's arm. "Come back when you're unpacked, and you can help me set up my Xbox."

Carlos smiled but said nothing.

Ralph wasn't sure if this was a 'say nothing' moment. When the silence got uncomfortable, he said, "We have nothing else going on. Thanks."

"Don't sound overly enthusiastic," Sheryl smirked and pulled out her phone. "What are your numbers?"

Carlos rattled off a series of numbers while Sheryl thumbed it into her phone.

"I don't have a phone," Ralph said when he realized they were waiting for him.

"You don't have a—" Sheryl stopped herself and put her phone in her pocket. "Carlos is your phone now. I'll text you a pizza place. Bring the food with you."

A sound emitted from Carlos's pocket. It sounded like the music from the original Twilight Zone theme.

"That was me," Sheryl said. "Now you have my number. Other than Levi, you're the only people I know. So be weird, just don't be too weird."

Carlos couldn't stop beaming while Ralph still wasn't sure how to feel. He had one friend who could numb his regular rage and another friend who was offering to help him fit in.

Perhaps college wasn't going to be as horrible as his father had implied.

CHAPTER 2

"Hello," Meredith flagged down another student walking by. Meredith was broad-shouldered and dressed in denim pants and a denim jacket. Under her jacket was a yellow button-up shirt with her smartphone in the shirt pocket.

"Hello," the student answered as she walked up. Shorter and quieter than Meredith, her hair was long and pulled into two braids. Her clothes looked like they could have been a Catholic school uniform with the white shirt buttoned up and tucked into black pants. "Is there something that I can help you with?"

Her voice was clipped and almost mechanical in her enunciation.

Meredith was surprised by her fellow student's ... well, everything, but did her best not to show it.

"My keycard was made today, and the doors haven't updated or whatever they do." She sighed, "I can't get in. Would you mind?"

Stephanie West eyed this other student suspiciously.

"You lack the build to expect any success in a mugging," she paused, "unless I am your target, of course. Although, I can assure you that I have nothing of value on my person. You aren't here to rob anyone are you?"

Meredith provided a slight smirk, not certain if this was a serious question or a joke. "If anyone is getting robbed, it's us. Tuition here is insane."

Stephanie continued to stare at Meredith until both of them were well into uncomfortable territory before she made up her mind.

"My name is Stephanie West." She thrust out her hand. When Meredith clasped Stephanie's hand she was surprised by the hard pumping that followed next. "I believe I like you."

"Meredith Johnson, archaeology major," she supplied and to keep things amicable, added, "I like you, too." She nodded toward the door and the pile of bags near the door. "Can you help me out?"

Stephanie withdrew her hand and nodded. Just as quickly, she pulled her own keycard from her pocket and slapped it against the card reader on the door. The door let out a buzz and Stephanie pulled it open.

Stephanie then held the door open as Meredith struggled to drag in her two bags and the laundry basket filled with tied grocery bags.

"Thank you," Meredith said over her shoulder as she began maneuvering her way down the hall toward where she thought her room was. She stopped just outside of the 107 door and jumped when she realized that Stephanie had been following her the hundred feet or so from the door.

"Oh," Meredith said, "hi, again."

"My apologies," Stephanie said. "It was not my intention to follow you." She pointed past 107 at the next room. "I'm 108."

"Oh," was all Meredith could think to say before quickly adding, "Thanks again for the help with the door."

Stephanie nodded and continued past Meredith and into her own room.

Fumbling with her keys, Meredith moved toward unlocking the door.

It sprang open seemingly on its own.

Standing before Meredith was a pink-haired woman in baggy clothing. She had a big smile on her face.

"You should see the look on your face," she grabbed the laundry basket filled with bags from Meredith and took it into the room. "I'm Sheryl Mason, your roommate."

The room was mostly bare except for the blankets on the bed and a large television under the long windows. The closets were to each side of the door when Meredith came in and had accordion-style doors. Sheryl's was closed, and Meredith assumed that anything else Sheryl owned must be in there.

"I claimed the right side," Sheryl was explaining after she

set the laundry basket on the empty bed, "but if you want to do bunk beds, we'll have to get a maintenance guy to get us the pegs. I know some guys upstairs that said they are going to do that and get a couch or a minifridge."

Meredith dragged the rest of her stuff in. "Meredith Johnson, but I'm guessing you figured that out already."

Sheryl jumped onto her bed and scooped up a controller. Almost instantly, the tv erupted into explosions as magical swords came crashing down on dinosaur necks.

"Yup," Sheryl didn't look away from her game. "Happy to meet you. I like to game, but if you don't like the sound, I can put my headphones on."

Meredith had to admit to herself that the tv was a little louder than she would have preferred but she wasn't going to make waves in her first few minutes with her new roomie. She said it wasn't bothering her and went to work unpacking.

"Where are you from?" Sheryl said at what Meredith assumed had to be a load screen.

"Upstate New York," Meredith paused before deciding to elaborate, "Syracuse."

"Ah," Sheryl smiled, "then you'll be into the basketball scene?"

"What?" Meredith was confused for only a moment before she remembered that everyone only knew Syracuse for its Orangemen. "No, actually. I'm majoring in anthropology. I've never been much into sports. Where are you from?"

"I'm a local," Sheryl answered. "Made any friends, yet?"

"Kind of. I met our neighbor. Little weird, but she helped me into the building."

Sheryl laughed. "Yeah, she's odd, but generally seems harmless."

"You'll have to give me more of a chance," a voice from behind them made them both start. "I assure you that I could be quite harmful when given the opportunity."

"Oh man," Sheryl paused her game and took a deep breath. "Damn you're quiet."

"I am from Stuart, Iowa," Stephanie offered, without being prompted.

"Wow," Meredith knew nothing about Iowa. "What brought you here?"

Stephanie frowned. "That is an excellent question. When I examine my initial reasons, they hold up to the most basic of scrutiny: Miskatonic University has a great veterinarian program, and I received a scholarship to go here. Both are excellent reasons to leave behind everything I knew and make the trek to the east coast."

"But?" Sheryl asked as she jumped back into her game.

"But," Stephanie continued, "the most satisfying answer that I can find is that I feel like I belong here."

"You have a funny way of talking," Meredith said.

Stephanie nodded. "Yes. I am a bit ... socially awkward." She grinned. "Please, don't let that scare you away."

Sheryl blew a raspberry and smacked the bed next to her. "Welcome to the family. I've got beer under the bed. Help yourself or don't, just don't tell anyone."

Stephanie hopped up onto the bed next to Sheryl and watched her play her game while Meredith continued to unpack her things.

Something was nagging at the edge of Meredith's mind. Finally, she asked.

"Veterinary medicine? I didn't know Miskatonic University had that as a major."

"It's a relatively new major," Stephanie explained. "For decades, Miskatonic has been the place to go for an advanced degree in mortuary sciences, yet their applicant numbers have been dwindling. Having the facilities at their disposal, they recruited several veterinary educators and have set the facilities to a dual purpose."

"And if any of the puppies die," Sheryl laughed, "then the guy next to you will know how to dispose of the body."

"Disposal won't be an issue," Stephanie commented in complete seriousness. "I am sure that they will have the crematorium up and running by the time classes start."

Sheryl was at first taken aback by Stephanie completely missing her sarcasm before she realized what her new friend had said.

"Miskatonic has a crematorium?"

"Oh, yes," Meredith's face lit up with excitement as the topic shifted. "The crematorium has been in semi-regular use since the campus was first built." She frowned. "It was listed on the website as a historical site. Did you not see it?"

"I must have missed that link," Sheryl said. "That's a random fact to know."

Meredith shrugged. "I like history and Miskatonic has a lot of it."

When Meredith had finished unpacking, she turned to her roommate and new friend and asked, "Now what?"

"I conned the two guys upstairs into buying us pizza," Sheryl set down her controller and stretched. "They'll be down here in a few minutes."

"Do you want to go and get your roommate, too?" Meredith asked Stephanie. "Always room for more, right?" Her last question was aimed at Sheryl.

Sheryl quickly nodded.

"I do not have a roommate," Stephanie hopped down from the bed. "I am aware that I am an acquired taste and didn't want to subject anyone to that random chance of us not getting along. Besides," she explained, "I prefer to not have distractions get in the way of my studies."

"You won't be a buzzkill, will you?" Sheryl asked.

Stephanie shook her head. "Not at all. Socializing is just as important as study. Likely more so, given how alien it can sometimes be." She tried to relax and shrugged. "Don't worry, I'm cool."

Sheryl and Meredith burst out laughing. It was loud and after a moment even Stephanie joined in.

Sheryl's phone buzzed and she had to force herself to calm down before she could check on it.

When she had finished reading the text from Carlos, her laughter was a distant memory.

"It's the boys," she rushed for the door. "They're in trouble."

Meredith and Stephanie were quick on her heels as she moved down the hall and up the stairs.

They didn't make it all the way up the stairs before they

realized something loud was going on. Carlos met them and, ignoring Meredith and Stephanie, spoke to Sheryl.

"It turns out that Levi is our neighbor," Carlos said. "He started getting verbal and I texted you when Ralph started reacting."

"Reacting?" Meredith asked.

"It would seem," Sheryl explained, "that our new friend, Ralph, has a bit of an issue with anger."

"You seemed to know Levi a little better than we did," Carlos said. "I was hoping that you could help."

"You're the one who sent him running last time," Sheryl pushed past Carlos. "Can't you do it again?"

"I tried," Carlos shrugged. "He brought friends."

Sheryl could see what was happening now. Levi, short as he was, was on his toes and pressing his forehead against Ralph's. Ralph, to his credit, was keeping his fists to his side while three other guys were chanting.

"Hey Big Tuna!" was the nicest thing Sheryl picked up. The rest of the remarks were overly descriptive regarding carnal relations between Ralph's mother and sea creatures.

Levi wasn't saying anything, but it was obvious that he was the one who instigated it simply by Ralph only focusing his attention on the little man.

Sheryl stopped near the confrontation. "Are you going to do anything, Carlos?"

Carlos shook his head, "Nothing I could say would deescalate this."

Stephanie stepped in front of both of them before squeezing directly between the men in mid-confrontation.

"Might I inquire as to what has you both upset?" Her voice was quiet but as firm as Ralph's form.

"Levi's a racist," Ralph said quietly.

"You're not even the same species, fish-freak," Levi shouted.

Stephanie shifted and faced Levi. "Sir, your words hold no meaning. This is obviously a man of rather large stature. Are you certain that you want to continue goading him into a physical confrontation? It is obvious that he would be the only one standing when it was finished."

Ralph smirked, never taking his eyes from Levi's.

"Listen," Levi forced his attention to Stephanie, "it ain't bad enough that I gotta go to classes with a Chomper, but he's in my hall, too? And he wants to play football?" He threw his hands up. "Come on. I just don't want a Chomper like him anywhere near me." He looked to his companions and corrected himself, "Us."

Stephanie looked over her shoulder to Ralph. "What is a Chomper?"

Ralph shrugged and pointed to the shark-like fish mascot on his coat. "My school mascot. He's using it as an offensive term to describe anyone from my home."

"Where's your home?" she asked.

"Innsmouth."

"Never heard of it." Stephanie returned her attention to Levi. "And you would do well to forget it. He isn't a Chomper."

"What?" Levi, Ralph, and Carlos all said at the same time.

"We are all fully enrolled in Miskatonic University. The mascot of this school is a Night Gaunt. A dream monster. If I am correct, I believe the chant at local events is 'We Will Wreck Your Dreams.' And the mascot himself is named Gaunty."

"What does—" Levi started.

"That means we are all Gaunties now," Stephanie interrupted. "Besides, what happens if," she turned to Ralph, "I'm sorry, what was your name again?"

"Ralph," he answered.

"Stephanie," she offered in return. "It's a pleasure." She turned back to Levi, "What is the worst that happens if Ralph joins your football team? He's huge. While I don't claim any familiarity with the sport, I am still an American and under the impression that anyone of his size would be welcome on any team."

One of Levi's friends laughed and said, "Fish boy's slimy hands will drop the ball."

"Then be better than him." Stephanie ignored who had said it and stepped closer to Levi, putting her face inches from his. "If you are worried that he will do bad, then let him and destroy him with his own humiliation. Unless that isn't it at all." She got quiet. "Are you worried he will be better than you?"

"What?" Levi almost shouted the word. "Better? Not at all. He's a fish-freak."

"Then let him compete and destroy him," a gleam filled Stephanie's eyes. "Raise yourself upon his ashes and stop looking like a bully in the dorm halls."

"You guys are all freaks," Levi said. "I don't have time for this." He reached past Stephanie and jabbed Ralph in the chest with his finger. Ralph's entire arm twitched but he didn't take the bait. "Go to tryouts and watch us smoke you." To his companions, he said, "Let's go get a beer. I'm over this."

Ralph and Stephanie didn't move as each of Levi's friends walked past them and through Carlos, Sheryl, and Meredith and down the stairwell.

Ralph's breaths were shallow, and his anger was obvious so no one said anything for a moment.

"That Levi guy just keeps trying to piss in your cornflakes, huh?" Carlos spoke quietly.

Ralph's eyes softened and he let the anger flow out of him. His shoulders sagged. "That's normal." He turned toward his new friends. "In general, people don't like folks from Innsmouth. You should probably steer clear of me."

Sheryl stepped forward. "I have a nose and I smell pizza. You bought that just because I told you so." She smiled and hooked her arm around Ralph's, dragging him back toward his room. "I'm not willing to relinquish that power, yet."

Meredith and Stephanie introduced themselves to the guys and everyone sat down on the one bed within reach and the floor. Carlos had the top bunk, as Ralph didn't want to stress test how strong the beds were. There was a large space on the left side of the room that Carlos claimed would be for a couch when they found one.

"Twice on the first day," Carlos said. "Is Levi going to keep being a problem?"

Ralph shrugged. "If you guys had let me handle it, he wouldn't even think about coming back."

"Yes," Stephanie frowned around her slice of pizza. "Violence is the only solution here. Then you will be expelled,

Levi will have the gratification of knowing that he won, and you will have to explain to your family back home why it is no school will take your applications."

Ralph smirked. "My family would be happy about it."

"Well," Stephanie interpreted his expression, "I'm guessing that you wouldn't be."

"Thanks," Ralph decided to again redirect the conversation, if only slightly, away from being the focus. "For what you did back there. That was incredibly brave of you to step between us like that. You don't even know us."

"I know bullies," she said. "In this case, it was obvious that you weren't the bully."

"Why's that?" Ralph asked.

"Levi was still standing when we got here," Sheryl laughed.

"Exactly," Stephanie agreed.

"What was that stuff about humiliating him on the field?" Meredith asked.

Stephanie shrugged. "Factual and Darwinism. I wasn't certain that Levi's tiny mind could handle it, but I was hopeful."

"That's pretty dark," Sheryl said.

"Necessary," Stephanie set her pizza down on the corner of the box that she was using as a plate. "The only piece of advice that I have for any of you is the same that my father gave me; don't defeat your enemies, destroy them."

"Your dad seems like he was a cheery guy," Sheryl mumbled.

Stephanie smiled. "He was kind. He knew that I was small. He gave me advice that made being small less of a weakness."

"My father would have told me to eat him," Ralph's voice was quiet.

Everyone just stared at Ralph, waiting for a punchline.

Finally, Meredith said, "As a joke, right?"

Ralph shrugged but gave a slight smile. "It wouldn't be the first thing he told me to do, but we would likely get there."

"Did all of our parents screw us up?" Carlos asked, only half-jokingly.

"Mine are cool," Meredith laughed. "You guys are the screwed-up ones."

Everyone got quiet and stared at Meredith until she realized that what she said might have been offensive.

Then they all let the escalating tension go as they laughed in unison.

"I hold no delusions about what the coming weeks might do to this new dynamic," Stephanie said as the room grew quiet again, "but if it is at all possible, I would like to continue this association."

Carlos nodded his agreement. "This feels right."

Meredith looked at him. "Why did you have to make it weird?"

Carlos looked confused, but Ralph answered for him.

"My roommate gets feelings about things," he shrugged. "He knew about mine and Levi's families just by looking at us." Ralph nodded to Carlos, bolstering the latter's confidence. "If Carlos has a good feeling about anything, then I'm on board."

Sheryl turned to Ralph. "After everything that happened today, are you still thinking about trying out for the football team?"

Ralph shrugged. "I'm good at football. Got a scholarship and everything." He grabbed another slice of pizza. "Besides, Levi and his friends don't scare me. If anything, trying out is actually going to be easier than I thought it would be."

"Why is that?" Meredith asked.

A grin spread across Ralph's face. "I was worried the team might not accept me because I'm gay."

Meredith snorted. "It's 2021. Gay in sports isn't the problem that it used to be."

"Obviously not," Stephanie added. "Being from Innsmouth in sports is surprisingly more offensive." She frowned as she pondered, "Will the average bigot ever fail to surprise me?"

"That's cool about the scholarship," Carlos changed the subject. "I got in on a full ride from a local grant. I'll have to reapply each semester, but I should have most of my school paid for."

"Odd," Stephanie said. "I received a Veterinary Sciences Federal Grant under the stipulation that I spend at least two years at Miskatonic's new program."

Meredith's eyes lit up as she saw imaginary threads being

pulled taught. "What about you Sheryl?"

"Yeah," she said. "Same story." She didn't look at anyone.

Meredith leaned in. "Is it? I got in after doing a report on how williwaw winds changed the course of religion in the Polynesian Islands. They gave me a grant for my paper." She paused. "What are the odds that we are all here and all have our school paid for?"

"Geeze," Sheryl leaned away and frowned. "Are you a conspiracy nut or something? I'll bet most of the students in Peasley Hall are on some sort of financial aid program or something. It's probably how they selected housing."

Carlos shook his head. "Levi made it clear that his dad paid for everything."

"Then he's lying." Sheryl seemed almost angry about this.

Meredith backed down. "It's just weird. That's all. Don't worry about it."

Sheryl's guilt finally overrode her misguided sense of self-preservation.

"I'm here on a math scholarship," she grumbled.

"What? So?" Carlos's eyes were wide with confusion. "Why is that a big thing?"

Sheryl glared at him. "I'm not just good at math. I can do complex equations instantly in my head." She rubbed her eyes, taking the moment slowly to hide her face. Finally, she added. "I hate math. More than anything. I didn't even want to go to college until the guy who wanted to give me the scholarship explained that if I wanted to get into game development a math degree would be an avenue for it."

"You're a dual major then?" Stephanie asked.

Sheryl nodded, "Math and Computer Sciences."

"Something isn't adding up," Meredith said it almost to herself.

"While the odds are low that five complete strangers would find themselves drawn together after each being, essentially, paid to be here," Stephanie stated, "there's no end-sum that explains why or why us."

Meredith pulled out her phone and opened the notepad application. "What's everybody's last names?"

Sheryl rolled her eyes. "You are a conspiracy nut, aren't you?"

Meredith squared her shoulders. "Too many things in this world don't add up and I'm tired of getting railroaded or manipulated just because someone thinks they can use me. Do you want to be used, Sheryl?"

"To what end, though? Say you discover someone is using us, so what?" Sheryl countered.

"I'll cross that bridge when I get to it," Meredith said. "Until then, it's just me being a little crazy." She raised her eyebrow. "Didn't we already decide that you guys are all weirdos? This is me joining you."

"Let your freak-flag fly," Ralph agreed. "My last name is Allen."

"Carlos Davies."

"Stephanie West."

Sheryl sighed. "Mason."

"And I'm Johnson," Meredith typed in with her thumbs.

"Great," Sheryl stood and stretched. "You have our names. Now what?"

Meredith shrugged. "I do some searches and see if anything pops up. I probably won't find anything."

"Do you guys want to do lunch tomorrow?" Carlos's eyes lit up with excitement.

Ralph nodded. "Tryouts aren't until three. I only have two classes before that. Meet you guys at Student Union at noon?"

"I need to take lunch at eleven-thirty if I am to make it to the Munoz Medical Sciences building by my twelve-thirty class," Stephanie said.

"Lunch at eleven-thirty, then," Carlos beamed when everyone agreed.

CHAPTER 3

Other than Stephanie and Sheryl, the group of new friends found themselves in mostly the same classes on the first day.

Ralph, who was yet undecided on what his major would be, still had to take the same General Education requirements that the rest of the freshman class needed. When he had selected his classes, he had signed up for a history class and through another strange coincidence that Meredith continued to insist wasn't a coincidence, he had ended up in the same history Gen-Ed class as Carlos and Meredith.

History 101—Introduction to Historical Thinking and Analysis was surprisingly less exciting than the title made it sound. It was still day one, so Carlos was still holding out hope that the class would pick up, but Ralph had surrendered. If he didn't fail this course, it would be by the grace of his friends.

Meredith, on the other hand, was absorbed. Introduction to Historical Thinking and Analysis focused on teaching students to source their documents and the differences between direct sources and indirect sources when doing research. Even the professor, Jane Schulenberg, seemed exactly the perfect level of engaging to keep Meredith from ever getting bored.

Ralph and Carlos were the first ones to the door when class was over and ended up waiting for Meredith as she introduced herself to Professor Schulenberg and drilled her on what kind of documents and research they would be running into in the coming weeks.

While Ralph, Carlos, and Meredith were getting their minds massaged in History, Sheryl and Stephanie were in their first shared class together.

Introduction to Macroeconomics was the first math class that they were both required to take. This one, while a Gen-Ed, was required for both of their majors, although, much like Ralph and Carlos, both women were equally bored.

On the one hand, the teacher, Professor John Timmons, was very engaging.

"The answer," he said at the beginning of the class, "to every question I ask will either be 'more money,' or 'money is good.' It will never be anything else."

Sheryl laughed, enjoying the statement, but finding the entire idea of an economics class as ridiculous. She spent most of the class running gear stats through her head for her most recent update in Wicked West, the new game that should be finished downloading to her system by the end of the day.

Stephanie had an entirely different experience. While Macroeconomics wasn't required for her Veterinary Sciences major, she did need a few math classes, and this met that requirement.

She had intended to spend the entirety of class paying complete attention, no matter how boring the curriculum. To her credit, she was taking notes and resisting the urge to correct the teacher when he was obviously incorrect.

That was all autopilot, though.

Since she left her room, she had been getting the distinct impression that she was being stared at.

Different students or pairs of students seemed to be whispering about her when they thought that she wasn't paying attention. She couldn't make out what any of them were saying, but it was obvious that she was the target of some sort of joke.

The classroom had seemed like a place of security where she could hide from whatever this was. That wasn't the case. Two rows in front of her a woman would take moments and stare at her.

When she stared at Stephanie, it was with hate.

On the outside, Stephanie always chose to show a cold façade with intellect and reason being what ruled her decisions. This didn't mean that Stephanie had no emotions, she just saw no reason to let them get in the way of how she perceived the world. Emotions were a private thing to her and always had been.

Inside, she was a hurricane of confusion and fear. Everything about this angry blonde two rows up was only causing Stephanie paranoia and despair. On the outside, she wouldn't give anyone the satisfaction of how distraught she was on the inside.

With the safe harbor of the classroom having been compromised, Stephanie was looking forward to the solace, and perhaps understanding, of her newfound friends.

Lunch couldn't come fast enough.

Stephanie decided that she didn't want to wait around to be confronted by the random student up front or to see who else might be joining in on her silent torment. As quickly as she could, she rushed from the room. Sheryl did her best to keep up.

They were halfway across the quad and to their next class, English 101—Composition 1, when Sheryl finally caught her.

"What's the rush?" she asked.

Stephanie stopped and turned, looking past Sheryl to see if anyone was behind them.

"For reasons outside of my understanding," Stephanie was speaking in a clipped tone, showing more emotion than Sheryl had seen her demonstrate before, "I have become the focus of several of the other students."

"Focus?" Sheryl was confused. "What does that even mean?"

"I have seen many students staring at me and laughing on several occasions today," Stephanie explained. "One such student, who was obviously angered by my presence, was a member of our Macroeconomics class."

Sheryl held up a hand. "Let's take a minute and try and calm down." She looked all around her and while there were students looking their direction, it seemed to be more of a passing glance at the two people having a discussion in the quad. "I'm sure you noticed something, but are you sure that it's negative?" Then she remembered who she was talking to and waved at Stephanie's outfit. Again, she was wearing a white button-up shirt tucked into black pants. "No offense, but could it be how you're dressed? You look like a Jehovah's Witness."

"Don't be ridiculous," Stephanie scoffed. "I don't have a tie. Besides, our classmate is not likely to have an intense hate for Jehovah's Witnesses."

Sheryl had to admit that Stephanie was right. Lots of people wore their pajamas to class, so it wasn't like there were fashion police roaming the campus to offer uncomfortable glares at people with questionable fashion choices.

"Do you want to skip the next class or something?" Sheryl suggested.

Stephanie shook her head. "Not at all. I am just not comfortable lingering where people can continue their visual assault."

"Let's go then," Sheryl pushed her long dark hair from her eyes and looked around. She saw one pair of guys standing near the library and watching them. She marched a few steps in their direction before flipping them off and shouting, "What are you looking at?"

That didn't help anything as the guys just started laughing before turning and heading into the library.

"Whatever," she returned her attention back to her friend. "I've got your back. Let's go."

With all the excitement of the previous day and moving into their rooms, the new friends never took the chance to compare their schedules. When Sheryl and Stephanie sat down for Comp 101, they were surprised to see Ralph, Meredith, and Carlos already there.

Other than a short hello, there was no time to talk, so their friends were left in the dark as to Stephanie's newest concerns.

The class started much as the others had, but this time there was a lot more back and forth with the students. The teacher, Kristy Malcom, went over her agenda and was more than pleased to discuss with her new students what to expect in the coming months.

That and the lack of anyone giving Stephanie distracted looks gave her the chance to relax as much as she ever did in an educational environment.

Not only did she relax, but she also became thoroughly engrossed in the conversation.

"All that I ask," Professor Malcom was saying, "is that you try to bring a new approach to the texts. You're going to have reading assignments that, to be completely honest, every class that has ever come through these doors has also had. Think about that when you're writing. Try to come up with something entirely unique. I will never fail a completely unique paper."

"That can't be true, can it?" Stephanie asked, mildly incredulous. "There have to be topics of taboo nature or where the view indicated some sort of underlying psychosis that you just couldn't pass."

Malcom laughed. "Well, I encourage you to use your reason, as well. If you are planning on using a review of *Of Mice and Men* to gratuitously explain the dissections of the human brain, then you've missed your mark. Even if it is unique." She nodded at Stephanie. "Thank you …" she paused indicating that Stephanie should provide her name.

"Stephanie West," she beamed. If Stephanie's psyche had a weakness, it was all forms of even the mildest praise.

"Well, again, thank you Ms. West …" Professor Malcom trailed off. She was suddenly staring intently at Stephanie before turning back to her desk and typing furiously at her computer.

"You said your name was West?" Malcom asked without looking up from her screen.

"Yes," Stephanie said with hesitation. "Have you heard of me? I'm new to the area."

"No matter," Malcom waved her hand. "What's your major?"

"What?"

"Your major," Professor Malcom stood, and all the color drained from her face as she stared directly at Stephanie. "What is it?"

Fear was suddenly filling Stephanie's mind as she recalled all the looks she had received earlier in the day. Suddenly, she was getting the same look from her teacher. A teacher who had seemingly enjoyed her company only moments before.

"Vet-veterinarian Medicine," she finally stuttered out.

"Over my dead body," Professor Malcom stated. She stomped toward the door and dismissed the class as she left.

"What was that about?" Meredith asked.

Stephanie couldn't help herself as she sobbed at her desk. Sheryl took the time and filled them in. Some of the other students, the ones who had as much clue as Stephanie about what was going on, stopped by to touch her shoulder and offer what minor comforts they could.

"It obviously has something to do with your name," Meredith said as her eyes drifted into thought.

Ralph was standing there with his arms folded, his anger at the teacher and Stephanie's situation evident. "I figured I would have to deal with the racism that's been following me around, but what does anyone have against a tiny midwestern girl?" He quickly added, "No offense."

Stephanie signaled that she wasn't offended before looking directly at Carlos.

"What?" he asked.

"Your intuition," Ralph guessed. "What are you picking up?"

He shook his head. "Sorry, guys. I've got nothing. I think Meredith is right, though. Something about your name and," he shrugged, "your major, too, I guess, is causing people to get upset."

"Lunch is in half an hour," Meredith looked supercharged by the questions on everyone's lips. "Let's each do our research and regroup then."

The half hour flew by. At eleven twenty-six, Stephanie's phone chimed to indicate that she had received an email. She looked at it and was surprised.

"Ms. West,

I apologize for my outburst during class. I applied an association with your name that is in no way related to yourself or your chosen major. I ask that you forgive me and will understand if you do not.

Either way, I hope to see you in my class on Wednesday.

Thank you and again, sorry,

Ms. Malcom"

It was such an impossibly quick turnaround that Stephanie didn't know what to think of it.

As they sat down in the middle of the cafeteria area, each

with trays from the various options provided by their campus dining hall, Stephanie read them all the email.

"That was quick," Carlos said.

Through a mouth of broccoli, Sheryl said, "She got in trouble."

"What?" Carlos was surprised.

"While you guys were going all Google on Stephanie's name," Sheryl explained, "I decided to try and follow Malcom."

Ralph laughed and slammed his hand down on the table. "Who knew you had it in you?"

"I did," Sheryl winked and continued her explanation. "I didn't hear what they were talking about, but she was mad. I mean screaming-at-the-dean mad." She took a swig of her drink. "The dean actually grabbed her by the arm and demanded she calm down before dragging her aside. He whispered a ton of stuff to her and then she started nodding her head. When he stormed off, she had pulled out her phone," Sheryl waved at Stephanie's phone, "to email you, I guess."

Stephanie had a bowl of soup, which surprised Ralph, only because he didn't know that any of the places were selling soup. She set her phone down and began sipping on it before asking what everyone else had found.

"Absolutely nothing," Ralph said. "I came here early to check out the food." He hooked his thumbs at Carlos and Meredith, "I was kind of hoping they would jump on this."

Sheryl rolled her eyes at him.

"Oh," Meredith had a huge smile, "I found something, all right." She pulled her laptop from her bag and propped it open. After typing in her password, she spun it around to show the screen.

Carlos almost threw up what little food he had eaten.

"What is that?" Sheryl asked.

"That is a series of corpses tied together," Stephanie said without giving the picture more than a passing glance. "Obviously." She waggled her fingers at Meredith, eager for her friend to explain what she found.

"Dating back to the nineteen twenties and with possible copycat cases as recently as a decade ago, a man named Herbert

West is believed to be a psychotic killer who made his home in Arkham. It turns out that he started his killing spree as a medical student at Miskatonic."

Ralph was getting angry on behalf of his friend again. "Because she shares a name and wants to study medicine, everyone hates her like she was the killer? For a college, this school is coming off as less and less enlightened every day."

"It goes deeper," Meredith continued. "These weren't just murders, these were mutilations, disfigurement, and much worse. People started going missing or their recently deceased relatives would no longer be in their graves." She pointed at the screen and the mutilated corpses. "That is several members of the Miskatonic staff. They take this attack personally, even a century later."

Carlos spoke up, "I remember seeing it getting covered on the news as a gruesome historical event." Carlos closed his eyes after taking a bite of his food.

Meredith nodded, "Anytime anyone dies locally, they compare it to their most famous killing spree."

"So, everyone is treating me like the devil because they think I might be related to him?" Stephanie asked.

Meredith nodded. "That's part of it." She let out a long sigh. "The other part is that you kind of look like him." She flipped the screen back to face her and scrolled to another part of whatever article she was reading before turning it to face the group again.

On the screen was a blonde-haired young man with round glasses and a thin face.

"His facial structure, in the cheek bones and the high forehead are incredibly similar, but," she pointed at her decidedly different colored skin, "might I point out the obvious?"

Stephanie might share a resemblance with this Herbert character, all the way down to the clothing even, as he was wearing almost the exact same outfit in the picture as Stephanie had on then, but he was white.

Ralph was the first to point out the obvious. "If you are related, it might not be directly."

Carlos's eyes shot open. "Sandra Finker?"

"What?" most of the table blurted in unison.

Stephanie did not. She only stared at Carlos.

"What about her?" she asked.

"I have literally no idea," Carlos said. "I just heard the name really loud. Does it mean something to you?"

"Nothing to do with any of this," Stephanie said.

"Alright," Meredith dragged it out, waiting for Stephanie or Carlos to elaborate before continuing. "Anyway, the most prolific victim of ole Herb was Dr. Allen Halsey, the dean of the medical school here." When no one reacted, she sighed and put her face in her hands. "One of the medical buildings is named after him."

"Oh," Sheryl rolled her eyes, "that guy?"

"And," Meredith ignored her friend's sarcasm, "his great granddaughter is on campus." She turned to Stephanie, "I'll bet that she was the angry girl in your math class this morning."

"I do not believe in having to pay for the sins of ancestors that people seem to think that I have," Stephanie said.

"Welcome to reality," Ralph grumbled. "I'm hated for being associated with an entire town that was accused of terrorist actions in the twenties. It's been a century for me, too, but I still get all the hate."

"Terrorist actions?" Carlos asked. "I thought everyone was hating you because they thought you were part fish or something."

"Yeah," Ralph agreed around a mouth of food. "That too."

"He is your ancestor," Carlos's voice was slow, like he was sleep talking.

"No," Stephanie's face was turning red, "and stop your weird psychic thing. My life isn't some book you can read from cover to cover."

Carlos opened his eyes. "He had a brother. His brother married Sandra Finker. Sandra Finker is your great grandmother. She's also Black. That's why you don't look exactly like him, but you have to admit, the family resemblance is uncanny."

"I am not a murderer," Stephanie hissed through gritted teeth.

Ralph reached across and touched her arm. "No, you're not.

You're related to some whacko. That's alright. We don't see you any differently, and we'll do our best to correct anybody that says anything about it."

Stephanie yanked her hand back and stood up. "My situation, as misread as you all seem to be taking it, is hardly similar to sharing DNA with marine life. Take your condescension and put it to better use dealing with your own problems."

She stormed away from the table.

Ralph's face was red, but he didn't say anything. He just put his head down and stared at his food.

"She's still processing some weird crap," Carlos said quietly. "Don't take it too personally."

Ralph stood, slung his bag across his chest, and grabbed his tray. "I've got to get ready for the tryouts. I'll see you all tonight."

"Care if I come and watch?" Meredith asked.

Ralph grumbled something as he walked away. Meredith beamed with optimism and decided that what he said was, "Whatever."

CHAPTER 4

The few hours before the football tryouts were anything but relaxing for Ralph. He tried taking a nap, watching television, gaming with Sheryl, and stretching. The most helpful thing was likely the stretches, but he was going to do that when he got to the tryouts anyway.

When three o'clock hit, Ralph had already been standing in line for half an hour. Even with the football scholarship, he would need to prove to the coach that he was worth the effort. If he wasn't playing football, he wasn't getting the money to go to school.

Ralph knew better than to wear his Innsmouth Chomper's jersey and instead wore his practice mesh over his pads. Half of the people trying out weren't even wearing pads and out of all of them he was probably the only one who didn't really need them.

The problem with being from Innsmouth was that he was already genetically different from everyone there. Before the nineteen twenties, Innsmouth had just been a place for people to avoid. They were weird and didn't like people from outside of town. This was just a cover to hide their real concern.

That the world would discover their secret.

Long before they were outed in the late twenties, the people of Innsmouth had learned of a religion that would offer them everlasting life and riches beyond their wants. They only needed to procreate with their deity's spawn and help keep the religion alive. In the grand scheme of things, it was an easy decision to make. So, they did.

When commoners called the people of Innsmouth "fish-people" or claimed that they had a "look," they weren't wrong.

It was infinitely more complicated than that, but for the feeble human mind it was the easiest and most honest answer to explain it.

To keep the religion strong, Innsmouth had created a rule of ignoring the outside world. Their children would only ever have two requirements in life. The first would be to mate with their progenitor's spawn. The second would be to undergo the change and migrate to the water to be with the rest of their generations of family.

When the federal government bombed their underwater home, the people of Innsmouth were worried that they may never recover. Suddenly, the two tenets of keeping their religion going were more important than ever. Replenishing their family numbers would take generations and mating was now the number one priority.

A century later, Innsmouth was a thriving port again and outsiders were generally discouraged outside of the general things that required interaction with the rest of the world. You couldn't have a school without sports, music competitions, and internships were a thing that helped create a sense of local pride and made the rest of the world see Innsmouth as less than odd.

Keeping the world out and not letting what happened before happen again was top priority. When the government had dismantled Innsmouth, the Innsmouthers didn't have the numbers to properly defend themselves. That wouldn't happen again. Mating with the progenitor race and making the change had become a requirement for the continued protection of Ralph's people.

Except Ralph wanted none of that. The things they used as tools to hide, like football, the internet, and social lives, all had come to mean a sense of independence for Ralph.

When he had come out to his parents, encouraged by society outside of Innsmouth to be his true self, they had reacted violently. Innsmouther genetics made them sturdier stock than normal humans and stronger, too. The ability to recover from violent actions made violence in the home the norm in that port city. Even with his hybrid genetics, Ralph took days to recover from telling his parents that he didn't want to be part of the mating ceremonies.

That was when Ralph began planning on how to leave Innsmouth. Even if he couldn't avoid the change, he didn't want to be part of whatever culture included his immediate family. He wanted out and until he could figure out how, he would live his life as a normal person.

What he was doing wasn't unheard of. Every generation of hybrids from the deep had a handful of people who didn't want to be what they were. It was part of what had led the Feds to Innsmouth in the first place. Just because you were born to a certain set of people didn't mean that you actually belonged.

So, when they looked at him, standing third in line for the football tryouts to join the Miskatonic Night Gaunts, with disgust in their eyes, they weren't seeing Ralph. They were seeing the stories that followed his hometown and the stories that came with those who escaped.

They looked at Ralph and saw everything that he saw. They saw what he didn't want to be.

The difference was that Ralph wished no ill will upon his family and friends back home. He loved them and wanted them to have what they dreamed of. He just didn't share their dreams and wished that they understood that.

A quick glance at the stands showed him that Meredith had ignored his grumbling and shown up anyway. He wasn't nervous at all about not being able to perform to the best of his or anyone's ability, so she barely registered in his brain as anything other than a footnote.

The footnote read: Surprisingly great friend.

Her presence offered nothing to assuage his years of not feeling good enough around his family, though, and he stepped forward as the line grew closer to offering him his chance to impress the Miskatonic University coach.

Ralph pushed all his fears and stresses to the side and readied himself.

Coach Flagstaff was a head shorter than most of the guys on the team, which made him about a foot beneath Ralph's height.

He was thin and wiry with a head and face covered with salt and pepper stubble.

"Ralph Allen," he shouted. "You're up." He blew the whistle.

Ralph knew how hard he could hit but, from his years being on a high school team, he also knew how hard he should hit. Humans were squishy.

One of the sophomores was standing a few yards off and holding a blocking bag.

"Hit it," Flagstaff yelled.

Ralph took off. When he got to the bag, he put his shoulder into it but also slowed his momentum. Whoever the guy was behind the bag bounced back, taking the bag with him. When he had stopped sliding, the sophomore was about ten feet back.

Meredith whooped and cheered and clapped for Ralph in ways that did start to bolster him emotionally. Is this what familial support felt like?

Weird.

Coach Flagstaff didn't look like he was even paying attention. He wrote something down on his clipboard and then waved to the cones offset from the main line of students.

"You can hit," Flagstaff explained. "Show me you can move."

This was how the rest of the tryout went.

The idea of the football tryout was to show basic understanding of the necessary skills of the sport while also showing that you had the endurance, speed, and strength to adjust.

Ralph had no doubts about his physical abilities and knew that if that was all that mattered, he would have a position on the team. Unfortunately, even in this modern world, he was concerned that his ethnicity might cost him his scholarship.

"Alright, Allen," Flagstaff shouted. "Hit the showers. We've got what we need."

Ralph couldn't help himself and ran to the coach then.

"Can you tell me anything yet, Coach?"

Flagstaff looked at Ralph with a raised eyebrow.

"Did nobody tell you?" he asked.

Ralph's fear leaped to the front of his mind. "Tell me what?"

Coach Flagstaff snorted. "Miskatonic University has never

said no to a man from Innsmouth during tryouts." He slapped Ralph on the shoulder. "You didn't even need to show up and we would have put you on the team. You're a rare opportunity for me. We haven't had an Innsmouth kid on the team in twenty years. I wasn't going to turn that down."

Ralph beamed.

It was true that his heritage left a bad taste in his mouth, but it felt both right and justified that he was able to get something that he wanted from it.

After he showered, he went back out onto the field to watch the rest of the tryouts. He planned to join Meredith in the bleachers but was distracted from his course by Levi.

While in no way intimidated by Levi, Ralph was relieved to see that the Dunwich man was alone this time.

"Just don't," Ralph raised the flat of his hand toward Levi. "I don't want to hear anything you have to say. At all." He moved to walk past the sophomore.

"Hold on just a minute," Levi grabbed Ralph's arm. Both men stopped and looked down to where the contact had been made. Ralph did everything in his power to keep his anger from flooding out of him.

"Let me go," he growled.

Levi realized his mistake and held up both of his hands apologetically. "Look," he said, "I haven't been the best, and I won't get better, but we're teammates now. I just wanted to say congratulations."

Ralph shook his head. "You haven't been the best and I sure as hell am not going to forget that." He pointed at the field. "We're teammates on the field. Nothing else." The larger man snorted. "You made it perfectly clear what you think of me and playing football isn't going to change that."

Ralph decided that was his cue to leave. He let his shoulder hit Levi with a little of that Innsmouth strength. He just wanted to remind Levi who he was dealing with.

When his shoulder hit Levi's, Ralph stopped. It was like hitting a wall. He looked down to see the shorter man smiling.

"You're not the only one who can hit hard," Levi said to him before making his way toward the locker room.

Meredith was more excited than Ralph was. She leaped up as he joined her, and they sat down to watch the rest of the tryouts.

"I already texted everybody," she said. "That was great! You did amazing."

"Hey," Ralph was distracted by his encounter, "keep away from Levi. Or," a new thought came to him, "you like research. Maybe find out what his story is." He looked her in the eyes, "But keep your distance. I'm his target and I can take it. Don't you go getting him angry at you next."

Meredith rolled her eyes, "I'm sure you're aware by now that bigots hate the friends of those they hate just as much as those they ... um ... hate."

"Huh?" Ralph was still too distracted to keep up.

"He already hates me," she explained. "I'm sure of that. I'll look him up. What's his last name?"

Ralph frowned. "I don't really know. It says Smith on the roster, but after talking with Carlos, I don't think that's his real name."

Meredith's mind was already working as she said, "I'll get with Carlos and work from there." She forced her attention back to the now. "You were great! I have never seen anyone hit the thingies as hard as you did. The other guys looked annoyed, but I think that's good because they mostly were thinking about how they couldn't get a spot if you did."

She was rambling and Ralph was not oblivious to this.

"Meredith," he said with a smile and a soft voice. "Why did you come here? You don't really know me, not yet, and I don't think you know much about football."

"Give me some credit," she waved at the field. "I know what a touchdown is."

He just stared at her.

"Fine," she sighed. "You're right. If I didn't know you, I would have been bored out my mind."

"Then why are you here?" Ralph pressed.

"It doesn't take someone like Carlos to pick up that you probably didn't get a lot of support back home." She tilted her head to the side, "Or have too many friends. None of us really know each other yet, but we're starting to, and I wanted to show you the kind of friend that I can be."

"I'm gay," Ralph laughed. "You heard me say that last night, right?"

Meredith punched him in the arm. "You are definitely not my type." She frowned. "Complete honesty?"

"You're the one saying you want to be besties," Ralph shrugged. "Friends should be honest with each other."

She let out a deep breath she hadn't realized that she was holding. "Everything I said about wanting to be your friend and give you the support that you might have been missing was true." She crossed her heart. "I swear it."

"But?" Ralph pressed.

"But," Meredith folded her arms, "I also want to learn everything you can tell me about Innsmouth," she paused before adding, "that no one else will tell me."

"Why?" Ralph wasn't sure if he was angry at Meredith using friendship to drudge up his past, or if he genuinely wanted to help this new friend. He held up his hand before she could answer, "Make it good."

"My name is Meredith Johnson. My family changed it about forty years ago from Johansen. They changed our name because they believed that we were being hunted."

"Johansen to Johnson isn't exactly witness protection," Ralph pointed out.

Meredith rolled her eyes. "We were from Norway. We moved to the states after we changed our name. Johnson is common enough that we could disappear."

"Who was hunting you?"

"My great-grandfather died unexpectedly after he made a report to police about something he saw in the ocean," Meredith said, seemingly ignoring Ralph's question. "He saw something in the waters. A lot of people died and when he tried to get justice for them by telling the authorities, he died. Most of my family just dropped it, but—"

"But you can't see a good mystery without investigating," Ralph interrupted. "Right, Velma?"

"Come on, dude," she smiled. "If anyone, I'm Shaggy." Her face turned serious as she returned to the story. "The report that my great-granddad said that he found a sunken city, raised from the sea. It said he saw something. I think his crew found the sunken city of R'lyeh." She stopped talking and stared at Ralph. He knew the name and his face couldn't hide it.

"There, that," she said excitedly. "I can't find anything other than stories and bad dreams that talk about R'lyeh, but you knew it just from the name. I think that R'lyeh and Innsmouth have a connection. Both have rumored sea cities and connections to, no offense, but cults."

"You think a cult killed him?" Ralph asked. "And is hunting you?"

"You would know better than I do." Her brow furrowed, "Would the Esoteric Order of Dagon do that kind of thing?"

In a movement faster than even Ralph knew he was capable of, his hand shot up and covered her mouth. "Don't ever say their name," he hissed.

When he removed his hand, she repeated her question. "Well, would they?"

She referred to the religious order that governed all life in Innsmouth. It was secret and, according to the government files, was dissolved when the Feds blew up Devil's Reef.

It obviously wasn't gone. If anything, it was stronger than ever.

He nodded slowly. "That sounds like something they are capable of."

Meredith shrugged. "That's it, then. I want to be your friend," she held up a finger, "because you're a kickass dude, but also," she held up a second finger, "because you might be able to give me some more information about R'lyeh. Or at least tell me how the religious groups around these cities function."

"To what end, though?" he asked. "Let's say you figure out what they did or that they were responsible for your long dead ancestor. Then what?"

"Mostly," Meredith nodded slowly, "I'll be satisfied, but then we can deal with the rest of my issue."

"The rest of your issue? What issue?" Ralph asked.

"They didn't just kill my great-grandfather," she explained.

"They've killed at least hundreds of people in the years since. I want to stop them."

"That's a lot of work for a college kid to do," he said.

"Well," she said. "I'm hoping that it'll be five college kids."

"That is a tall order."

"I think it is all tied together," she said. "I think there's something to us all getting full rides to college, and I think it has to do with who we are. On the surface, I'm nobody. Just a kid who likes a good mystery, but if someone here knows who I really am, then suddenly it all starts to come together."

"How so?" Ralph hadn't bought this idea the previous evening and he still wasn't sold on it.

"You're a kid from Innsmouth," Meredith explained, "that's something that you and I both know," she waved at the football field, "is more than just being from a town. My entire family is being hunted by cultists because my long dead ancestor might have seen something."

"The others are just normal people," Ralph didn't say it convincingly.

"Carlos just knows things and Stephanie has a serial killer in her family tree. Not Ted Bundy or the Zodiac, but the worst killer and corpse mutilator to ever exist."

"And Sheryl?"

Meredith waved. "Sheryl likes to keep her secrets. I'm sure we will figure out why she's here in time. Until then, I've got enough evidence to assume that something is up."

"Again," Ralph shrugged, "what do we do with that information?"

"We need to gather more until a path forward makes itself visible. Right now, that means two things—"

Ralph threw up his hands, "Being besties and learning more about each other."

"Exactly."

He sighed and smiled. "You showed up."

"What?" Meredith was confused.

"My family only ever cared about my destiny. About changing who I am to be who they want me to be. They never came to my practices and they never took an interest in who

I already was." A tear formed at the corner of Ralph's eye. He wiped it before it became anything. "You want to be my friend? Well, you already are. You did more than anyone else ever did for me."

"I showed up?"

"Yes," Ralph stood up and started to walk down the bleachers. "You showed up."

When he got to the bottom and she was still sitting there, he shouted up to her.

"I just ran and hit a bunch of stuff. I'm hungry and you're buying, bestie."

CHAPTER 5

A text from Carlos suggested that everyone meet back at the Student Union for an early dinner. By the time that Meredith and Ralph joined their friends it was past five, and right on time for dinner.

They spent the next fifteen minutes letting the lines die down as they each explained their days. Carlos had nothing too exciting to talk about. Stephanie was obviously still frustrated about the revelations at lunch and did her best to sit the furthest from Meredith and Carlos.

The rest of Stephanie's day had been her only introductory class that was specific to her major. It was Biology 101, and a general education course for most students, but she needed it. What she didn't need was all the looks, including those from the teacher, as she tried to pay attention to the course.

"How does everyone here know more about my family history than I do?" She was staring at the line at the salad bar. She wasn't entirely sure that she wanted a salad, but that's where she recognized several of her classmates from Biology standing.

And whispering.

Stephanie liked to believe herself above such petty things. Her behavior, odd as it was, had been the subject of ridicule her entire life. Before high school, people had thought it cute and endearing. As she got older, people found it stuffy and annoying. She understood, and mostly ignored it.

This felt different. She wasn't being judged for her behavior, talents, or accomplishments. This time, she was being judged for being related to a psychotic killer. It was out of her control. Why should she suffer because someone who shared a few genetic markers with her turned out to be a complete monster?

"It's still the first day," Meredith said. "Once they get to know you or get used to you, they'll stop. We just have to get through the first day or two."

"None of it is logical," Stephanie muttered.

"Pasta line is moving," Ralph said. "We going?"

"I didn't hear anything after 'pasta,'" Carlos smiled and started to get up.

Then his face contorted with pain. He fell forward and into the table, screaming incoherently as the table slid away under him. Ralph and Sheryl were on the floor and next to him as soon as they noticed he collapsed.

"Why is he screaming like that?" Meredith shouted.

Carlos rolled onto his back and his screams went silent while his face continued to twist. He gripped at the side of his head as if he was trying to stop something from exploding out of it.

Whether in answer to Meredith or to describe what he was feeling, Carlos shouted an answer.

"Our world is cracking apart!"

As if his words had summoned something, half of the students in the Union vanished. Two of the walls, specifically the one near the exit and the wall touching it, also disappeared. In their place was a vast field of swaying blue grass and a pink sky.

In the field, and moving at incredible speed, a herd of … something … ran at them.

The things in the field ran on two legs with brown, meatball-shaped bodies. Instead of mouths, or perhaps covering them, tentacles writhed as they caught the scents of food.

Throughout the cafeteria, students and staff screamed in terror and confusion. They scrambled to get out through the service doors or over the food counters. The only people who didn't run or scream were the five friends.

Stephanie and Meredith were trying to get Carlos up so that they could move him to safety. He had gone limp, and it wasn't making things easier for them. Ralph knocked their table over and slid it in front of the girls and Carlos as a sort of shield.

Sheryl was beyond terrified and wanted to run. Beyond her understanding, she fell into math equations. She started chanting equations she had never thought of before and solving them as quickly as they came to her mind. It was either dive into the mathematic reality of her mind or accept this horrific reality in front of her. She chose her mind.

Ralph was the only one who seemed entirely unfazed by any of this. The only thing that seemed to bother him was his roommate collapsing. The rest was all just in the way of helping his friend. Innsmouth folk knew they weren't alone in the universe. They were wizards and warriors and even their most untrained youths knew to not fear the dark depths of the oceans.

To fear the dark made you prey.

Be a predator for Dagon.

Ralph leaped over the table and ran at the small herd of animals. As he came across whatever furniture remained, he hit them with his genetic strength. Tables, chairs, and garbage cans hurdled out and into the oncoming monsters. A trashcan hit one of the creatures and it popped, exploding gore everywhere.

The merman ripped a leg from a table and began swinging it like a club. The monsters were coordinated enough to know they needed to take him out, and focused their lashing face tentacles on securing his arms.

Doing so was harder than they anticipated and three of them were thrown and popped before the rest decided to go after the other students.

One ran straight at the mumbling Sheryl as her hands covered her head. Its tentacles stretched out, ready to pull her into its gaping maw.

Ralph spun and threw the table leg like a trident, aiming to pierce the creature before it got to his new friend.

The leg hit the creature in its center mass and impaled it, sending it back and away from Sheryl, but not before Sheryl noticed it and screamed.

Vocally she screamed, but internally, Sheryl noticed where the math had been leading her. The math had been that of the angles of the room around her and how they connected to the angles of everything else in every universe. She reached a mathematical understanding of the fabric of reality that had only ever been achieved by one other.

As she screamed, her math released itself and she fell through the corner of the wall she had been leaning against.

Gone from this world.

Ralph didn't know how to help his friend or even if he could and that didn't stop him from staring at where she had been. She had been there and then she just wasn't anymore.

One of the students nearest him that hadn't made it over the counters in time was struggling as one of the meatball monsters nibbled on his leg. He howled and shrieked in pain as it began devouring his flesh.

Ralph ran over and tackled the thing. He grabbed it by its tentacles and pulled until he tore its face wide open. Gore splashed over him. He twisted, swinging the creature by its torn face, and slammed it into the ground.

He took a moment to help the student up and over the counter.

When Ralph returned his attention to the monsters, they all seemed to have made it into the cafeteria and were struggling to get over the counters and at their pinned-down prey. At the table that had Meredith and Stephanie behind it, the latter was swinging a tray to keep the monsters back while Meredith yelled at Carlos to get up.

Suddenly, a burst of light came from behind the table. Ralph didn't know what it could have been and ran at the table to check on his friends. Meredith and Stephanie let out a yell in surprise and even the monster trying to get past Stephanie took a leap back and stood there in its own form of shock.

A man stood up from behind the table. His sudden movement sent Meredith staggering back as she stared at him. He wore Carlos's clothes, although they were tight on him. Unlike Carlos, this new person had a full head of grey hair with a salt and pepper beard.

Seeing Meredith trying to stutter something out, the newcomer tried to calm her.

"The veil is weaker here and I have only borrowed your friend." Despite his rugged appearance, there was softness in his eyes. "He will be returned to you."

The softness was suddenly replaced by a fierce look of rage. The newcomer thrust his hands outward and shouted, "I am the Key."

A wave of golden energy burst from him and through everything. The meatball monsters each exploded, and the gore showered over everyone nearby.

Then he shouted again.

"He is the Gate."

The world returned.

As reality resumed the five, now four, were surrounded by a new, yet more familiar chaos.

The first thing that any of them noticed was that Carlos had returned and collapsed. Whoever the man who had taken his place had been, there was no sign of him.

As a matter of fact, there was no sign of anything they had just experienced. All the gore and monster corpses were gone. All that remained were the confused students and staff behind the counters and the mess of tables and chairs.

Stephanie moved to help a student up. Reaching for her, the woman was about to take her hand until she saw Stephanie's face. She yanked her hand back and slid away, using the nearest chair to help herself up.

Stephanie couldn't help but feel hurt.

She decided to focus her efforts elsewhere.

"Where did Sheryl go?"

Meredith started looking around. "We didn't leave her … uh … there, did we?"

Ralph shook his head. "No, she disappeared in the middle of the attack."

Stephanie looked at Ralph incredulously. "Disappeared?"

He shrugged. "It looked like the corner of the wall sucked her up."

"What was that?" Meredith hissed.

Before any of them could attempt to answer, one of the faculty did for her.

"An earthquake, obviously," the server said.

"That," Stephanie said loudly, "was not an earthquake. I believe it is required that you remain on Earth to experience an earthquake."

The server looked confused.

The friends looked around at everyone and noticed that none of them seemed overly concerned. They straightened tables and chairs and picked up fallen bags and books but mostly went about their business as if nothing happened.

"And we are the only ones who remember what we just saw," Meredith said quietly. Almost instantly, she was typing into the notepad application on her phone.

"Is he alright?" Ralph knelt beside his roommate.

"He will be fine," a new voice said.

They each looked up to see one of the faculty standing over them. They had seen her around the administration building but none of them knew who she was. She was thin with silver hair, but she didn't look more than ten years older than any of the friends.

"We cannot talk now," the staff member said, "but we will soon. Right now, I'll let you know what I can."

"And you are?" Ralph set up the table that had been Carlos's shield and started putting the chairs around it. When he was done, he picked up his friend and stood there holding him while his friends sat. They all looked eagerly at the newcomer.

"I am Carol Berg," she said. "Administrative Assistant to the Dean."

"Great," Meredith was still shaking from the ordeal. "What the hell was that?"

Carol stayed standing. "The short version, and the short version is all that you're going to get right now, is that it was exactly what it looked like. Parts of the campus shifted to another reality."

"That is not possible," Stephanie said. "I would more likely believe a mass hallucination."

Carol nodded toward the nearest students, all of whom were returning to whatever they were doing before the event.

"The mass hallucination is the earthquake they all think they experienced. We have wards in place to keep the weirder stuff from affecting the general populace. You five are special. The wards won't affect you."

"How are we special?" Meredith blurted out.

"Wards?" Stephanie scoffed. "As in magic?"

Carol shook her head, ignoring Stephanie's skepticism to answer Meredith. "It is incredibly important that I not tell you that. You're on the right road, though, Ms. Johnson."

"What happened to our friends?" Ralph asked.

"The … voice … in Carlos's head manifested itself and saved you." Carol explained.

"What does that even mean?" Ralph demanded.

"Again, at the risk of our entire reality, I cannot tell you that either." She shrugged. "Carlos is going to need to discover that on his own."

"And Sheryl?" Meredith asked.

"She activated her gift and escaped," Carol smirked. "She's in her happy place."

"Quit being cryptic," Ralph said through gritted teeth. "You're saying you can't tell us anything and then you stand here telling us half things. Talk straight with us. What the hell just happened and where is Sheryl?"

"The campus had an unmooring incident," Carol explained. "We temporarily broke from reality. It happens, and for it to stop happening you all need to figure out a few other things on your own." She shrugged. "I want to tell you everything, but I cannot. The unmoorings will keep happening. Most of the school will remain unaware." She saw the annoyed expressions on their faces and added, "Look, the powers in charge of whatever is going on didn't want me telling you this much. I don't think that's fair and neither does the dean. You should at least be allowed to know that this will happen again, and you aren't going crazy."

"That reality, or whatever you want to call it, had monsters." Ralph's anger and adrenaline hadn't come down yet. "People got hurt. What's to stop this unmooring crap from killing us?"

Carol shrugged, "I am hoping that won't happen."

"Hope?" Meredith demanded. "We could die on some other world, and you hope that doesn't happen? Thanks for nothing."

"And Sheryl?" Stephanie repeated.

"You're all gifted," Carol said. "You know that, right? You all have something about you that makes you uniquely qualified to be in Arkham. Sheryl is no different. When her unique quality activated, it took her out of that hellscape and to her dorm room with a video game controller in her hand."

Carol's phone buzzed and she looked at it. "My time is up. Reality has fully reasserted itself and you're on your own again." She smiled. "That's alright, though. You just keep being you, going to classes, and doing the things that make you uniquely you and this should all work out."

She turned and walked out of the Student Union.

"What the hell was that?" Ralph mumbled.

"Let's get Carlos back to your room and check on Sheryl," Meredith said. Controlling the things she could control was her only recourse at this point.

They all started to march out of the Union, Ralph still carrying Carlos.

Stephanie slid in next to Meredith.

"Very well," she said. "It would seem that I need to know everything that I can regarding my psychotic uncle. You seem uniquely qualified to assist in that research. Would you mind helping me figure that out?"

Despite the crazy of everything that just happened, Meredith couldn't stop herself from grinning.

"Absolutely."

CHAPTER 6

They had only been through their first day of school and already the five students were exhausted.

While the rest of the campus spent the evening seemingly unaware of the events that transpired, Ralph, Stephanie, Sheryl, Meredith, and Carlos all struggled to find some form of understanding.

Ralph mostly stayed nearby for Carlos. First, it was a matter of monitoring Carlos's state while he rested on his bed. After that, it was a matter of trying to help Carlos remember what happened.

"We were about to have lunch," he explained, "then I was … somewhere else."

"Dinner," Ralph corrected. Sudden concern filled him for his friend's mental state.

"Whatever," Carlos waved it away. "All that weird stuff happened?"

Ralph nodded. "All of it," he shrugged, "and then some member of the faculty came up and basically told Meredith she was right and that was all she would tell us. Who was the old guy that … uh … you turned into?"

Carlos shook his head. "I don't know. I didn't pass out, I went somewhere else. There were yellow skies and weird creatures flying above. I was on another planet, but the ground was made from a smooth black material, like obsidian but it flexed under my weight. It didn't make any sense."

Sheryl's explanation for what happened to her was as useless to the students as Carlos's.

Meredith and Stephanie cornered her in the room when they got back. Sheryl was just sitting at the edge of her bed with a controller in her hand and playing a game. The only difference between then and whenever else they had seen her playing games was that she didn't seem to be paying it any attention. Her mind was focused on something else and somewhere else.

"Please," Meredith pleaded with her roommate. "Tell us what you know."

"I told you," Sheryl brought her attention back to the now and anger filled her face. "I don't know what happened. I was trying to focus on anything that was more real than whatever the hell that was. I figured I must have gone insane, so I tried to bring my mind back into focus. That was when I saw the dorm room through a hole in the corner that I was staring at." She shrugged. "Between hell and here, I choose here. I dove through the hole."

It was Stephanie's turn to shake her head. "Your sanity is perfectly fine. We were all in that place. We escaped soon after you left."

"Good," Sheryl turned her eyes away from her friends. "If I had known it was real, I wouldn't have left you behind."

"What made you think this wasn't real?" Meredith's voice was soft. "Has this happened before?"

Anger filled Sheryl's face. "It didn't look real, Meredith. What made you think that it was?"

After that, Sheryl shied away from the conversation every time it was brought up.

As the days progressed, so did classes and distractions that helped to hide the traumatic effect of being the only ones to remember the unmooring. Combined with Carlos and Sheryl mostly avoiding any mentions of the topic, it led to a generally peaceful first week.

Except for Stephanie.

When Stephanie wasn't at class or sitting silently in the corner of one of her friends' room while they talked or played games, she was obsessing.

Stephanie had two things to obsess about. The first was her heritage and the constant whispers happening around her wherever she went. They were almost non-existent when she was with her friends, mostly because Ralph had made it clear that he wouldn't put up with anything being said in their presence and the word spread quickly enough. Of course, Stephanie didn't always have Ralph right next to her and the leers from faculty and students was beginning to wear on her.

The second thing that she obsessed about was related to the first.

Alicia Halsey.

Alicia had made it her duty to know where Stephanie was at all times. After the first day it had been in subtle ways, but by the end of the week she could be seen running to catch up to Stephanie. She never got too close, but she was always there. As much as Stephanie obsessed about not being seen, Alicia obsessed over seeing her.

So, when Meredith texted Stephanie to come over first thing on their first Saturday morning as students at Miskatonic University, Stephanie leaped at the chance. Meredith might have discovered something about Herbert West that could be used to free her from the taint of his last name.

At the very least, Meredith could provide the social distraction needed to, for a while, forget about Alicia Halsey.

When Stephanie walked into Sheryl and Meredith's room, she was surprised to find that her friends weren't alone.

"Hey Steph," Meredith said. "This is Chris Gaines. A friend from my Anthropology 101 class."

He shook Stephanie's hand.

Sheryl broke from her game, pulling back her headphones and looking at Stephanie with a smirk. "Don't be shocked. It's true. He's real."

"What?" Stephanie said.

Chris shook his head. "It's a nineteen nineties Garth Brooks joke. Never mind."

Stephanie, still confused, chose to ignore the attempt at humor and Sheryl returned to her game.

Chris was taller than Stephanie, but not by more than an inch or two. He had shoulders broader than Carlos's and dark hair that reached down to touch them. Stephanie saw him as generally plain looking, yet he held himself confidently.

"What is going on?" Stephanie prodded.

Chris and Meredith were standing over her bed with papers and notebooks cast about all over it. Stephanie's structured mind struggled with the scene. It was a mess and Stephanie hated messes.

Meredith pointed to Chris. "Chris is a history buff and has spent a lot of his time producing a podcast that focuses on Arkham legends. He knows quite a bit about Herbert West."

Stephanie was angry. "Did you go and recruit more people to spread rumors about me, Meredith?"

Meredith held up her hands calmly. "No, I did not, and I was worried that you would see it this way." She pulled a notebook off the bed. It looked older than anything Stephanie had seen and as if it was held together by only Meredith's willpower. "This is my great-grandfather's journal. He did an episode on the surprising surge of cultists in the area in the early twentieth century and I asked him to help me figure out what my great-grandpa knew. Why was he killed?" She set the book down on the bed. "When I asked for his help he said," she stopped and waved at Chris.

"I said," he continued, "that it would have to wait until I was done with my notes on my Herbert West episode."

"Oh no," Stephanie's mood sank.

"Oh no?" Meredith was surprised by her friend's reaction. "We have an expert. You wanted information, and he has it all."

He shook his head, "I have a lot of it, I think. Not all."

"You're going to do an episode on Herbert West," Stephanie calmly explained, "and people will hear it, at which point the number of people staring at me and accusing me of century-old atrocities shall double."

Chris shook his head. "That's the opposite of what I have planned."

"Explain," Stephanie pressed.

"You're the only known descendant of Herbert," Chris said. "You're only getting looks and whispers from people because you look kind of like him and definitely act like him if the descriptions are accurate. If you went with me and helped me confirm some of the stories, or even if you just tagged along while we investigated his past, letting me interview you at the end, you will get the answers you're looking for, and I'll have an episode of my show that breaks records." Stephanie's unreadable expression made Chris keep going. "More importantly, it will humanize you. It is literally your only chance to get as many of the jerks at this school off your back as possible."

Stephanie looked at Meredith. Meredith's expression showed hope and excitement while Stephanie was only feeling fear and dread.

"Fine." She decided that she could use some hope and excitement.

"Great," Meredith turned back to the bed. "We have a ton of information to go over and a lot of it is probably not true at all, but," she yanked a piece of paper out from under a pile of more and held it up, "we have an address."

"To what?" Stephanie felt her heartbeat quicken.

"His house," Chris explained. "It's right against the Arkham Cemetery and has been mostly left alone since he owned it." He grabbed another paper that looked to be a photocopy of a signed document. "Do you know a Jacob West?"

"That is my father," Stephanie's dread grew.

Chris's face blanched just a little, "He's the still current owner. It looks like the place fell to the next of kin when Herbert disappeared and has just been passed on and on until today. Nobody ever tried to sell it."

"Wonderful," she said, "we can find where he buried all of the bodies."

"About that," Meredith said. "We don't think Herbert was actually a murderer."

Chris held up his hand. "I didn't say that. I just think he killed way fewer people than everyone thinks."

This intrigued Stephanie. "What do you mean?"

"There was an interview with a student who shared a class with Dr. West," Chris explained. "In the interview, the classmate claimed that West was obsessed with the processes that happen after death." He paused in his excitement as he explained. When he continued, he used air quotes. "Specifically, he wanted to know about 'reversing' those processes."

"My murder-happy uncle wanted to make a zombie army?"

Stephanie smirked and raised her eyebrow at Meredith. "Are you telling a joke?"

Meredith shrugged. "It fits. He lived next to the cemetery and everyone he was accused of killing had an obituary days before the assumed murder."

"Not everyone," Stephanie said.

"What?" Sheryl's voice surprised them all. It turned out that Stephanie's suspect past was entertaining enough that Sheryl had removed her headset minutes ago to listen in.

"Alicia's ancestor and the reason she and her entire family hate me was murdered by Dr. West," Stephanie explained. "I did my own research this week. Or at least as much as I could do with her following me everywhere." She jabbed at a picture on the bed of Dean of Medicine, Allen Halsey and Alicia's great-grandfather. "Dean Halsey was sick with typhoid and he was taken to Uncle Herb for treatment. Whatever treatment he gave to the dean led to his subsequent madness, several murders, and his eventual death."

It was Chris's turn to jab at things on the bed. He found a folder and pulled it up. Medical records from Arkham Asylum. "Except he didn't die for a long time," Chris said. "Without typhoid and with a healthy lifestyle, the dean probably had another twenty years in him. Instead, he was institutionalized for another fifty years before he died of blunt force trauma in a violent escape attempt. If he hadn't died there was nothing in his file to indicate that his life was nearing completion. Even at one hundred and twelve years old."

That made Stephanie balk. She grabbed the file and opened it, reading through it quickly to confirm that everything Chris said was true.

When she was done verifying the document, Stephanie returned her attention to Meredith.

"You are trying to convince me that Uncle Herb succeeded in reversing the effects of death?"

Meredith lifted her shoulders. "We don't know. He did something to Halsey. It could have just been an experimental cure for typhoid. Whatever it was, we won't know more until we do the foot work."

The foot work, of course, being going to the house that it turned out was entirely owned by Stephanie's dad and investigating anything that remained of Herbert West's life.

"You are aware that this is entirely ridiculous?" Stephanie asked them. "The dead do not rise and sometimes men are just evil."

"Women, too!" Sheryl shouted as she placed her headphones back on her head.

"Yes," Stephanie agreed. "Men and woman can just be evil, and the sweet dreams of George Romero are not stalking our streets."

"Not today," Chris countered with a huge smile. "But we all saw what happened earlier this week. Things aren't normal around here. Or do you guys think that was just an 'earthquake' too?"

Sheryl took her headphones off and all three girls stared at Chris.

"How do you know about that?" Meredith asked in a hushed voice.

"A lot of people know about that," Chris said like it was nothing. "Whatever magic the school uses doesn't work on everyone." He shivered. "I was playing racquetball, then the walls were gone and I was standing in a river of blood. There were," he closed his eyes and swallowed hard, "things in the water. I almost didn't make it out."

The girls had no idea what made someone exempt from the magic or how they were able to keep their memories of the event. It was somewhat relieving to have found someone else who could verify what happened to them.

Sheryl just stared at them. Pain stretched across her face. She had been denying what happened and questioning everything as another of her moments. Another time where her grip on reality had slipped and only overclocking her mind on math that was so advanced to her that it seemed fictional allowed her to fall back into the real world.

Someone that wasn't part of her world just agreed to seeing the same thing. Was it real? If it was, what did that say about her other 'events'?

"Very well," Stephanie was the first to break the prolonged silence. "Let us get to this West house."

Ralph had been to one practice that week. The rest were going to start in earnest on Sunday night and become a nightly thing. They needed to get caught up before their first game. Until then, he was focused on playing hard and ignoring Levi and his crew.

Carlos was reading something from what looked like an older book, some sort of eighties sci-fi thing, while he lay on his bed. It was still early in the morning and they both had yet to get any sort of motivation.

That being said, their biggest motivation was breakfast.

"Food?" Ralph asked, without looking up from the social media feed on his recently purchased mobile phone.

Carlos smiled and leaped to his feet. "I could eat a horse. Let's go."

"You're eating for two now," Ralph joked.

"Shut up," Carlos hadn't talked much about his replacement the other day, but that hadn't stopped Ralph from trying to make it a conversation.

"Do you think that guy who replaced you the other day was the same guy who puts ideas in your head about things?" Ralph asked when they got out into the quad.

Carlos shifted uncomfortably but surprised Ralph by answering. "I think so. I think he even has a name."

"A name? Like John, or something weird or alien?" Ralph was laughing.

Carlos shook his head. "I think he calls himself Randy. Maybe. Or something like that. He doesn't have a lot of opportunity to tell me much." He threw his hands up. "If he's telling me anything. I always thought it was just me knowing things. It's that knowing things that tells me he has a name."

"This would be a lot easier if he would just talk to you like a normal person," Ralph said.

Carlos silently agreed.

"Duck," Carlos suddenly said and then turned and pushed Ralph out of the way.

A football flew through the space where Ralph's head had been and hit the ground. Carlos went after it while Ralph spun in the direction that it came from.

Nate Peasley, another member of the team, and Levi came running up. Nate was a lanky guy with powerful looking arms and served as the Gaunts' quarterback.

"Sorry about that," he said, laughing. "I didn't see you there."

Levi glared at Nate, "What are you talking about?" He pointed back the way they had come. "It was a mile over my head." He saw Ralph. "Hey man, I know this looks bad, but I had nothing to do with this."

For whatever reason, Ralph believed him.

He didn't acknowledge Levi. Instead, he looked directly at Nate.

"What is it with you guys wanting to pick a fight with me?"

"Calm down, mermaid," Nate smirked and looked to Levi for backup. His teammate did not come to his assistance. "We're all on the same team, right?"

Carlos came up with the ball. "Really? We're doing this, again?"

Upon seeing Carlos, Levi tensed. "Come on, Nate. Let's just get the ball and get out of here."

"Is this the weirdo?" Nate asked. He stepped toward Carlos and tried to grab the ball. Carlos shifted his hand to the left a little and Nate's hand swiped past, catching nothing but air.

"Total weirdo," Carlos smiled. "Wanna see?"

"Yeah, show me." Nate was eager to see the party trick.

Carlos reached up to Nate's forehead. The football player flinched and stepped back.

"Do you want to see the trick?" Carlos asked.

Nate nodded and stepped closer. "No funny stuff."

"It is all funny stuff," Carlos's voice was different, but only Ralph noticed. It wasn't Carlos, it was the voice of the man Carlos had called Randy.

Laughing, Carlos pressed his palm to Nate's forehead.

Nate's mind propelled out of his body and across the stars. His spirit rode the waves of the crystalline fire before confusing the Yith of eons past and stopping the wind on the plateaus of Leng. Hyperborean soldiers worshipped his passing while gaseous Nerms residing in the Crawling Caves of the Dream Lands begged him to stay.

In the blink of an eye his mind saw what Carlos dreamed, and then returned to his head.

He fell over screaming.

CHAPTER 7

"What did you do to him?" Levi was shouting.

Carlos stepped back, mildly surprised at Nate Peasley's collapsed form. On the ground of the quad, Nate was twitching as drool came out of his mouth. All three of them stood around him, trying to figure out what to do.

"We don't have any time," Ralph said, smacking Carlos's arm a little harder than he intended. "People are going to see this. They are going to run over here."

"What do you want me to do about it?" Carlos said. "I don't even know what I did."

"Fix it or something," Levi hissed.

Carlos shook his head quickly. "I can't." His face went blank, and the other voice spoke through his mouth. "I am a child of the Silver Key. Only the Gate and its children can fix this." His eyes were focused entirely on Levi.

"What the hell does that mean?" Levi's concern over his friend was replaced by anger. Anger at what, Ralph had no idea. Much quieter, Levi added. "Don't."

Carlos was himself again. "I can't do it. It has to be you."

"Whatever you guys are talking about, hurry it up," Ralph whispered. He could see people already starting to look this way.

"If you know who I am," Levi was pleading with Carlos now, "then you know why I can't do this. I left Dunwich for good."

Carlos' eyes were filled with empathy toward his fellow student. "I don't know what just happened to him. He could be like this for a few minutes or for much longer. Either way, he won't be himself when he comes out of it."

Levi grabbed at his head and spun in place before coming

back around and jabbing his finger at Carlos.

"I need something from you if I am going to do this."

Without hesitation, Carlos said, "Anything."

Levi pointed at his friend on the ground. "I know Nate started this, but this is your fault. He wouldn't be like this if you hadn't touched him." Carlos didn't argue the point. "That means whatever happens to me is now your responsibility to deal with. You're the reason the Gate is here now and you're responsible for keeping the Gate closed."

Carlos nodded.

"Great," Ralph said. "Can we save the asshole now?"

Levi let out a long sigh and got to his knees. Placing one hand on Nate's chest and raising the other into the sky, he started chanting.

"Y' l' uln r'luh ot yog-sothoth. Nogephaii fahf shuggoth l' h' mgep y'nah." His voice was quiet but something in the ether heard Levi. The previously empty sky darkened, and clouds came in from every direction. Energy surged from the hand touching Nate's chest and suddenly the quarterback's eyes fluttered open.

Nate was confused and dazed. He looked from each of them and then to Levi.

"What happened? Did they hit me?"

Levi looked like he was burdened with hiding great pain. He was struggling to stand up as Nate climbed to his feet.

"No," Levi answered. "You just fell over. You said something about feeling dizzy."

Nate scooped up the football and nodded to Levi. "Let's get out of here."

"Go ahead. I'll catch up." When Nate didn't move, Levi added, "I need to tell the mermaid about practice."

Nate was still confused, but he was also still coming back from whatever fainting spell he thought he just had. Instead of staying and remaining the focus of everyone's scrutiny, he nodded agreement and left.

"What's happening to you?" Ralph asked.

"It doesn't matter," Levi said and glared at Carlos. "It's his problem now."

"Levi," Carlos said. "Before you go, you should know that this school is a magnet for the unusual. You aren't alone. You should try to remember that we are all, in one way or another, on the same team."

"Tell that to the guy who's mind you just tried to fry." Levi's words were harsh, but not wrong. Then, in a softer voice, he added, "This is only the beginning. I'll get your number from Ralph later. We'll have a lot to talk about."

Levi turned and followed after Nate. As he moved, it was obvious that he was beginning to feel better.

Ralph's eyes were wide, which was saying a lot for a guy from Innsmouth.

"What was that? What just happened?" His curiosity at another freak event on Miksatonic University grounds piled onto the rest in his already-overwhelmed head.

"I really just don't know." Carlos put his hands on his hips and stared after Levi before focusing on his friend. "That Gate and Key stuff was all Randy, but this time Randy left a little bit of information for me to sort through. Levi's real last name is Whatley. They forced his grandmother to be part of a ceremony that bound her offspring with Yog-Sothoth."

"Oh," Ralph had heard of the alien deity from his own religious leaders. More than just time and space, Yog-Sothoth was the beast who animated all of reality. He was also known as the Gate. In that way, part of the previous conversation made a little bit of sense.

Seeing that his friend understood, Carlos continued. "Like you, Levi doesn't appreciate the roles his family has thrust onto him. He wants out. He shunned it all to come here and by casting this one spell to reverse the damage that I accidentally caused, he made his family aware of his growing power, and worse."

"Worse?" Ralph asked.

Carlos nodded and turned toward the breakfast hall. "He had to take some of that power into himself. There's no telling what will happen to him now. He could begin to change, or his entire soul could be devoured by the days he already lived." Carlos shrugged. "We won't know for a while, and when we do it will be too late."

"And you just took responsibility for those changes?" Ralph pieced together.

"I had to," Carlos said more to himself than to Ralph. "I asked him to betray everything he was because I couldn't control Randy's sense of justice. Now Levi could become, well, horrible. That's on me." He sighed. "Besides, I think Randy has more secrets he can use that might help. This Gate and Key thing sounds important to some sort of balance."

Ralph scoffed. "No, it sounds like you stole it from Ghostbusters."

Stephanie's heart raced faster with every mile they drove toward the West place. She had texted her father a handful of times to ask if he knew anything about the house and details of what she should expect.

He only responded with admission that he knew about it and that since no one will buy it's just a hole that taxes go into.

Then he encouraged her to look for anything that might be worth something and to take lots of pictures.

Stephanie sighed. Her parents never understood her or the things that concerned her. This was just another example of that. She had access to the house of a serial killer that was part of their family. The only bit of fame that their family had ever known was as the terrors of an east coast town and all they wanted to know was if the house had any secrets that they could sell and be rid of.

On the opposite side of that spectrum was her driver, Meredith, and their new friend Chris. While Meredith tended to take all her notes in an app on her phone, Chris was a little more old-school and hadn't put down his wire-bound notebook since they left the campus. He had a million questions for Stephanie, but she didn't have any answers. In this, Chris was giving way more than he was getting.

Chris came across as some beach kid from California, but he knew way more about the local legend around Herbert West than the actual facts of the murders.

"What if we find his original laboratory?" Chris's voice was dripping with excitement.

"His laboratory?" Meredith asked. "When you say it like

that you make him sound like a mad scientist."

He raised his eyebrow at her. "He was attempting to cure death from a basement next to a cemetery. How does that not sound like a mad scientist."

"Mad or not," Stephanie said plainly, "if any of this is true, which I still doubt, then it is probable that we will find some sort of laboratory. Or at least whatever could remain of such experiments after a century of age and decay."

"She's a little morbid," Chris said.

"What you call my morbidity is only my factual look at the situation as we currently understand it." She let out a small sigh. "I am currently grappling with emotions of discovery and horror, both of which no one tends to successfully juggle. Therefore, my response is to fall deeper into my examination and understanding of facts."

"I'm sorry," Chris turned to look her in the eyes as he said it. "You're right. This has got to be hard to hear. The last thing you need is the local fanfiction about your recently rediscovered uncle."

"I'm sorry, too," Meredith added. "You asked for my help and now we're on some last second discovery mission."

"Neither of you has anything to apologize for," Stephanie said. "On the contrary. I am grateful for the stories as well as your excitement to investigate my past. I am only explaining my previously-described morbid tendencies. I do tend to come off as morbid or odd from time to time, but that is mostly as means to compartmentalize my incoming flow of information. If emotions are too much for me to deal with, as they sometimes are, I lock them down and force myself to confront the facts without emotional bias until those same facts can make the emotions more manageable." She shrugged. "It does not always work and might not be the best means of moving through the world, but it is what comes naturally to me."

"A lot of interviews from the time of the murders described Herbert the same way," Chris continued.

"I am increasingly concerned about our similarities." Meredith turned into the driveway for the place as Stephanie spoke.

"Just because you share some traits," Meredith countered, "doesn't mean anything. You have more differences than the handful of things you're noticing are the same."

Chris nodded in agreement. "Yes, definitely. Fiction or fact, every story states clearly that Herbert couldn't even socialize. On the contrary, you're downright pleasant."

Stephanie raised an eyebrow. She had never been referred to as sociable or pleasant before. While her demeanor tended to alienate people, her recent group of friends was obviously proof that Chris made a valid point.

"We're here," Meredith interrupted Stephanie's self-evaluation.

The driveway was paved, but not recently, and was incredibly short. Any of the landscaping that might have been seen as beautiful or more than just a 'front lawn' was a result of the proximity of the house to cemetery. The lawn was grown over with patches showing that it had been worked recently, but not diligently. The tall grass intermingled with plants that the three Miskatonic students hadn't seen before. Weeds grew into a century's worth of urban jungle that was only broken by the path from the driveway to the front door.

The path was made of stones, but that wasn't readily evident. With no one having taken care of the estate for so long, dirt and weeds had done their best to obscure the path, too.

The house was nothing to brag about. Being turn of the century, each of the students had expected the house to be classical in style. It was not. Instead, it was a simple two-story house with wood siding and graffiti marking up the walls. Most of the windows were knocked out and even the front porch was nothing more than a crumbling stone pad where one could rest a welcome mat.

Exiting the car, Chris and Meredith held back while Stephanie approached the door. Whether she was feeling intense emotions or simple curiosity, nothing changed the fact that this was her mission of discovery and neither wanted to take that from her.

"In our excitement," Stephanie said as she examined the door, "we might have forgotten to discuss how we plan to enter the house." She jiggled the handle to indicate the issue. "It is locked."

Chris shrugged. "If you're not against climbing through the broken windows, I'm sure that there's a way in. This is definitely a place that the local anybody uses to get high or drunk."

"Why?" Stephanie asked with her eyebrow raised.

"Broken windows," Meredith fell into her naturally investigative state, "people come here. The graffiti implies that they wanted to customize the place in some way." Then she shrugged. "Somebody visits."

Chris said, "Arkham is also a place where people try to avoid the weird or invite it in. Drugs and spooky places help with that."

Stephanie did not care outside of whether they might run into someone deep in the throes of a high. Even then, her curiosity in seeing what that might look like overrode her precautions.

"I do not fear the broken windows, and the dilapidated siding should allow simple enough purchase," she waved Meredith over. "Would you mind giving me a lift, please?"

Once all three of them had scrambled through the window just left of the front door, they took in their surroundings. The front room still had the remains of furniture. Even with those remains, the place was sparsely furnished. Whatever Herbert had been, it wasn't a home maker. There were two ancient chairs near the fireplace that had been pushed back to make room for a torn and soiled Scooby Doo sleeping bag. The fireplace mantel was covered in dust, and it was obvious from the shriveled roll of toilet paper sitting on top of the ash pile that there hadn't been a fire there in a long time.

The floorboards creaked with the threat of catastrophic failure as they moved deeper into the house. They migrated through the living room and into the kitchen where there was more of the same. A sink was filled with a nest of some sort, and a small table with no chairs was coated in an uneven mix of browns and reds inviting dark assumptions from Stephanie and her friends.

They continued like that, moving slowly from room to room

for the better part of the next half hour. The upstairs was even less decorated than the downstairs had been, and the stairs had to be taken slowly. Every step bowed in a way that felt like it was a matter of time before one of them fell through.

It was just as Stephanie was coming down the stairs when Chris gave a shout.

"Over here," his voice came from somewhere further back in the house.

Meredith joined Stephanie as they followed their newest friend's voice back through the kitchen and to an old icebox against the wall.

Except that it wasn't just an icebox. The icebox in question had been in place to hide the true nature of a secret entrance into an otherwise unknown basement.

Chris pointed at the floor. "I saw those scratches and wondered why someone would need to move this so much. I guess Herb didn't want people finding something downstairs."

Still cynical about the entire prospect, Stephanie countered, "Or we found the winter hideout for Arkham's vagrant population."

Meredith frowned. "It's your house. It is up to you if you want to go down there."

Stephanie knew as much and was using her negative emotions to hide her fear at what could be at the bottom of the stairs.

There weren't a lot of possibilities of what could be in a murderer's secret basement.

Chris and Meredith were visibly excited.

"Are you certain that you wouldn't like to go first?" Stephanie asked.

Chris held up his notebook. "I'm going to take notes on your reaction for my podcast."

Meredith shook her head. "No. It has to be you." She let out a nervous laugh. "That way if there's a bunch of zombies walking around down there you can let us know."

Stephanie frowned and squared her shoulders before ducking into the hole. "Very well, then. Let us see what Uncle Herbert kept in his murder hole."

The stairs leading down to the basement were obviously built as an addition to the house by someone, likely Herbert, who knew nothing about carpentry. They held her weight, but she wasn't about to start bouncing on them.

When Stephanie's feet touched the dry earth of the basement level, she brought up her phone and turned on the flashlight application.

The basement was about the same size as the kitchen and there were poorly built tables and several lanterns around the room. In the center was a surgery table that looked as if it would have barely fit through the hole she had just climbed down.

The back wall of the basement room was completely collapsed, and bones could be seen mixed in with the dirt and rocks. Stephanie aligned herself with where the front of the house was and determined that the collapsed back wall butted up to the cemetery.

The tables around the room had every sort of scientific apparatus that Herbert could have smuggled down there. Beakers, stethoscopes, microscopes, Bunsen burners, and books.

Lots of books.

Stephanie was entirely distracted, taking it all in, and was only reminded that she wasn't alone when Meredith's voice came down to her.

"Is it clear? Are you alive? Can we come down?"

"Uh," Stephanie forced herself back to the here and now. "Yes, all is clear."

Meredith and Chris climbed down the makeshift stairs and joined her as she began poring over the books. The books fell under only two categories. They were either medical texts that were likely cutting edge back in their day, or they were Herbert's journals.

Stephanie ignored the medical texts and was flipping pages through her estranged great uncle's journals before Meredith and Chris were in the room. They were a mixture of vitriolic reviews of his daily activities and interactions with the rest of the people of Arkham, especially those from the medical community at Miskatonic University, along with his notes and formulae for something he called the 'reagent.'

Her friends had taken to examining the equipment and the various other oddities scattered around.

"Be careful around the needles," Stephanie warned as Chris leaned over a set on the table closest to the caved-in wall.

Chris leaned away from them and gulped. "You don't think they still have whatever chemicals Herbert used on them, do you?"

Stephanie frowned. "No, I just don't think a podcaster should risk tetanus. Lock jaw would ruin your career."

He nodded, appreciating her concern.

"What's this?" Meredith called over her shoulder.

Stephanie scooped up the journals and put them into a large leather bag discolored by time and other things that she preferred not to try and label. She slung the strap over her shoulder and joined her friend.

Chris and Stephanie hovered over Meredith's shoulders to see what she had found. On the table against the wall across from where Stephanie had found her estranged uncle's journals had been a jar. It had a peeling label on it that was too aged to read, and the jar seemed to be sealed with wax.

Inside the jar was the most interesting discovery. A viscous chemical clung to the sides of the jar as Meredith tipped it.

"Where is the light coming from?" Chris asked.

"The chemical itself," Stephanie answered as a faint green light was emitted by the jar and onto each of their faces.

She was reminded of something from Herbert's journals. It had stuck out because he had underlined it and circled it.

I have discovered something oddly fascinating and perhaps a sign of my imminent success at finally creating a cure for death: The reagent GLOWS.

CHAPTER 8

Sheryl had opted out of joining her friends on their hunt for the West heritage and instead had headed back to her room. Everything just felt too big for her, and she wanted to do what she always did when things got too big and shrink into one of her video games.

The rules made sense there and she never seemed to black out or go to 'other' places when she played games. Life was simpler with a controller in her hand.

As she sat on her bed and booted up Wicked West, Sheryl couldn't stop shaking.

The flashes of other, terrifying, places had cursed her for as long as she could remember. Her family had come to despise her for what they called her 'episodes.' By the time she was in her teens, she had learned to hide her complete horror at whatever thing her mind had conjured up in the moment. She couldn't stop being afraid, but she could stop letting others see how afraid she was.

She could try to control their judgment.

Then the campus blipped out of existence, or maybe her episode bled into the reality that was the cafeteria and her friends, but that didn't make sense, either. They saw it. For the first time in her entire life someone else had seen her nightmare.

Except that's not how it felt.

Normally, she would be letting her mind drift and an equation or problem would surface in her mind and by the time she solved it she would be witnessing alien nightmares from whatever dark places her soul still had. This time, it was the solace of those numbers that woke her from the nightmare instead.

For whatever reason, Sheryl had been cursed with an exceptional understanding of mathematics. Even figuring out the correlation between her mindless computations and her episodes didn't stop her from naturally wanting to solve those kinds of puzzles. She had to actively keep her mind from not doing math. She had gotten into gaming, first, as a means of distracting her mind from the math that would send her head into other realities. Then she learned how much math and coding went into game development and decided to use her curse to her advantage.

The math scholarship got her into college, but hopefully math and games could cure her.

But Chris saw what her and her friends had, too. Someone she had never met had seen what had happened in her head, while being in an entirely different location.

Does that mean it didn't happen in her head?

Who even was this Chris guy? Was he just a figment that her fractured mind had created to convince her that she wasn't crazy? A means to advance her madness into full hysteria.

Her palms were sweating so badly that she almost dropped her controller when the two shotgun rounds went off to signify the game had finished loading her in.

Sheryl continued to try and calm down. She squeezed her eyes shut and tried to focus. Automatically, her mind drifted to math again. This time the equation looked entirely different to what she normally gave herself. Much like the last equation that seemed to wake her up, this one had the implication of something new and perhaps more to her liking. Instead of fighting it, she continued down the path.

The surge of exhaustion that ran through her snapped her from her hopes. That was always the feeling she would get right before one of her episodes. Sheryl squeezed her eyes tighter begging reality to have remained the same. Begging her sanity to stay in place.

These things always worked the same way. She couldn't keep her eyes shut because she had no idea what fake world her mind had conjured up. Those worlds had creatures or environments that could hurt her, or at least convince her to hurt herself. She wasn't sure how it worked, but she would sometimes come out of an episode with a weird bite more, or a burn where the nightmare world had rained on her. That was why she wasn't even sure if Chris was real. If her brain could convince her that these fictional worlds were hurting her than she couldn't trust anything anymore.

"What the hell did we just walk into?" Ralph's voice came from behind Sheryl.

Carlos's voice was filled with excitement. "The Wild West, obviously. Sheryl," he asked, "how did you do this?"

Confusion and terror mixed with hope and Sheryl opened her eyes.

Her dorm room was gone and in its place was an entirely different, yet recognizable world. She sat on an old porch at the front of a building. The bench she sat on was made from the same aged and rough wood that made up … well, everything. The sun warmed her face and blinded her as Sheryl took everything in. The porch faced a street made of mud. Horses marched back and forth in front of her, carrying riders somewhere else.

Ralph and Carlos stood next to her, absorbed entirely by the sight in front of them. All around them were cowboys, stable hands, farmers, and grocery clerks. A man with a badge and a thick Sam Elliott-style mustache leaned against the porch railing and waved a hand in front of Sheryl's face to get her attention.

"Never seen you," he snickered, "or those weird duds you have, in town before. Are you lost?"

Sheryl snapped out of her confusion. She knew exactly where she was, just not how she had arrived or how Ralph and Carlos were also there.

She ignored the Sheriff and turned to her friends.

"This is the town of Easter in the game Wicked West."

"How is that possible?" Carlos asked.

After years of avoiding uncomfortable situations with his family and friends back home, Ralph was more in tune with when people were getting impatient with him, and it was obvious that the Sheriff didn't like to be ignored.

"Sorry, sir," he stuck his hand out and shook the Sheriff's

hand. "We were just passing through." He looked to Sheryl and then to Carlos and tried to gauge just how different their clothing was to the rest of the scenery. "We're with ... the circus."

The Sheriff raised an eyebrow that was almost as thick as his mustache. "Circus? Easter doesn't get much in the way of entertainment around here. Maybe y'all can give us a peek tonight? I know the saloon could use some livening up."

Ralph forced a smile. "Of course. We'll see you there."

The Sheriff seemed pleased with the turn in the discussion and left to, Sheryl assumed, go and let everyone know about the circus show that would be happening that evening.

Sheryl stood and grabbed both of her friends' wrists before dragging them into the building they stood in front of.

"Haven't seen you around here before," said the doctor of the empty clinic she had stepped into. She continued to march past him and directly into the back room where she shut the door and slid the lock into place.

"I think I did this somehow," she made herself say.

"How?" Ralph asked.

Before she could attempt to explain, Carlos cut her off. "Like you did when you left the event the other day." His eyes glazed over a bit, "You have an innate ability to manipulate reality."

"What does that mean?" Sheryl shook him. "My entire life I thought that I was crazy or broken. I thought ..." she stopped suddenly, tears forming.

Carlos came back to himself. "The universe is a series of successful geometries with algorithms steering destiny and shaping physicality. Someone with an impossibly strong grasp of mathematics could manipulate it."

"So," Ralph asked, "she made this place? Did she make that place we all got pulled to before?"

Carlos shook his head. "She made this place, but that is a lot harder to do than to just move between points in reality. The woman from administration, Berg, said that the event in the cafeteria was real and when Sheryl left that, the place remained."

"It's the numbers," Sheryl wiped her eyes and explained. "When I want something and close my eyes, I focus on math to distract me. That was how I left the cafeteria." She waved her hands around, "Why did I conjure this, though, Carlos?"

"Carlos?" Carlos asked. "Oh, right. This body."

"Are you kidding me?" Ralph said. "Listen, Randy," he grabbed his friend by the collar, "I'm getting tired of your shit. Bring me my friend back, now."

Randy in Carlos's body pushed against Ralph and made the larger man let him go.

"My apologies for the Peasley boy, but I am not the enemy," Randy said. "I'm trying to help." He turned to Sheryl. "When we are afraid, we instinctively reach out with our minds for comfort and home. Most just think of a safe space or hum a tune of a song that gives them relief from memories. You, on the other hand, subconsciously activate your gift, which, it would seem, is to use math to manipulate the reality around you. In the cafeteria, that was to open a doorway to somewhere safe." He frowned. "Odd that it was your dorm room and not your actual home." He shook his head. "Never mind that. This," he ran his hand down the wood of the door, "was something different. In your moment of stress, you decided to dive into something familiar and comfortable. You obviously can't fit yourself into the ones and zeroes of a game, so you used your innate gift to parse out a piece of reality and reshape it into this safe space that perfectly mimics your game."

"How do you know all of this?" Sheryl's voice was just above a whisper. She couldn't verify what Randy was saying but for whatever reason his words just felt right.

"I was once a man," Randy explained. "I learned how to dream. Like what you do when you sleep, but I could stay there, I could travel the universe. I learned so much …" His eyes fell back into memories, mostly pleasant, and then he came back to himself. "I missed all of this, so I came back. The same, but different. I was no longer Randolph Carter but was instead Carlos Davies. Carlos has the power of dreams and as he learns my gift, I will become a silent partner in his life. Until then, I assist more directly."

Anger flashed over Ralph's face. "Tell that to Nate Peasley."

"Peasley was a pissant. He won't bother you again."

Sheryl believed Randy completely. Relief washed over her with realization.

"I'm not crazy?"

"No," Randy shook Carlos's head. "Just gifted."

"Or cursed," Ralph waved around to indicate the game they were still in. "We are still stuck in an ultra-violent take on the Old West."

"Sheryl can get us out," Randy said. "You know how you got here, and you know how you escaped the cafeteria. Focus and do it again."

"And don't leave us behind," Ralph added.

A loud drum sounded. It was two deep beats, but it echoed around them.

"What was that?" Ralph ran to the window to look see what was going on. "Men with guns are outside."

"We're wanted," Sheryl explained. "We are trespassing in the doctor's office."

"This is your world," Randy spoke calmly to Sheryl. "Your math created the place where you were safest. You have the power here."

Sheryl closed her eyes. When she opened them, she was wearing her gear from when she played the game on her console: a large-brimmed hat with a snakeskin band, and a multicolored poncho.

"What the hell?" Ralph jumped back.

"What's going on?" Carlos looked around, confused. "Randy?"

"Yes," Ralph stepped back from the door. "Take cover. I think Sheryl is going to fight the law."

She unlocked the door and stepped out into the rest of the doctor's office. The doctor was nowhere to be seen and men with guns and badges were running in one at a time through the front door while others tried shooting her through the window.

Quicker than she could have pretended to attempt in her home reality, Sheryl drew her pistol and hip-fired repeatedly. When her gun ran empty, she dropped it and drew another from her other holster and continued her barrage of bullets.

When she ran out of ammunition on that pistol, she was surrounded by dead bodies.

The double beat of the wanted drum went off again and she turned to face her companions.

"We should probably get out of here," Sheryl explained. "If this thing I've created works like the game, then they won't stop coming until they can't find me."

Carlos and Ralph both nodded enthusiastically in agreement.

"How do we do that?" Carlos asked.

"You were telling me how and then the drums went off," Sheryl shrugged. Then an idea struck her. She spun and went to the desk the doctor had been sitting at. Grabbing a pen and a sheaf of paper, Sheryl started scribbling numbers. Halfway down the page, she closed her eyes and kept writing.

A lawman stepped up to the window and aimed a rifle at the side of Sheryl's head and fired.

She was back on her bed and still holding her controller. The Wicked West game had a warning box across it that she had been disconnected for being idle for more than fifteen minutes.

Carlos and Ralph were standing where they had been when they had walked into the room.

"Math magic is a thing?" Carlos asked.

"Does Randy tell you nothing?" Frustration leaked from each of Ralph's words. He turned to Sheryl. "Are you good? You aren't going to drop me into the middle of Fortnite or something, are you?"

Sheryl shrugged. "Anxiety has always been my trigger, but," she held up her hand, still clutching the paper from the Wicked West world she had conjured, "I might be able to control it now."

Carlos was still shaking his head. "Math magic is a thing."

CHAPTER 9

Their dorms had a lounge near the front of the building with couches and a television to encourage students to socialize. This is where Stephanie, Meredith, and Chris found Carlos, Sheryl, and Ralph sitting and discussing everything they had just been through.

"What did he mean by dreams?" Carlos was asking his friends.

Sheryl shrugged. "He made it sound like he traveled places through his dreams."

"I got the feeling he was saying that you got your intuition thing from the dreams," Ralph added. "Like how you know so much about Levi and his family." He shrugged. "Maybe you talked to someone in your dreams, and they told you about him?"

Carlos frowned. "I just assumed that Randy was the one telling me those things."

Sheryl shook her head. "I think he's why you dream, or he has been helping you learn more about dreaming. I don't know. I wish he wasn't so vague all the time. It would be nice to know more about this math magic stuff."

"Math magic?" Stephanie asked as she came in.

"Sheryl's a wizard," Carlos's excitement was almost contagious.

"A wizard," Meredith's eyes lit up.

"Don't be ridiculous," Stephanie mumbled.

"Long story," Sheryl noticed the jar of glowing goop that Stephanie was cradling. "What is that?"

Silently kicking herself for suggesting a wizard as a ridiculous concept, Stephanie sheepishly said, "A reagent to reanimate the dead."

It was Carlos's turn to light up with excitement. "Reanimate the dead? And it glows? That's awesome."

"Who's the new guy?" Ralph asked.

"This is Chris," Meredith said. "He's helping us learn more about Stephanie's family."

"He has a podcast," Stephanie added.

"Great," Ralph wasn't sure how he was supposed to react to that and instead shook Chris's hand.

"He also remembers the thing that happened the other day in the cafeteria," Sheryl no longer exuded her earlier terror over what was real.

"You remember it?" Ralph asked. "I thought no one did."

Chris shrugged. "Some of us did."

"Not many," Meredith's curiosity found a new target and she found herself wondering why Chris hadn't been affected. "We were actively excluded from whatever wiped everyone's minds. Why weren't you?"

He shrugged again. "I really don't know."

Chris wasn't meeting her eyes.

Carlos clutched his head and screamed. He fell off the couch and began to seize. A gap in reality opened beneath him and closed once Carlos fell through.

"Where did he go?" Ralph shouted before anyone could move. "Where did Carlos go?"

Levi, some kid from the football team that they hadn't met yet, and Nate Peasley walked into the lounge at that moment.

"There you are," Peasley stomped toward Ralph who hadn't taken his eyes from the floor where his roommate had just been. "What did you do to me?"

Nate grabbed Ralph and pulled him to his feet before pushing him.

"Not now, Nate," Ralph growled.

"Especially not now," Stephanie spoke up. "I believe one of Ms. Berg's unmooring events is about to take place."

That cut through to Ralph. Last time he had to fight for his and his friend's lives. Now he might have to do that again all while wondering if his friend was still alive.

"Nate," Levi said, "don't do this."

"Do what?" Sheryl asked.

The new guy, shorter than Nate but not as short as Levi, spoke up then. "Your boys bumped into Peasley earlier. He thinks he is having blackouts, but we saw it. He stops what he's doing and then he starts speaking in tongues." The new guy was obviously bothered by this.

"I don't remember anything," Nate hissed. "I know you did something, though."

Ralph got to his feet and looked to his friends, "We have to find Carlos."

"No," Nate pushed Ralph again, "you need to get your ass kicked."

He moved to push Ralph a third time, but this time it was like he was hitting a wall. Ralph didn't move.

Fury radiated off Ralph as he turned and walked over to the brick wall of the lounge. He leaned against his forehead against it for a moment.

"Nate," Levi pleaded. "Let's leave him alone for now. Coach won't like a fight."

Nate ignored Levi and walked toward Ralph. The way Ralph was standing he could punch him in the back of the head and bounce his head off the wall. It seemed like a convenient way to start his payback.

Ralph didn't move from the wall as he pulled his arm back and punched the brick.

Chipped brick blasted in every direction as his fist impacted and pushed through the wall creating a small hole.

Nate stopped in his tracks and stared as Ralph brought his fist back. Turning, Ralph was smiling when he looked on Peasley.

"Where were we?" he asked. "Do you still want to fight?"

Nate grabbed at his friends and ran out of the lounge.

Levi didn't go anywhere.

"She said it was happening again?" Levi didn't seem at all phased by the Innsmouth native's display of his natural abilities.

"My name is Stephanie West," she frowned at Levi. "And yes. I believe that it has already started." She turned to Ralph. "Randy will protect him."

Ralph knew she was right. Randy could protect Carlos better than anyone, even a fishboy from Innsmouth, could.

Thunder, so loud that they all clutched their heads, shook the building.

"Come on," Chris shouted, grabbing Meredith's hand.

She didn't move.

"Where?" she asked.

"The library," Chris explained. "There's a forbidden texts section locked down. If we can get in there, maybe we can stop these things from happening."

Stephanie saw her friend's reaction and caught on to her concerns. It was suddenly occurring to them both how Chris was conveniently available when they needed answers and now that there was a crisis approaching, he wanted to take them off the field.

Except that Stephanie and Meredith didn't really know the rest of their group very well, either. Why were they both so hesitant to trust him now?

"I will go with you," Stephanie volunteered.

Chris was confused for a moment before nodding. "Alright, let's go."

Before they could leave, Meredith stopped and looked to the rest of her friends.

"Are you guys going to be alright?"

Sheryl nodded, "I've got Brick-Smasher with me. We'll be fine."

She accepted that and followed Chris and Stephanie out the door and into a hellscape.

"What do we do about Carlos?" Ralph asked.

Sheryl shrugged. "We don't even know where he is."

They both looked out the windows and watched a red liquid rain from the sky.

"What about your math magic thing?"

"Math magic?" Levi asked. "Like Nahab?"

"Like who?" Sheryl turned away from him.

"An old witch my family had to deal with once in a while," he frowned. "She claimed to travel between worlds through what she called 'geometries.' I think she was just crazy."

"Until a half an hour ago, I didn't even know I could do it," Sheryl explained. "Is she still around?"

Levi shook his head. "She was old as dirt when I was a kid. There's no way she would still be alive."

Sheryl felt her small flame of hope die. She returned her attention to Ralph. "I don't even know where he is or how I would get to him."

Ralph was clenching and unclenching his fists. "We have to do something." He turned and stomped toward the door. "Let's help Meredith and Stephanie in the library."

Surprisingly, Levi followed them out into the red rain.

The skies had turned to a tumult of fire and smoke, as if the earth had been turned upside down to roast over an inferno. A few more steps into the thick substance that was coming down and Levi yelled for them to stop.

"Look," he pointed up at the raging storm.

"Are those," Sheryl strained her eyes, "dragons?"

Carlos gasped when the pain finally resided. Dry grass brushed his face as he lifted his head. It was another full minute before Carlos climbed to his feet and took in his new surroundings.

Frozen plains stretched as far as his eyes could see. The only blemish to this frozen expanse of grass was the hill of black obsidian that stretched toward the sky. Stairs carved into the glass-like stone were covered in people falling over themselves to reach the top.

Carlos couldn't make out what was on the top but that wasn't his immediate concern. Instead, his mind registered that he should be cold and growing colder as the wind tore at his face and robbed him of his heat.

He wasn't.

"The elements won't affect you here," a voice from behind him said. "Not as you are now, anyway."

Carlos spun around and found a man standing in front of him. He was taller than Carlos by a few inches and gaunt. He didn't look unhealthy, just thinner than most. He wore a turtleneck shirt, much like Carlos was wearing, with a dark suit jacket over it. He knelt and swept his hand through the snow. It moved, but his hands came away dry.

"Randy," Carlos guessed.

The man shrugged as he stood back up. "Randolph Carter."

"Where are we?"

"We are dreamers, and we are where we dream to be," Randy said. He waved at the expanse before them. "This is Hyperborea. It is a world of dry cold that is very close, as these things go, to your world. Over the years, people have fallen through the cracks. Their descendants have populated this world and, as humans do, survived."

"Why can't I feel the cold?" Carlos asked. "I don't know what it means to be a 'dreamer.' Am I here, or is this just a dream?"

Randy frowned as he struggled to find the words. "I have been moving through the realms of the Dream Lands for over a hundred years in your world, and longer in my own experience, and the explanation is not an easy one. The most simplistic explanation is astral projection. Your mind can go anywhere, and you can control whether people see you or not." He bent and scooped up some snow and grass. "You can even interact with the world in many ways."

"My entire body came with me," Carlos countered.

"It is similar to astral projection," Randy rolled his eyes. "That was to give you an idea. In the Dream Lands, your body and your mind are not entirely separate entities. You also get all those intuitive flashes of information. Dreamers do not always need to go out in search of information as it can sometimes find them. Here," Randy turned and started to walk away, "come with me."

As Carlos made the choice to follow Randy, the world changed. They were in a bog, walking across the soft ground as steam rose from the patches of swamp. The time of day had changed as well. Whereas Hyperborea seemed to be experiencing noon, this new place was experiencing midnight.

Strewn across the bog were large fungal growths. Generally shaped like trees, these giant mushrooms had vines hanging from their tops that rhythmically dipped into the marsh.

"Now where are we?"

"Use your gift," Randy suggested. "Let the dream tell you."

Carlos looked around the area and tried to pull data from his surroundings and got nothing. When that didn't work, he broke from Randy's wake and approached one of the large fungal growths. He placed his hand against it and attempted to let his intuition tell him what was going on here.

"Is it a graveyard?" he asked.

"Very good." Randy followed Carlos to the tree. "Tell me more."

"We aren't in our time anymore," Carlos continued. "We are in the distant past." An image of a creature or thing appeared in his mind, and he fell back, landing in the mud, yet remaining dry.

The thing had been fungus and flesh, with crab-like pinchers and a bug head on a long neck. He had never seen anything so absolutely alien before.

"An ancient Yith," Randy explained. "The ideal organism for traversing the cosmos and time. Of course, at this point they had yet to have their minds supplanted by the species that would give them that name."

Carlos got to his feet as reality changed again. Large insects that looked like bees with heads on both ends of their bodies crawled everywhere. They were passing both around and through the pair of dreamers as they worked to keep their enormous hive functioning.

"How does this help me, or my friends, now?" Carlos was excited to finally have answers to some of his major questions throughout life, but he didn't know what good any of it could do.

"Every major revelation, religious text, the Necronomicon, the Book of Eibon, the internet, were all brought into existence by dreamers like us. At this point, you have been gone from your world and your friends for less than a full second, yet we have traversed three worlds, different timelines, and experienced at least fifteen minutes of personal time. This is the information superhighway the internet dreamed of being." Randy sat down on a larva the size of a futon. "Learning how to use it will determine how you use it. I made a choice to go beyond the Gate and learn that final knowledge. I became more, much more, but

I can no longer move through the world of man. I could have chosen to remain in my world, dipping my toes into this font of knowledge. I would have lived out my normal life, transcending human awareness, while staying tied to my physical form and dying at a ripe old age of 89." Randy winked. "I checked. Every parallel version of myself dies at 89." He straightened back up and continued. "Or I could have chosen to continue as a man of dream and never gone through the gate. How far you go, what you do with this, is entirely up to you."

"All information?"

Randy frowned. "Yes, but are you wise enough yet to understand that not all things should be known?"

"What does that mean?" Carlos asked. "You seem normal, undamaged, and you passed through what sounds like the 'point of no return.' How could being aware be bad?"

Randy stood and the hive vanished. They stood in stark black, nothing around them except for unattainable void.

"Were you not listening?" Randy was angry. "I cannot ever return to my mortal form simply because of what I learned beyond the gate. My knowledge in your reality would shatter my soul and shred the flesh from my body. I would become an infectious puddle whose knowledge would be a curse on the land. Simply returning to Arkham in my true form would result in the extinction of all life on your planet in a matter of days." Randy calmed. "And that is only the threat of the gate. Some worlds have protections from dreamers, some people live entirely in the Dream Lands. Everything has a cost."

"Say that I am not wise enough to know which information will cost me," Carlos's own anger was starting to flare. He didn't normally show it, but in the Dream Lands emotions were manifest. "Say that I only just discovered that I was a dreamer. How do I learn?"

Randy smiled. "Time is different here. There is much I can teach you before you return."

The library at Miskatonic University had a handful of people huddled in a corner toward the checkout desk.

Chris was leading the way when Meredith and Stephanie

saw what they were hiding from.

The floor of the library had turned into a funnel, angled down in the center with a hole that consisted of a series of bladed tentacles thrashing about to gain purchase anything they could.

As they came into the room, the friends had to slow down, so as not to slide and get grabbed by the alien being.

"We need the forbidden tomes," Chris said before starting around the outside of the funnel toward the back of the library.

"Why?" Meredith demanded. "If there is a book that can counter this, why hasn't the school already used it?"

"They are too afraid," Chris countered as he climbed over tables and chairs toward the back. Out of a complete lack of knowing what to do, Stephanie and Meredith continued to follow him. "They fear making it worse, but we can make it better."

"How did you meet him?" Stephanie asked her friend.

"Here," Meredith said. "I was looking into our names on the computer here and suddenly he was asking me about you."

"And then?" Stephanie demanded.

"We went and found you." Meredith realized that she hadn't properly vetted this new friend.

Stephanie stopped, jumped to the slanted ground, and grabbed Meredith before she could hop to the next table.

Then she kicked it.

Chris fell flat on the surface of the table as it started to slide down the funnel and toward the horrific creature. Stephanie grabbed the edge with one hand, obviously struggling to stop the slide of the table.

"Who are you?" she demanded of Chris.

"Dragons?" Ralph shouted as the wind and red rain picked up in violence and volume. "What can we do about dragons?"

"The dragons aren't attacking," Levi pointed, "but the rain is."

Several of the students getting hit by the rain were suddenly screaming and grabbing at their faces. Almost as quickly as the screaming started it stopped and each of them was writhing in rage. Their eyes were as red as whatever the rain was. They each took off in different directions and began attacking students.

"We have to stop them," Sheryl said.

Ralph grabbed his phone and tossed it to her. "There's calculator on that. Do you think you could math us back to our own reality?"

Sheryl tossed the phone back. "I think the math has to be in my head." She held up the game controller that she brought with her. "I think this is all that I need." Sheryl closed her eyes and tightened her grip on her controller.

"What do we do?" Levi asked Ralph.

Ralph shrugged. "Can you do anything that won't require Carlos to, um, fix you?"

Levi frowned. "I think we're beyond worrying about that right now."

"Then we stop the other students from fighting each other." Ralph squared off against Levi. "I need you to hit me."

"Hit you?" The request surprised Levi.

"Obviously, you are less like them and more like me," Ralph nodded. "I need to know how hard you hit."

A grin spread across Levi's face. "As much as I would enjoy hitting you, no." He nodded back toward the dorms. "Let's just say that if I had punched that wall, it would have come down."

His voice and the look on his face told Ralph that Levi wasn't just posturing for bragging rights.

He was strong.

Knowing where the other stood, they each broke up and ran after some of the rabid kids, doing their best to keep Sheryl in their sights while they did.

Sheryl struggled with her own concerns. She needed to figure out how to do that trick with her math magic that pulled her back to her dorm room the last time this kind of event happened, but she needed to do it to the entire campus.

Figures flew through her mind as she tried to focus her thoughts on the world around her. Her grip tightened on the video game controller and her thumbs found their places of comfort on the buttons. The equation presented itself before her. It was massive. This wasn't going to be a quick solution.

For assistance, she pulled out her own cellphone and opened

the calculator application. Her brain could handle the individual calculations required to move a person through space and time but moving all of campus was going to take a lot of work.

Ralph grabbed the young woman trying to gnaw the throat out of a band student and tossed her away.

He looked back to where Levi had been doing something similar and was greeted with an impressive sight. Levi had been attacked by one of the dragons. Up close, they weren't dragons in the traditional sense. Instead of lizards with wings, only their torsos had the lizard look. Four lizard legs and a lizard neck led to a large squid head with no eyes and a gaping maw of razor-sharp teeth. The wings were those of a dragonfly and the gusts of wind coming from them scattered several other students. Levi was gripping several of the thing's face tentacles while its front legs swung for his belly.

Ralph quickly grabbed the same woman he had just pulled off the band student and threw her in the direction with the least number of students and faculty. He wasn't sure what the plan had been before, but if dragons were entering the fight, he would need to rely on the people around him to handle the possessed folks.

He ran to Levi's aid.

"What are you doing?" Chris was screaming as he clutched the edges of the table. It was obvious that Stephanie was struggling to hold the table still. Meredith stepped up and grabbed the edge, but with the angle and the weight on the table she wasn't much help.

Chris only had moments before the tentacled monster devoured him.

"Unless you wish to be devoured by the almighty Sarlacc," Stephanie said, "then I suggest that you tell me who you are and what you are really after."

"Sarlacc?" Meredith eyed her friend.

"I am not naïve to popular culture," Stephanie grunted, "and now is not the time."

Chris let out a small chuckle. "I am part of a group that has been following Meredith."

"What?" Meredith's face turned red with anger. "The cult that has been after my family?"

"Your essence was tainted by your grandfather's vision," Chris was trying to climb up the table toward them. "It was always believed that the taint would lead one of you out of hiding and to Arkham."

"Why?" Meredith demanded. "Why would that happen?"

"Arkham holds the book. The Necronomicon. It can be used, with the proper sacrifice, to awake the sleeping god."

Stephanie's grip was slipping. "And Meredith is that sacrifice?"

"She is strong in the scent of that place," Chris explained. "The madness that attaches itself to blood only existed in her grandfather. It was a mistake to kill him when we could have used him, but he was going to talk. When we discovered that he had family, it only made sense to eliminate him and seek the others."

"For clarity," Stephanie said, "you tricked Meredith into believing you were her friend so that she would help you steal a book you would use to sacrifice her and raise this," she winced as her grip slipped some more, "sleeping god, correct?"

Chris smiled. "Now that we found her, it doesn't have to be Meredith. You have a brother, don't you? We could—"

"I don't think so," Stephanie said, and gave the table a push.

The tentacled maw at the center of the library didn't hesitate to grab the table and crush it and Chris into a pulpy mess.

"We need to get back to the others." Stephanie grabbed Meredith's hand and dragged her back toward the door.

CHAPTER 10

Carlos gasped as they stopped spinning.

"That was a longer journey than most, although not in the physical sense," he could hear Randy saying. "Distance is different in the Dream Lands. It isn't so much about how far away something is, as it is about how difficult it is for you to open your mind to it."

By this point, Carlos knew better than to ask where they were. He opened his mind and let the dreams fill him. Sand whipped around him as the wind had its own dreams of knocking over the non-corporeal entities.

What was this place?

No.

"This is home?"

Randy nodded. "Yes and no. Mostly yes, but a little bit of no."

"This is home if something changes?" Carlos was still feeling out what the dreams were giving him.

"This is your home and many roads lead to this point," Randy attempted to explain. "Some of them are even favorable, as this could be a distant point in time." As he said it, the sun shifted from the bright yellow ball that Carlos knew to a smaller blue orb of light. "This is the world when it is introduced to the alien notion of the Great Old Ones, the Elder Things, or the—" he gargled out a noise that didn't sound anything like words Carlos had heard before.

The dream translated it for him, and he was afraid.

"Many in your world are already aware of what lives beyond the border of the veil of dreams, but none have yet succeeded in bringing down that veil." Randy sat down in the dirt. "You and your friends are living in a moment that will likely bring down the first of many pillars holding up the veil."

"The veil must remain," Carlos couldn't stop himself from saying it.

"Yes," Randy agreed. "It must. When the others cross into your world, they will devour everything you know and leave a barren husk behind. If it happens after an enlightenment or evolutionary advance, humanity can survive, but to happen now, at your moment, would catch the world unprepared."

Another dream came to Carlos then and he found himself in the Miskatonic University Library. He watched as Stephanie came to her unfortunate conclusion and made a potentially hazardous choice.

"Right now," Randy said from behind him, "your mind is beginning to realize that there is a much bigger picture. When others see just the thread, you are starting to see that there is, or could be, a tapestry. Your old self is asking how Stephanie could have committed such a heinous act while also knowing that she had no other choice. The Carlos of Dreams knows better. He is telling you that that boy's path ended in someone's death, and that this is the best possible course that would have led to the least amount of bloodshed," he paused before adding, "for now."

"How could she?" Carlos didn't know if he was asking Randy, himself, or the universe of dreams.

"This does not taint her as you might suspect," Randy attempted to explain. "She inherited many things from her horrid ancestry. Those genetics have always been able to see a little more of the tapestry than anyone else, through sheer force of will. She could see that not every choice is black and white." A hint of a smile touched Randy's face. "Unlike her unfortunately famous uncle, she is also plagued by conscience. She will face the hard choices, but she will not escape their cost."

"Ancestry?" Carlos asked. "Her uncle?" Dreams and conversations resurfaced in his memory. "Herbert West." He gasped as the rest hit him and he knew the truth of the contents of the leather bag slung over her shoulder.

"The reanimator."

Stephanie threw up as soon as they were outside of the library.

"You killed him," Meredith was saying.

"I am aware," Stephanie replied when she was done spitting. Tears were fogging up her glasses. "It is not something that I wished to do."

"Then why did you do it?" Meredith screamed, unable to hide her own tears.

Stephanie looked at her friend. "There was little else in the way of options." She stood and used the logic behind her choice to ground her back in the now. "He had already sworn that you were to die. More than likely before that happened, I would meet an untimely accident. Nothing would stand between him and his cult's drive for that book." She wiped her eyes and then pulled a napkin from lunch out of her pants pocket to wipe her mouth. Pulling another out, she handed it to Meredith. "I was not going to sit idly by and watch as he murdered my friend."

Meredith didn't know how to feel, and the napkin was soaked by the red rain before she could wipe her own eyes.

She grabbed Stephanie and pulled her into a tight hug.

"I don't know that it was the right choice," Meredith whispered into Stephanie's hair as they embraced, "but thank you for making it for me."

Stephanie let the hug linger before pulling herself away and straightening her shirt.

"Yes," she said as if nothing in the last ten minutes had happened. "In the spirit of that choice, let us find and assist our friends as best we can."

"The red skies," Carlos was saying, standing beside Stephanie and Meredith as they embraced, "this is another event like in the Student Union. The school has become untethered from reality." He stated the last bit with confidence, trusting the knowledge that the dreams imparted to him.

Randy nodded. "This is one of those events, yes. It will not be the last." He took a deep breath, and they were back in the dust and wind of the barren Earth.

"What are you trying to do?" Carlos demanded. "Are you

trying to 'Wonderful Life' me into changing the future? Are you inviting me to escape an inescapable nightmare by joining you in the Dream Lands?" He threw his hands up. "What is the point of all this?"

"The point," Randy and Carlos were suddenly standing in what the dreams told Carlos was a library larger than the moon, "is to show you what this gift of yours is capable of."

The walls and shelves were all reminiscent of any other library, yet instead of books filed neatly away on them there were only blinking lights. Alien creatures, some unfathomable to even Carlos's open mind, approached the lights and touched them, flooding their minds with whatever data they had been searching for. Silver and stone greys toned everything in the room, even the lighting, and no seats were visible.

"If knowledge is power, then the power of dreams is omnipotence," Randy explained. "Your friends are partaking in an event that could change the course of your world's history. One of many events that will, unfortunately, plague your life if you and they make it through this one." He sighed. "And more events will always be around the corner for the rest of time, but you now have access to the most powerful search engine in the history of the world."

They were back in the red rains on the grounds of Miskatonic University.

"It is a tool with infinite uses," Randy was no longer visible, but his voice was just as loud. "You can use it to escape, to aid, to prepare, to provide comfort, and to change the course of reality, but you must always be looking to broaden your understanding of the universe so that your choices don't make things worse."

His warning struck Carlos differently than Randolph Carter had likely intended.

"Is that why you're not part of this world anymore?" Carlos asked the air. "You keep calling it my world. You said you can't come back once you went through the gate and you imply that you went through the gate for the ultimate understanding, but I don't know that I believe you. All this information at your fingertips and the vastness of humanity needing every bit of help that anyone can provide, and you found the largest door you could and ran through it." He laughed, but there was no humor in his voice. Only irony and understanding. "You escaped the burden for personal enlightenment and now you're back. Why? Out of guilt."

Silence answered Carlos as he stood there, watching alien dragons attempt to tear apart the campus and kill his new friends.

Finally, Randy's voice answered.

"I did run. Out of greed for more. An eternity in the Dream Lands taught me to feel guilty for that decision." He paused. "I came back out of that guilt to do for you what no one ever did for me."

"What's that?" the student demanded.

"Show you that greed isn't your only choice. Be a student, a friend, a dreamer, even. Don't go through the gate. Not yet anyway. Wait and enjoy the life you live. Perhaps save the world while you're at it." Almost too quietly to hear, Randy added, "Perhaps in showing you what you can do, I can find my own redemption."

The rain passed through Carlos as he walked toward Ralph. His roommate was struggling to stop a dragon thing from eating a pair of terrified students. He held it by its hind legs as it alternated between snapping at him and dragging itself forward to snap at the two snacks.

When Carlos was directly beside his friend and the dragon thing, he reached out and placed his hand on it. The dragon fell into the Dream Lands. Carlos hoped that this monster of fire and blood would end up in Hyperborea, but he had nowhere near the amount of control over his newly-explained gift that he hoped he would. Instead, he settled for pushing the dragon to 'not here.'

As the dragon shifted out of the current reality, Carlos shifted into it, essentially taking its place.

Ralph fell to the ground and red mud as the force he had been struggling against vanished. Levi, whom Carlos hadn't realized had been on top of the beast, fell flat with a splat at least ten feet to the ground. He looked around, confused as he tried to figure out what had just happened.

Ralph looked up from the ground and saw Carlos standing there, already drenched in the red rain. He questioned nothing, jumping to his feet and pulling his friend into a tight hug.

"Where the hell did you go?" he demanded.

Carlos sighed. "Randy took me on a walkabout. I learned a few things."

"Like what?" Ralph asked while Levi helped the other two students to their feet before joining them.

"Mostly that Randy is an omnipotent coward," he smirked, "and how to get a little bit more information from my intuition when we need it." It wasn't the full story, but they had enough going on that it would do for now. "Stephanie and Meredith are on their way here."

Ralph didn't question how Carlos knew that or if it was even true. His friend had been reliable in his information before.

Levi and Carlos acknowledged each other with a nod, each choosing to avoid the conversation of the earlier issue with Peasley.

With the dragons mostly remaining hundreds of feet above their heads and almost everyone having made it inside at this point, they made their way back toward where Sheryl sat in the rain. She was soaked in the red rain, her eyes closed and hands gripping the game controller.

Stephanie and Meredith joined them just as they reached Sheryl.

"Now what do we do?" Ralph asked.

"I think," Carlos furrowed his brow, "this is where I help Sheryl."

He looked at his hand, wondering if this was something he was capable of. Randy had been his guide, but most of this power of dreams stuff came with intuition, not explanation.

Trusting his intuition, he touched Sheryl's hand.

They stood in a house that seemed to be decorated by a grandmother stuck in the fashion sense of the nineteen seventies. The curtains were closed and no light was coming in, so Carlos had no idea if it was day or night. He saw doilies and bright orange knitwork draped over the furniture. Against the wall was a console television with a VCR on top. He had no idea

where he was, but that didn't matter. Sheryl is what mattered.
"Where are we?" she asked.
"The Dream Lands," Carlos smirked. "I think so, anyway. It pulled this from one of us. It's a place of comfort and control."
"I don't recognize it," she said, completely ignoring that he pulled her into a weird adjacent reality. Then again, she had already shown that she could do something similar, so perhaps nothing surprised her anymore.
"Weird," Carlos looked around. "I don't either." He shook his head. "That doesn't matter. We're here so that I can provide you anything you might need to put reality back to the way it was."
"Years," she grabbed her face and let out a moan of frustration. "I need years. The math for this is too big. I can see all of the equations and know what I need to do, but to solve it I need more time than we probably have."
"Well," Carlos's smirk broadened into a full grin, "I think I might be able to help with that."
To the outside group still in whatever reality plagued them and not in the Dream Lands solving all the world's problems with math, it looked like Carlos touched Sheryl's hand, the rain stopped, and they opened their eyes. They both gulped at the air as if they hadn't breathed in minutes.
Looking up, they watched as the skies shifted back to the greys and blues that Arkham was accustomed to. The red that soaked everything remained, but the rain itself was replaced by clear skies.
Reality had reasserted itself.
"Did you guys do that?" Ralph asked Sheryl and Carlos.
Carlos nodded. "It wasn't easy." His face showed exhaustion.
"How did we do that?" Sheryl asked him. "We were in there for," she paused as if the scene around her denied all that she understood, "years."
"Time is different in the Dream Lands," was all that Carlos gave by way of an answer. If he wanted to explain further, he couldn't. He only knew what he did from his brief conversation across time with Randy.
Levi fell to the ground, clutching his gut.

"Carlos," Ralph called out to his roommate.

Carlos leaped to his feet and went to Levi's side. Levi groaned and took on a sickly green coloring.

"It's part of his metamorphosis," Carlos said.

"His what?" Meredith's eyes were wide.

"I don't know," Carlos answered, hoping that his dreams would give him some idea of what to do next. "We need to get him back to his room." He turned to Ralph, who had started to help Carlos lift Levi to his feet. "You go with them. You guys can fill me in when you get back."

"Go with who?" Ralph asked.

"I think," a tall man with dark hair and a brown suit jacket surprised them all by standing just outside their circle, "Mr. Davies is referring to us."

Beside him stood the administrative assistant from earlier.

"There is much to tell you and we don't really know how much time we have left."

CHAPTER 11

The group of friends followed Dean Ward and Ms. Berg as they led to the administrative building. No one said anything as the red liquid evaporated from the grounds and their clothing like it had never been there. It was another example of the reality they were home to reasserting its influence.

In silence, they climbed into an elevator and rode three floors up. Meredith didn't want to be more than an arm's length away from Stephanie, who was clutching her stained leather satchel. Ralph's hands were deep in his pockets as he tried to shrink his large frame. All of them were tired.

They had all just experienced another unmooring event that would have exhausted anyone. Yet, none of them were as tired as Sheryl, who leaned against the elevator wall. She began to wobble until Ralph put his arm around her. Not even thinking about it, she let him hold her up.

When the door finally opened, it was to a hallway that looked as old as the campus was. Carol finally broke the silence when they saw the doors open.

"The campus received a facelift about fifteen years ago," she explained, to anyone who was paying attention. "The dean's office, as well as mine, have been on different floors over the years."

"Carol's job has always been more of a babysitter role," Dean Ward explained. "She keeps the dean accountable while also managing the type of protections that have stopped the campus from spinning off into a different reality."

"Fifteen years?" Stephanie asked. Carol didn't look much older than her early thirties. "Did you get your position directly after graduating?"

The dean raised an eyebrow at Ms. Berg and left her to answer the question.

"You, of all people," Carol said softly, "are aware that not everything, or everyone, here is exactly as they seem." She let that hang in the air as they migrated through a large wooden door and into an office decorated more as a turn-of-the-century library.

Bookshelves lined the walls anywhere there weren't windows. The floor was hardwood with a weathered rug in the center. Near the far wall and windows overlooking the campus was a broad desk made of wood. A couch that matched the greys of the rest of the building's décor, and not the office it was in, was situated directly in front of the desk.

"As you can likely tell," the dean explained, "the couch was brought in for you and this meeting. Please," he waved toward the furniture, "have a seat."

Ralph opted to remain standing while his friends collapsed on the couch.

Carol pulled a straight back chair closer to the desk so that she could face the dean and the students with minimal effort.

"Obviously," Dean Ward said once everyone was seated and looking mostly comfortable, "something terrifying is happening to the campus." He spread his hands wide. "The clinical explanation is that Miskatonic University was designed as a lock on the cage that is our reality. That lock is breaking. These unmooring incidents are cracks, other realities leaking in or our reality leaking out. This cage, to continue the metaphor, is for our protection. Outside forces have sought to bring things into our reality that our reality is not designed for."

"What do you mean by, 'not designed for?'" Stephanie asked. "What happens if these 'things' get through?"

"It entirely depends on which 'thing' makes it through," Ward said. "Some might devour everything and leave our entire reality a barren husk. Another might infiltrate different cultures and create madness or chaos. In the worst-case scenario—"

"Those aren't worst-case?" Ralph interrupted.

"In the worst-case scenario," the dean continued, "their very existence could stop the mechanism of our reality from working.

A stick in the spokes, a wrench in the engine. Everything stops, explodes, and we are not even forgotten. We just cease to be."

Stephanie was frowning. "Obviously, that won't happen."

"Why is that, Ms. West?" he decided to see where her acute mental faculties were taking her.

"The destruction of our reality, and thus time as we know it," Stephanie explained, "would eliminate our ever existing. This is a fundamental case of existence. I think, therefore I am. We exist, therefore all of time and space must not cease to ever exist."

"Very astute," the dean commended her. "Unfortunately, that does not take into account the effect of other realities on our own. It is highly likely, if the studies are correct, that we exist within a dream in the corner of the impossible mind of an ancient and unknowable beast. If that is the case, then if he wakes, or if our reality goes away, does that mean we never existed?" He spread his hands again, "Do we even exist now?"

"You are being ridiculous," Stephanie dismissed him.

"Either way," the dean continued, mildly entertained at having derailed the West girl, "the fact we have unmooring events shows that the protections we have in place are no longer capable of holding back those outside forces."

"You mean people," Meredith pieced together. "You mean there are people trying to bring things over here and it could kill us all."

"Yes," the dean admitted. "You met one of them. The recently missing Christopher Gaines. A fictional name to cover up that he was here on behalf of the Cult of Cthulhu to open the door to returning the Old One to our reality."

Stephanie felt sick at the implication that the dean knew Chris was missing already. She looked to Meredith and saw that her pale face hadn't missed it either.

"Neither of you need concern yourself with him, though," he added. "It is my understanding that while his society is still operating on the belief that they can open the door for their dread lord, that he has been removed from the board."

This shared knowledge did not, in fact, calm either of the girls down.

"What does any of this have to do with us?" Sheryl asked.

"That is where Ms. Berg comes in," the dean waved toward his administrative assistant. "We have a plan in place, and it involves this," he placed his hand on an old leather journal. "She can better explain your role in all of this than I can. She was there."

They all turned their focus to the secretary sitting beside them.

"Before I explain everything, and your role in it, you need to understand something about myself and my own role within the campus. Remove that impatient look, Ms. West. My time is valuable to me, and I would not waste it on small talk.

"Simply put, I am unnaturally, or perhaps supernaturally, long-lived. That does not mean that I am just old. It means that I am very, very old. By any measure of the natural human lifespan, I am historic. Accept that as fact now, because that's the easiest part of this story to swallow.

"Very well. With that out of the way, I can dive to the heart of the matter.

"The two events you have experienced are by no means the first unmooring incidents. They are becoming more frequent, though. For that reason, all our predictions have been moved up to accommodate.

"The first unmooring event that I witnessed was in 1943. Dean Doran was many things. Aloof, stubborn, prone to aggressive outbursts, and likely insane. He was also my friend.

"The semester had only just broke, and he had started to become restless. To understand Andrew, you had to know that he was not in his element unless he was in a shady alley, three men, or half-men, about to kill him and the fate of all humanity weighing on his success. He was a man of action and being dean to a prestigious school only fulfilled his needs some of the time.

"His assistant had only just passed, and he was still getting acquainted with his replacement. He was entirely outside of his comfort zone.

"The unmooring event knocked us all for a loop. The world vanished and we ceased to be corporeal beings. We were bursts of sentient light in an endless void of greys.

"I don't know what he did or how, he was just energy, but Andrew, Dean Doran that is, somehow righted us and returned the university and everyone to our home dimension. He then disappeared into his office for two weeks. "He didn't actually disappear, not like Sheryl did. No, he locked the door to his office and did not leave. Of course, he must have left at some point. Even that mad man needed to eat. When he did finally let me in, there were hundreds of books from the campus library scattered in various states of research. Every surface was covered with tomes in languages that I had never heard of.

"His two weeks were not wasted.

"He came to me with a leather-bound journal. The book, that book right there, is filled with the only method of anchoring Miskatonic University to our reality permanently in the considerably more-likely event that the campus becomes lost in a different reality. Or, at least as permanently as ever before.

"You see, Andrew spent the first week reading the past notes taken by his predecessors regarding the unmooring events and what they knew about them. He learned that Miskatonic, and the land that it is on, was enchanted, for lack of a better term, to protect our world from the others. The other worlds, other dimensions, seek to bleed into our reality. They are apex predators and will devour everything. We cannot co-exist and Miskatonic makes it so that we do not need to.

"There are some who believe otherwise. The dean already explained that Chris was a member of one of those groups. The unmooring in '43 was caused by a local cult hoping to summon their sex god and promote a world of pure ecstasy. They did not realize that ecstasy means something entirely different to beings with different minds and physical processes than humanity. Before they could invite in the reality they believed they wanted, they first needed to open the door. In this case, that means breaking the spell that makes Miskatonic University the lock on the door to Earth. The unmoorings are not the university going to another place, they are our home reality becoming untethered and driving away from the safety of Miskatonic.

"For obvious reasons, it is imperative that we not allow this to happen. Andrew recognized that, and his second week of seclusion was focused on developing a plan of action. That book is a comprehensive list of spells to reverse an unmooring event. Most are simple enough and, as most events are caused by a person or group, simply finding and stopping the aggressor halts their spells and the event.

"That brings us to what Dean Doran referred to as 'The Final Break.' He wrote that as the unmoorings continued, we would begin to see them starting without an instigator. They would come more frequently, preludes to a main event. Once we reached that point, it would only take a single event caused with purpose to completely sever the anchor point.

"When that happens, he detailed a final spell that could reset the anchor and the original stability. It would save the world and buy us hundreds of years before we would need to consider restabilizing the anchor again.

"The spell is called the Scion Cycle. A decade ago, Dean Ward and I cast it. We used up all the protective magic of the secret armory of the university. It will be years before priceless and protective artifacts kept within these halls will have their powers built back up enough to be useful again.

"The scholarships that you each received were our final piece to the spell. The spell itself identifies and guides five bloodlines with incredibly strong ties to Miskatonic University and Arkham. It brings those bloodlines here and pushes into motion a fate machine that puts each of you into the correct place to enact the re-anchoring. It does not make it happen, so much as it collects you and provides the opportunity.

"Once the spell was started, it drew the five of you in. Ralph, the flesh of the Deep Ones. Carlos, the dreamer incarnate. Meredith, the one touched and hunted by madness. Sheryl, the witch. Stephanie, the blood of the reanimator.

"There is not enough in my friend's book to say what happens next, but the spell is already in motion. The five of you are here, and you are the pieces that can lock down our reality.

"Before you can even ask, I don't know what this means for you or if you will even survive this. Arkham is a nasty place with dark secrets. It only makes sense that this damned city would need dark and terrible acts to save the world."

CHAPTER 12

When Carol had finished her explanation, no one said anything. The dean dismissed them to give them time to absorb what the administrative assistant had explained.

They grumbled about their day so far before splitting up to go to their respective classes, promising to meet up in Sheryl and Meredith's room when they were done.

It took much of the day for them to figure out their individual thoughts on the unmooring events and the Scion Cycle that had drawn them all to the campus. Stephanie was so distracted that she completely ignored Alicia Halsey's attempts to goad her into a confrontation.

Of course, Stephanie was also distracted by what she had been reading in the journals.

When she got tired of spinning her wheels on what the Scion Cycle meant for her and her friends, she kept returning to the fact that she had been referenced as the 'reanimator.' She spent much of her classroom time deep in her uncle's lost journals.

Each page told a similar horrific, yet intriguing, story. Herbert's formula, in each of the iterations the reagent went through, worked but only with varying levels of success. For whatever reason, he was incapable of figuring out the correct percentages for each of the formula's components. For that reason, each of his experiments ended in the patient being mad or tearing themselves apart. By the time that classes had ended, she had decided what she could do to make the project successful, and it brought a smile to her face.

Carlos had spent the day with Levi, who was struggling with the pain of his body being forced to contain more otherworldly forces than it had been designed to hold. The more he pulled at his lineage for power, the more of himself Levi was going to lose. Nate Peasley came to find his friend and cuss him out for not having his back earlier, but Carlos would not have any of it. Nate experienced a very realistic scene of no one being in Levi's room before surrendering and searching for his friend elsewhere. Having already been in Nate's head once before, it was a simple task to make the man dream again, this time of something much less horrific.

Carlos continued to check his phone until Ralph finally messaged him to make his way to Sheryl and Meredith's room when he could. Levi had seemed to stabilize in the last few hours. The Dunwich man's pain was residing, and it wouldn't be long before he awoke. Carlos left him a note of where to find them, and left to join his friends.

Aside from Meredith, Carlos was the first to arrive. She immediately went into explaining everything that had happened since the unmooring, and everything Carol has told them about their role in what was happening. He did his part to best explain the walkabout that Randy had taken him on.

"So," Carlos was attempting to understand, "the only thing keeping all of reality in place is one campus on the East Coast? The vast infinite realm of planets and species spanning everything we know and this tiny speck of nothing is the lynchpin to keeping it all in place?" He paused, frowning as the Dream Lands whispered something to him. "Even with all the evidence being whispered to me from different worlds, I find that hard to believe."

Meredith nodded. "I think that's why we all need to talk."

"Where is Sheryl?" Stephanie's voice came from the door.

"Hello to you too," Carlos smiled.

"Hello, Carlos." She turned her attention to Meredith. "Where is Sheryl?"

"On her way." Meredith raised an eyebrow, "What's going on?"

Stephanie was clutching her new leather bag. She sat on Sheryl's bed and hugged it. "I have a math problem," she explained. "Something that I believe only she can help me with."

"You think she can help you make a better version of that

formula we found, don't you?" Meredith's excitement was obvious.

Stephanie gave a small nod. "Herbert West was clearly not a mathematician, and for all of my gifts, neither am I. Herbert didn't have Sheryl."

Ralph and Sheryl walked in at the same time. Sheryl went directly to her television and booted up Wicked West.

"So," Ralph started, "we're all chosen ones and need to sacrifice ourselves to save the world?"

"Sacrifice was not stated," Stephanie countered. "It was made clear that the results of this," she made air quotes, "'spell' are entirely unknown."

"That's implied, though," Ralph countered. "Right?" His voice was filled with agitation.

Meredith frowned. "I got that vibe, too."

"None of what we were told matters," Stephanie gave by way of response.

"What makes you think that?" Carlos asked.

Stephanie squared her shoulders before she answered. "Clearly, since the Scion Cycle spell was started a decade ago before putting into motion a series of events that brought us all together, there is a level of preordainment implied." When the only response that she received was their blank looks, Stephanie continued. "Our options are clear. Either Carol Berg is telling us the truth and we have no free will and the Scion Cycle will pull us along no matter what we do, or the entire story is fabricated, and we should just ignore it. It doesn't matter whether or not we believe it, because even if we ignore it, the outcome will remain the same."

Ralph's voice was low as he answered. "That's not how these things work."

It was Stephanie's turn to be confused. "No? Then how do they work?"

"Destiny and spells tied to fate are never predictable," Ralph's anger was confusing everyone. "My entire life has been tied to a destiny that I didn't ask for. Fate demands that I go home and continue to propagate my family with babies to fill the empty cities of the god my parents chose to worship. All because a fisherman decided he liked gold two hundred years ago." He looked directly at Stephanie when he said, "Even if it is preordained, we have a choice. If they are right, our choice could mess this all up."

"That isn't how I understand it," Stephanie said.

"Then you do not understand it," Ralph countered.

The room was silent as everyone felt the tension.

Sheryl paused her game and turned to the group. "They didn't tell us what to do next."

"What?" Carlos asked.

"They dropped this huge bombshell on us and never told us what we were expected to do."

Stephanie nodded. "That was my point. Obviously, they expect this spell to guide us in the right direction and solve their problems without any knowledge on what we need to do."

"Or they don't know what needs doing?" Meredith's gaze turned distant.

"What's that look?" Ralph asked her.

Meredith came back to herself and turned to grab a notebook on her dresser. "Ms. Berg told us about our roles in the Scion Cycle, but we still don't know who we are." She clutched the notebook. "Maybe I can help. I took all your names and did basic searches. Stephanie was easy enough to figure out, but the rest of us not so much. I'm the hunted one who is tainted by whatever my grandfather found in the Pacific Ocean. Then she called Sheryl the witch," she flipped a few pages in the notebook. "I found a person with Mason as their last name, in Arkham, who was also called a witch." She looked to Carlos, "Sorry, Carlos. I haven't been able to find anything about your name."

Carlos shook his head. "I found out plenty. I'm a dreamer, someone who can travel between worlds through the Dream Lands. Randolph Carter was a powerful dreamer who chose to give up his humanity to learn what lies beyond the edges of knowledge." He shrugged. "Randy got bored and decided to latch onto me to teach me how to be like him."

All of them stared blankly at him until Ralph broke the silence.

"That's what I was figuring."

The group of friends laughed, relieved at the tension finally loosening around this topic.

"Who was the witch?" Sheryl asked.

"Keziah Mason," Meredith tore the page out of the notebook. "I knew there was something crazy going on here, and now with this Scion Cycle stuff we can't just ignore it."

"Incorrect," Stephanie said. "I intend to ignore it to focus on my studies. If at any point a clear path presents itself, I will readily make myself available."

"Same," Ralph said. "I've had enough with destiny thinking it controls me. I left home to escape destiny and now this school is trying to tell me that my leaving was part of destiny's plan? No, it isn't."

Carlos touched Meredith's shoulder. "Perhaps this is a problem with stages, and right now is yours. Do what you do best and keep hunting the answers." He turned his head as more of his Dream Lands intuition came to him. "They said that Chris wasn't the only one. There will be more of whoever sent him. Maybe you should find them first."

The group finished with their conversations and catching each other up. Carlos filled everyone in on how Levi was doing and where his dream quest had taken him. He left out the piece where he saw Stephanie kill Chris, opting instead to talk to her about it privately. Ralph was relieved to hear that Levi was doing better. Steph obviously wanted to talk to Sheryl about her estranged uncle's journals, but Sheryl was torn between Meredith's notes and her phone as she did internet searches for anything with the name Keziah Mason.

As the group broke up, Ralph, Carlos, and Meredith headed to the Student Union to get food, while Stephanie lingered, waiting for her opening with Sheryl.

When Sheryl finally closed her game and stood up to follow her friends, Stephanie stood in her doorway.

"What's up, Steph?" She eyed her friend suspiciously, as the unreadable expression that Stephanie normally wore had been replaced by a nervous look that was decidedly out of place.

"As you are aware," Stephanie clutched her bag tighter to

her chest as she spoke, "Meredith has been assisting me in discovering information about my notoriously famous ancestor. To that point, she has gone above and beyond anything that I could request of her." She patted the satchel, indicating that it and its contents were relevant to the conversation. "I now have Herbert West's journals, explaining how he made his reagent and each experiment he conducted. I can see where he made his mistakes, and I can correct them. With help."

"You want my help making zombie juice?" Sheryl crossed her arms and smirked as she spoke.

Stephanie's embarrassment was evident.

"It is not zombie juice," she spoke slowly, with a sharpness to her voice. She was obviously offended. "It is a chemical meant to reverse the effects of death."

"Look," Sheryl realized her mistake and backpedaled, "I'm sorry. I didn't mean to offend you. I'm just surprised. Before today, you hated the idea of everything about that man. Now, all of a sudden, you want to pick up his work?"

Stephanie nodded and her features softened. "I understand your confusion, as I also experienced it upon self-examination. At first, my interest in Herbert West was a morbid curiosity with my family history. Something I can only liken to being a distant relative to Jack the Ripper. I am aware and offended by what he was accused of, but then I also wanted to know everything about it and perhaps see if any of it were true. When it turned out that it was only half-true and he had been developing a means of reversing death, my morbid curiosity turned to mild obsession." She smiled and it looked awkward on her, but entirely genuine. "I am in veterinary sciences for a reason," she explained. "I don't want animals to hurt. To a further extent, what could this mean for humanity?" She straightened herself and squared her shoulders. "While my great uncle might have been unorthodox and unethical in his monstrous approach to science, I believe that his research had validity. To that extent, I wish to conduct it in a much more ethical and scientific way."

"But?" Sheryl was waiting to hear why Stephanie was asking for her help.

"But," Stephanie agreed, "his percentages were never right.

Most of the monsters he created were because he didn't know how to portion out the ingredients. It is more than just math, it's—"

"Math magic," Sheryl pieced together.

"Correct." Stephanie reached into the bag and pulled out one of the journals. "I believe that with your special skills and my uncle's notes, we can put together a formula that does exactly what it says on the label: Cure Death."

"Only if you'll help me," Sheryl said without hesitation. From the moment she realized that Stephanie was standing in her door waiting to ask her something important, Sheryl knew that she would need to ask her friend something similar.

"Of course," Stephanie returned. She looked mildly curious, but remained her stone-faced self. "Friends help each other. What do you need?"

Sheryl held up the pages from Meredith's notebook. "I want to learn everything I can about Keziah Mason."

"Wouldn't Meredith be better suited toward that endeavor?" Stephanie was confused. "She has done much of the work already."

Sheryl nodded. "Didn't you see that look in her eye? She's going to hunt down the cult Chris was part of. She wants to solve this Scion Cycle mystery. This," she shook the papers, "is a scary old witch and if she's dead…" Sheryl trailed off.

"Ah," Stephanie understood. "If we can't find answers, then perhaps we can revive her with the reagent and talk to her directly. Except," Stephanie frowned, "if she is dead, she won't be in any state to be a candidate for my ethical experiments. I have no interest in retreading my uncle's bloody path."

"If it even comes to that we would be entirely humane about it." She saw the look in Stephanie's eyes. "I promise, we won't even think about bringing her back unless it is a last resort and not until after we have reached an ethical means of doing it."

"What about her consent?"

"What?" Sheryl was stopped by the question.

"Ethics, experimentation, human involvement, all require consent, or we are back on the path of my uncle."

Sheryl nodded, understanding the dilemma. "If the dreamer

and the math witch can't figure out how to ask a likely-dead witch if we can revive her from the dead, then we won't use your reagent. I promise."

"You are only causing me more confusion," Stephanie admitted. "If you can ask her consent, then why would we need to revive her. Ask your questions at that time."

Sheryl threw up her hands. "I don't know. Look, I will help you figure out your serum-thingy. You help me find out more about Keziah and my powers. We probably won't need to revive her, even if we can find her, and we won't even discuss it unless I can do it without giving either of us a guilty conscience." She was both frustrated and winded from the outburst. "Agreed?"

"Of course."

CHAPTER 13

"Like a Jedi," Ralph said around a mouthful of chicken.

"What?" Carlos was frowning. "A Jedi?"

"He's not wrong," Meredith agreed.

After their meeting in Meredith and Sheryl's room, the three had headed off to the Student Union for dinner. They didn't know where Stephanie and Sheryl had gone, but if they were hungry, they'd show up.

"How is anything I described to you 'like a Jedi?'" Carlos didn't see the connection.

Meredith took a stab at it. "You get visions and intuition about events. You have powers that help you calm people down and a Force-ghost is training you."

"Alright," Carlos admitted, "but Jedi can't teleport places or go to the future or past."

"Dude," Ralph laughed, "have you even seen The Clone Wars?"

"The what?" Carlos asked. "The cartoon? No, I haven't seen it."

"Obviously," Ralph leaned back. "Go watch it. It's good, and you are a Jedi."

When Ralph had leaned back, his vision came into line of sight with the door, and he saw Levi entering.

He still wasn't certain on where he and his friends stood with the Dunwich boy. Were they friends, allies, or just people trying to survive? Ralph gave a quick nod that Levi returned, and waited to see if the football player made his way toward their table or not.

To the entire table's surprise, Levi came directly to them and sat down across from Meredith.

"Hey guys," was all he said as he sat down.

"How are you feeling?" Ralph asked before Meredith and Carlos could greet the new arrival.

Levi's appearance was unchanged from the last time they had seen him. The red rain had evaporated from his clothing, leaving no trace behind. The only difference between then and now was that Levi looked worn out.

"I can hear him," Levi's voice was a whisper. "There's a burning in my chest and I can hear the voice beyond the Gate. I can't tell what he's saying, but he's there and he's calling to me." He looked at Carlos, "Can you close the Gate?"

Carlos was surprised by the question. "I don't think anyone can close the Gate," he said, after a moment of introspection. "There was one who had the Silver Key. He could have done it, but it would have cost him everything." Carlos shrugged. "Even with the key, I don't think that I have that kind of power."

Ralph realized that he was concerned for Levi. He didn't understand it at first. This was the same guy who labeled him with his own ignorance before getting to know him. The person who made it clear that he wanted nothing to do with the 'fishboy.'

Then it struck him. They were the same.

Ralph was concerned for Levi and what Levi was going through because he broke away from his own family to try and live a life outside of what destiny had planned for him. Whatever this Gate and Key thing was that he and Carlos kept discussing didn't sound much different than the change that Ralph was expected to go through. Ralph's change wouldn't be for a few more years and there were things he might be able to do to halt it entirely. Ralph's empathy went out to Levi, who seemed entirely incapable of avoiding his destiny. His family had chosen their path, and now Levi was forced to follow them down it.

And perhaps Levi was sensing something similar in Ralph and his friends. All with destinies larger than themselves, they each had someone else telling them how to live their lives, against their own wishes.

"You're a beacon of light," Carlos was explaining. "The … thing beyond the Gate wants into our world and the more you use your inhuman abilities, the brighter you burn for him to see."

"What do I do?" Levi asked through gritted teeth. He was getting frustrated that in helping his five new friends he had sacrificed himself.

Carlos shrugged. "Using your inhuman abilities causes you to burn brighter to … him. So, maybe doing things uniquely human will change that."

"Such as?" Levi started to relax at the idea that doing normal things could make him less monster and more person.

"It's college," Meredith laughed. "Play football, get drunk, meet a girl. You know," she held her hands up indicating everyone around her, "be a reckless person in his late teens."

A vibration in Ralph's pocket went off. When he pulled it out and read the message his mood soured again.

Football field. Now.

Somehow Magnus, his older brother, had discovered his new phone number.

When he left the table, he told his friends it was a personal matter and that they should continue without him. Then he made his way to the football field. There were no practices going on and with dusk settling it looked like no one would be heading to that end of campus either.

The football field wasn't some large stadium like at some of the other schools. There were bleachers, but it was mostly open to the air, and anyone could walk up to or onto the field. This meant that when practice wasn't in session, players or people who just enjoyed the sport could go on the field for whatever reason, be it football or flying kites.

Magnus stood in the center of the field. It reminded Ralph of something he would see on some afternoon special about bullies. Based on what he was expecting his brother to say, it wouldn't be too far from the truth.

Magnus wasn't alone. Ralph recognized Adrian Pulner and Joe the bus driver, both Innsmouth busybodies who couldn't mind their own business.

All three, much like Ralph himself, had the physical description of just about everyone at Innsmouth.

Larger-than-average eyes, flat noses, and wide mouths. Their skin was pale and, in Joe's case, glistening.

Ralph stopped five yards from his brother.

"What are you doing here, Magnus?"

Magnus licked his lips. His tongue was wider than Ralph expected it to be. His change had started.

"This playing at being one of them is over," Magnus's voice was deeper than Ralph's. "Mom is worried. You need to come home."

Ralph shook his head. "You never did understand me. This isn't about playing at being one of them. This is about me, doing what I want."

"Our people don't get that luxury, boy," Joe spit as he shouted. His rage seemed too large for the entire field.

Magnus held up his hand and Joe stepped back.

"You're wrong," Ralph's brother said. "I do understand. Do you think I wanted to join Father on the reef?" It was his turn to shake his head. "It doesn't matter what I wanted, because once the change starts you won't have a choice."

"It hasn't started yet," Ralph said. "And until it does, I do."

"No, you're going home tonight." Magnus waved at Adrian. "Adrian here is going to help you gather your things and Joe is going to give us all a ride home. Let's get a move on. We ain't got all night."

Ralph was furious. "No."

Magnus was suddenly inches from his face. This far into the change, Ralph wouldn't be able to take him. He wasn't like Joe, who wouldn't convert fully because of some birth defect. Magnus was on his way to becoming a full Deep One.

"This isn't a choice, Ralph." He shoved Ralph and the younger Allen brother fell back and to the ground. "Now get your stuff and don't make me tell you again."

Ralph climbed to his feet slowly, never taking his eyes from his fellow Innsmouthers.

"I said no, and I meant it." Ralph was quieter than he intended. "I want to give this a try. I need to give this a try. If you or Mom or anybody wants me to come home, then you need me to fail here first. Otherwise, I will always be trying to get away from you."

"Well," Magnus smirked, "you don't have to come home conscious."

He swung at Ralph. Ralph flinched.

The hit never came.

To him anyway. One moment the fist was flying at Ralph's face, the next Magnus and his fist were both gone. He turned to see where Magnus went and found him on the ground several feet away.

Magnus grunted in surprise and pain as Levi punched him. Repeatedly, Levi dropped inhuman fist after inhuman fist into Magnus's face.

Joe and Adrian were slow to react, but anyone would have been in comparison to how quickly Levi had moved. They ran at Levi to grab him, and Levi just ignored them.

Levi only stopped when he heard Adrian shout.

"It's a Whatley."

Hearing his birth name, Levi stood and started toward Magnus's friend. A quick glance at his beaten brother and Ralph stepped forward, placing himself between Levi and Adrian.

"That's probably enough."

Levi had to force himself to look away from Adrian and to Ralph. When he did, his eyes softened enough to show that whatever alien power he had summoned to brutalize a man in the middle of his transition to a warrior for Dagon had left him. He took a deep breath and nodded. Ralph could see the pain in Levi's face as he felt that thing beyond the Gate reach out to him again. The sailor looking for his lighthouse.

"Fine," Magnus shouted as he stood back up. He spat blood on the ground, but his face was already beginning to heal from the damage it had sustained. "Living with humans and getting rescued by Whatleys. This will break Mom's heart." He spat again, this time directly at his brother. "It'll probably kill her."

Magnus turned and, without saying another word, left. Adrian and Joe followed, walking off the field and into the darkness.

When they were out of sight, Levi fell to his knees and gasped. He was shaking violently.

Ralph didn't know what to do and knelt beside him.

"What do you want me to do?" he shouted.

Through gritted teeth, Levi said, "Carlos sent me. Said you would need my help."

Ralph thought the world of Carlos, but he shouldn't have sent Levi. He could have handled Magnus.

Of course, if Carlos hadn't sent Levi, Ralph would be on a rickety bus back to Innsmouth.

"Levi," Ralph was pleading with the pained man, "how can I help you?"

Levi grabbed Ralph by the side of the head and stared at him through tears in his eyes. The moment seemed to last forever, and for a second Ralph worried about what would happen next.

Then Levi kissed him.

Carlos smiled to himself while he waited for Meredith to finish her dinner.

"What are you smiling at, Master Kenobi?"

"Bite me," Carlos sniped back. "I'm smiling because I might have inadvertently saved Levi's life."

"Huh?" Meredith said around a mouthful of parmesan chicken.

"Never mind," he dismissed any thoughts of Levi and Ralph, and changed the conversation. "Do you know where to start with this search for Chris's cult?"

Meredith shook her head. "I don't know anything about it. It's the same cult I have spent my entire life trying to understand, and I think Ralph might know something about the sea god they worship, but that's about it."

"It isn't Dagon," Carlos countered. "That much I can confirm. Dreams aren't specific, but if Ralph was the connecting tissue between you and the answers you're looking for, it would have made itself visible to me. No, this is something else."

Meredith smirked. "You sound like you're volunteering to join my Scooby Gang."

"Maybe I am," he returned her smile. "But I would rather you call me a Jedi, then Shaggy."

"Nice try, buddy," Meredith stood up with her empty tray, "but you are definitely a Fred."

CHAPTER 14

It was a little over a month before Meredith found a lead in her mysterious cult. She had been desperate to at least locate the name of the group hunting her and her family before they sent someone to investigate Chris's disappearance.

"Change your name on social media," Carlos had suggested a week prior to her breakthrough. "Chris found you, but we don't know how. If he didn't share his information with the right people, they could be starting from scratch. So, instead, make yourself a bigger target."

"If they are hunting for Johansen," Meredith put together, "then I need to stop hiding."

Once she changed her name to the more traditional Meredith Johansen, and dealt with the freak out from her parents who assumed she was going through some sort of college rebellion against her family, the friend requests started coming in.

"If they aren't someone that you already know," Carlos had said, "then every one of them is someone we need to be investigating."

"Why can't you just reach out and investigate them with your fancy dream weaver thing?" Meredith asked her friend.

"It's not as easy as it seems," Carlos explained. "Not everyone dreams every time they sleep, and I can't always turn it on and off. It seems to be easier when we're closer to one of those unmooring events."

Meredith had a thought. "Maybe it has something to do with how close to our world the other worlds are?"

Carlos shrugged. "I've been trying to learn more, but Randy has been unusually quiet and there isn't a lot of information on the internet that's useful to my unique take on dreaming."

As Levi and Ralph worked on figuring out exactly what they were and with football season getting under way, Carlos had a lot less time to visit with his roommate. Instead, he had been spending that time either trying to better understand this gift of his or assisting Meredith with her research.

He knew what Sheryl and Stephanie were working on, and it made him entirely uncomfortable. Carlos wasn't sure about Stephanie's motivations and recognized that Herbert West had been driven by what he thought were good intentions as well.

He wasn't about to tell Meredith what he knew. She didn't need to worry about her friends any more than she already was, but he was going to keep an eye on them, nonetheless.

One of their cult suspects who actually went to school with them became their first target. They needed to get this person alone and get information from them.

Friending someone on social media was one thing, but they needed to meet with this person. Carlos and Meredith shifted their usual Student Union meetings to the library. There, they would take over one of group study rooms for an hour and work on ideas.

The rooms were small, with a single table and four chairs. Outlets were built into the table and the rooms were meant to stop whatever sounds a group of rowdy college students might make while studying from getting out into the rest of the library. For that reason, they didn't have to be quiet. The only thing they needed to be concerned with was the large window in each study room. The windows were there for a simple method of seeing if the room was already occupied. It was the most private place they could meet that also gave them a view of anyone who might be trying to listen in.

Carlos thought this was overkill. They had only friended someone who might be an evil cultist. That same someone, an Erin Rathert, didn't even know they were looking into her or where they might be meeting.

Meredith's response was that Chris had managed to locate her when she hadn't friended him and had been careful about her identity.

He couldn't argue with her logic and decided that there was

nothing wrong with being a little over-careful.

The first two meetings were entirely on brainstorming how to get all of them into one room together, and where that room should be. They didn't want anyone to interrupt the interrogation.

"If only you could create some sort of bubble world or something like you did for Sheryl at the last unmooring event," Meredith was getting frustrated. As much as getting Rathert into a room with them was step one, she didn't see the point on focusing on that part if they couldn't figure out how to detain and interrogate their suspect.

"The more I test the limits of what I can do," Carlos explained, "the more I learn that that entire day was a fluke. Randy had to have been helping me or the unmooring event supercharged me, or something." He shrugged. "Right now, I can commune with voices that aren't all Randy and when I am asleep I can enter the Dream Lands, but the place I enter in is never the same and finding the nearest city is nearly impossible." Carlos shuddered. "The things that dwell in the forests of the Dream Lands are hungry. I spend most of my visit trying to survive."

Meredith raised an eyebrow. "Alright, maybe we don't use Dream power to make this happen." She gave him a serious look. "And please, don't get eaten."

Carlos nodded. "Dying in the Dream Lands is just as bad, and arguably worse, than dying in the real world."

A flash of insight came to Carlos then, as he remembered something that could help them.

"We need to get Sheryl," he said. Then he explained his idea to Meredith.

Stephanie was angry.

"What do you mean we can't test it?"

Sheryl shook her head and squinted at the glowing green jar in front of her.

"Until we find Keziah Mason," Sheryl explained, "I can't be certain. All I can do is tell you what my math tells me." She pointed at the jar. "There's something wrong with it."

"Your logic is failing you," Stephanie countered. "Keziah is likely dead, and we would need a working reagent to reverse that condition. We, therefore, cannot ask her to fix a serum that would be required to reverse the condition that the serum is designed to cure."

Sheryl held up her hands in surrender. "I get your point. This is our fourth attempt—"

"And getting some of these ingredients has been a less than ideal experience," Stephanie said. She was referencing both the chemicals that she had to steal from her veterinarian studies lab class, and the illicit substances she had been forced to locate and purchase from less-than-reputable sources.

Sheryl nodded. "I get it, but this," she sat and picked up her game controller, but she didn't turn on the game, "won't be any better than the stuff Herbert used."

Stephanie frowned and picked up the other controller.

About a week after they had started collaborating on the reagent, Sheryl had begun demanding break time. Stephanie's work routine tended to be nonstop until she reached a solution. Unfortunately, there was no easy solution for what they were trying to do and with Stephanie's mentality she would work herself to death. Breaks were instituted for classes, social life, and gaming, which Sheryl had put her foot down about. If she was going to be stressing out about her new job as cafeteria attendant of the zombie juice, then she was going to get her de-stress on the best way she knew how.

When the game booted up and they were both in, Stephanie remained uncharacteristically, at least to Sheryl since they had started working together in earnest, quiet.

Stephanie had taken to Wicked West quickly enough. The mechanics of using the controller were difficult for her to master at first, since she had never played a video game before, but most of the world interactions were intuitive and she was able to fall into the role of a cowboy hunting pelts on the open range with minimal effort. In the few weeks they had been playing, Stephanie had already reached half of Sheryl's level 176.

"My next question," she spoke quietly while she concentrated on a buffalo that had just crested a nearby ridge, "puts into doubt my ethical convictions to do better than Herbert."

"I know what you're going to ask," Sheryl killed a highwayman who tried to steal her horse.

"I am sure that you do." Stephanie paused before continuing anyway. "What if we tested it on an animal?"

"Why?" Sheryl's voice held a hint of disgust.

"Perhaps observation and comparing those observations with Herbert's notes would help us to figure out which components are in the wrong quantities." Stephanie stopped her character from moving in a relatively safe place in the woods and looked to Sheryl. "Herbert's journals specify which reactions are a result of which ingredients. If we see adverse reactions, we can line those up with the specific ingredients and adjust the quantities." She paused before adding, "We work with animal cadavers regularly in my lab class. Acquiring a specimen would not be too difficult."

"You mean, acquiring one with math magic wouldn't be too difficult," Sheryl corrected her.

Stephanie nodded. "You could get us in and out during the locked-down hours and we would have our specimen."

Sheryl put her controller down and met Stephanie's eyes. "And then we would force a defenseless creature back into our world in what could be the most painful experience of its life."

Stephanie deflated. "Unfortunately, yes."

Sheryl let out her breath slowly before settling on what to say next.

"You are going to do this anyway, aren't you?"

Stephanie started to nod before stopping herself. "I do not want to be him." The way she said 'him' left no doubt about who she was talking about. "I want it made entirely clear that, unlike my estranged and weird uncle, I care about life. I have empathy." She frowned as some other player on their server ran up to her and shoved a knife in her stomach. That was Stephanie's sign to put the controller down. "Unfortunately, I also realize that we have hit a wall in our research and that we will need to either advance it through traditional methods, such as animal testing, or by finding Keziah, of which we have no leads."

Before Sheryl could voice her response to Stephanie's examination of their current situation, the door burst open, startling them both.

Meredith came through, with Carlos close behind.
"We need your help," Carlos said to Sheryl.

Once it was confirmed that they had a way to detain and interrogate Erin Rathert, it was just a matter of getting them all in the
same room together. That turned out to be easy now that they
knew they would need Sheryl for part two of the plan.

With the plan mostly figured out, Carlos was still feeling
less than enthusiastic about it.

"Can't you do something subtle," he asked Sheryl, "like
convince her that you're part of her secret cult and let her give
you all the secrets that way?"

"Subtle would be better," Sheryl agreed while they tried
to spot their target in the Student Union. "Like I keep telling
Steph, though, I'm not Hermione. None of what I can control is
intuitive and the stuff that I can is entirely useless."

"Not entirely," Meredith countered as she recalled the plan.
"We can still use your gifts, just without any subtlety." She
shrugged. "Assuming she shows up."

"Everybody eats, drinks coffee, glares menacingly at their
enemies," Carlos nodded toward Alicia Halsey off in the corner
of the Student Union. "Does she do that often?"

"More so as of late," Stephanie admitted. "It is my belief that
she has made assumptions about what Sheryl and I are doing in
our spare time."

"Where did she get that idea?" Meredith asked.

Stephanie frowned and avoided everyone's looks by twisting
to look at the door behind her.

Sheryl took up the answer. "Someone," she tossed a glance
at Stephanie, "gets a little too excited sometimes and might have
asked the dean if human corpses are something that the campus
ever has to deal with. Obviously, that isn't something a Halsey
would want to hear anyone with the last name of West say."

"Sheesh," Carlos mumbled.

"Besides," Meredith said in an attempt to return to the
original reason they were waiting patiently in the Student
Union for Erin Rathert, "I invited her to hang out with us."

"I have been your friend for over a month at this point,"

Stephanie said, "and I don't even know what your idea of hanging out is."

"Erin won't either," Carlos countered.

Meredith shrugged, "I laid it on pretty thick. I told her that we are all outcasts looking to make friends." It was her turn to hide her eyes from the group. "I might have said that it seemed like we must be cursed, since so much weird stuff happens around us."

"The pity play," Sheryl nodded. "I like it."

Meredith suddenly stood up and waved before sitting down.

Erin was about Carlos's height with dark hair and brown eyes. There was nothing about her that stuck out. She wore a t-shirt and jeans, with no logos. She carried a bag with the strap over her shoulder and wore no jewelry or makeup. If they were wrong about her being a cultist sent to the campus to find Meredith, then Erin was the type of person who didn't wear their personality. Otherwise, she was a plant trying too hard to blend in.

While Stephanie and Carlos both stiffened in anticipation, Sheryl remained calm as Erin sat at the table. She took the only open seat that was purposefully left beside Sheryl.

Meredith was a natural. She fell into her role as a person desperate to people-please immediately. She introduced each of her friends and started talking about lunch options.

Sheryl had no patience for any of this.

She tore a page from her notebook and started jotting numbers down on it. When she had mostly filled the page, Sheryl folded it twice before unfolding it and sliding it directly in front of Erin Rathert. The creases in the page created angles that lifted it off the table.

"Erin," Sheryl asked as she twisted to face the newcomer, "do you like math?" She nodded toward the page.

Erin frowned and eyed the paper in front of her. "Not especially." She took the time to try and read it, but it all made no sense to her. "I'm an anthropology major for a reason," she said. "Anthropology means I just have to write a ton of essays. No math required."

Then her eyes lit up as she recognized something on the page.

Erin's hand shot forward to push the paper away, but Sheryl was quicker. Sheryl's hand found the back of Erin's head and slammed her face down into the page and through the angles of reality folded into the paper.

CHAPTER 15

Nobody on the team cared about whether Levi and Ralph were together. It was the modern day and homosexuality was only shunned by backwards people or in backwards towns like Innsmouth, that put more value on producing offspring and following tradition than on the happiness and well-being of individuals.

The team was more confused by the pairing than anything. They didn't know the similarities in the demands their families put onto them or the battles they had already fought together. All that Peasley and the other players saw was their friend siding with the fishboy. Levi and Ralph weren't the types of people to care much for what their companions on the football team thought, but even they were finding the doubled-down effort to make their lives miserable annoying.

Levi had mostly been accepted before this had happened. Since he still looked human, people didn't know he had a heritage as questionable as Ralph's. Showing affection for Ralph in front of everyone might as well have turned him into a fishperson too, in their eyes.

The first game changed that.

Coach Flagstaff was smarter than any of his players were. Having already worked with Levi in the previous season and knowing more about the people of Innsmouth that the average racist in Arkham, he knew exactly what both were capable of. For that reason, once he realized his players weren't going to be coached out of being assholes, he decided he would make Levi and Ralph sit out of the practices and start during the first game.

This wouldn't be a concern for Levi, as he was familiar

with the plays and had known how his team played. For Ralph, that was another story. Instead of practices, Ralph was made to watch previous games on Youtube while also going over the playbook.

This didn't mean that Ralph or Levi were out of shape when the first game against the Pike University Knights started. They practiced on their own as well as ran every evening. Their unique physiologies made it so that the acts of exercise were less than necessary, but they did it anyway.

When the coin was tossed, the Miskatonic Gaunts were given the first possession of the ball. This meant that the surprise Coach Flagstaff had in hand wouldn't be seen until MU went on the defensive.

The downs turned and Pike University got the ball and Coach sent both of his defensive linemen out with the rest of the team. Peasley tried to psyche them out. He got a few of his friends to join him in ruthless ribbing of the two men, but coach put an end to it as the play started.

Pike University hiked the ball, with the quarterback stepping back to find an open receiver, but he was greeted by something entirely unexpected.

A large Innsmouth man knocked back his offensive line.

Even if the entire team had rallied to stop Ralph from breaking their formation and tackling the quarterback, it would have left the rest of the team and Levi to rush him or block the receivers.

The entire team did not run to stop Ralph. After he shook off the two that had tried to stop him, he leaped forward and slammed bodily into the quarterback.

That was the first sack of six that would bring that game to an end score of 35 to 3 in the Gaunts' favor. By the end of the game, Pike University was struggling to outthink the wall that was the Miskatonic University defensive formation, but it was too little, too late with a field goal that gave them their only points for the entire game.

Peasley wasn't going to change his tune any time now, but he was certainly singing quieter. He couldn't fight the tide that was the acceptance everyone on the team showed when they won clearly because of their overwhelming advantage in trusting the fishboy and his fish-loving boyfriend. Everyone on the team seemed to shape up to the coach's way of thinking by the end of that game.

That didn't mean things were going swimmingly for Ralph, though.

"My life is too complicated to put labels on us," Levi had said. "Today is fine because we're both, mostly, human," he explained, "but the minute we forget that we aren't human is the minute I turn into the gateway for a cosmic entity that could tear this reality apart."

"Being human," Ralph countered, "forgetting that we aren't, is what's saving you. That's what Carlos said."

Levi nodded as they sat across from each other at lunch in the Student Union. "Yes, and keeping this complicated is part of that." He crossed his arms defensively. "I think that we can both agree that labels have ruined our lives. So, if I don't want to call you my boyfriend or whatever, that is how we avoid being like those who demanded we have labels."

Ralph couldn't help but feel like this was them holding back, but he was also only a month into whatever this relationship was and couldn't deny that Levi made a point. In his eagerness to be different from what his parents wanted, perhaps he was rushing his emotions.

"That makes a lot of sense," he conceded.

"Great," Levi said. "We're good?"

Ralph stood up and collected his bag, "We are definitely good."

"Where are you headed?" Levi stayed sitting, his food wasn't even done yet. Human or not, Levi's appetite was becoming increasingly concerning. At his previous sitting he ate at least three people's worth of meals. He was only a third of the way through his second plate, but Ralph knew from the ravenous look in Levi's eyes that he was only getting started.

At first, Ralph wanted to blame the increased cardio from their exercises, but that quickly dismissed itself as an option. Something was clearly happening underneath his no-labels-boyfriend's skin. Levi was originally a shorter and stockier person than most and looked better shaped for wrestling. Now, he was both taller and wider than when they had first met by several inches.

"I have a phone call with my dad," Ralph explained. "It's the first time he's reached out to me since I left."

Levi started to stand up. "You want someone there?"

Ralph shook his head, "No. Unlike my brother, he wants me to make this choice of my own free will. He won't be nice about it, but the rituals require that I take my place by his side on my own."

Levi sat back down, and Ralph headed toward his room. When he got there, he started dialing his cellphone. It rang before he finished.

"Hello," was all he said before he fell into an endless ocean.

Shore was nowhere to be seen as Ralph waded in a starlit night. A splash behind him made him turn and see his father, in his fully transfigured form.

His dad looked much as Ralph did, with the same wide eyes and wide mouth and wisps of what had once been a full head of hair. Now, his spine had protruded into a large fin to aid his already natural swimming prowess, and his human teeth had all been replaced by sharp ones meant for tearing at fish or other meat.

Ralph's father, Jonathan, had a mix of green and blue skin and scales covering his entire body with webs stretching between his incredibly long fingers. The only surprise that smacked Ralph was that his dad had finally decided to forgo the last of his human habits and was finally before him without pants or clothing of any type.

"Have you changed your mind?" Jonathan asked his son.

Ralph took in a deep sigh. He couldn't deny that the feeling of the water on his skin was the most blissful thing he had experienced in a while. There was something to be said for surrendering to your biological calling, but he knew what that meant. He knew that there was more to what his biology demanded than the feeling of belonging the ocean provided for him.

"Why would I?" Ralph was still emotional from his short

conversation with Levi regarding what they even were, and now the best punching bag possible was floating before him. Not his father, but a Deep One sworn to the laws of Dagon. "You don't want me anyway. You want a loyal dog to join the armies of Y'ha-nthlei."

It was his father's turn to sigh. "No," he said. "I only want my son beside me. I want your mother happy, and I want our family whole."

"Is that why you sent Magnus to collect me?" Ralph spat.

Jonathan shook his head. "He was meant to talk to you." It was clear that he was getting frustrated. "What he did was on his own." Jonathan's mood shifted. "He said you were with a Dunwich boy?" The way he said boy made it clear that he was being generous with that term. "The Whatleys have made it clear that the pathways are closed to us. We are not to be associated with the Gate."

"He's a friend," Ralph countered. "Not someone who's trying to open pathways to spells for me. That world is behind him now."

"You cannot escape who you are, Ralph," his father was pleading with him. "Whether you want to be one of us or not, you will still change. If you wait too long, you will change alone."

"It's not who I am that's the problem," Ralph only half-lied. He didn't want to undergo the change, but he didn't fear it. "It's all the religion and not having a choice. Whether or not I become a Deep One or not, don't you want me to make my own life?"

They had gone over this discussion a hundred times at least and Ralph could see that his father was already getting frustrated with the direction they were headed.

"There is nothing up there for you," Jonathan explained again. "At least with us, once you change, you can be somewhere that the people accept you. I want the best for you, and I want a life where you are not alone." Suddenly, his father's face shifted to something new. Sympathy and pleading stretched across those wide eyes. "I swam to the reef and communed with the Elders. You don't have to mate to keep your station in our family. You don't have to do anything except come back and join us in worship. The rest is entirely up to you."

Ralph was shocked. Never before had he heard of the Elders allowing anyone to forgo the procreation ceremonies. They never allowed someone so obviously different to stay within their ranks. At first, Ralph was surprised and perhaps even a little hopeful that he wouldn't have to spend his eternal life as a Deep One alone, but then another idea struck him.

"Why?" he asked. "What is happening?"

Jonathan's hopeful expression soured. "Wiser than your years. Perhaps that is the real reason." He sighed and bubbles formed on his gills. "You are not wrong. Something is coming. They will not say what, only that it rivals the expanse of Leng into the Dream Lands."

The expanse of Leng had been a reality-shattering event spoken about only in hushed tones.

"The unmooring events," Ralph said out loud.

"Unmooring events are happening?" Jonathan's attention was sharp. "At Miskatonic University? Are you certain?"

Ralph nodded. "Someone is trying to break the anchor and spin reality off."

"Then you must come home immediately. Y'ha-nthlei is the only place safe for you. You must be home if reality shatters, otherwise you may be lost to us."

"Lost how?" Ralph had an idea from the conversations he had shared with Carlos and his friends, but also from the story he heard from Carol Berg.

"This reality is touched by several other realities, and that bleed allows us to all coexist. The Dream Lands touch here in the minds of the people and Dagon stretches across the stars to let us live in his home, Y'ha-nthlei. If this reality is torn apart or cast aside, there is no telling where or when Y'ha-nthlei might land. Your people could be lost to you."

"I have a chance to stop it, all of it," Ralph explained.

"A chance is not worth losing your family over."

"My family made that choice for me," Ralph countered his father.

"Don't be like this," Jonathan said. "Don't fight now, when you could lose everything."

"That's when I should fight." Ralph was almost yelling.

"Excuse me," a voice called out from the darkness.

Both Innsmouth natives turned in the water to see where the voice could be coming from that had the power to interrupt their call across space and time.

Where there had previously been no shore and only the vastness of endless ocean, now rested a small island of obsidian, no bigger than would be required to fit a rotten corpse.

And that was exactly what was calling out to them. A corpse of skeleton with decades of rot was sitting cross-legged on the volcanic glass.

"My apologies for interrupting what looks to be an emotionally-charged call across the Dream Lands, but I am in desperate need to speak with you, Ralph."

"Who are you?" Jonathan demanded. The spines on his back had raised in anticipation of a confrontation.

"That is neither here nor there, Deep Lord Allen," the dead thing said. "What I am is a messenger attempting to reach Sheryl Mason."

"What do you want with Sheryl?" Ralph asked.

"You know this thing?" Jonathan turned back to his son.

"No," Ralph answered, "but Sheryl is my friend. What do you want with her?" he repeated at the corpse.

"To help her," the thing spread its hands, "of course. I wish to give you something to give to her."

Ralph spread his hands, indicating the ocean and everything around them in the land of Dreams. "There is nothing you can give me here that I can take back with me."

"Wrong," the corpse shouted. The echo was eaten by the vastness of their open world. "Clearly not the smartest child? No matter. I can give you an idea or an impression and you can take that back to her and she will be eternally grateful."

"How?" Ralph pressed.

Jonathan touched his son's shoulder. "Do not make pacts with things that you do not know."

His father's unwanted advice only frustrated Ralph further.

"What do you want to tell her?" he demanded.

"Give me your hand, child of the sea," the corpse said.

Jonathan's hand clenched where he still held his son's shoulder. "Don't."

Ralph twisted away and gave his palm to the dead thing.

Searing pain lanced through his hand and up his arm as the rotten corpse touched his palm. When the pain finally subsided, his hand was covered in numbers and equations.

"There," the dead thing said, "the deed is done. Give that to your friend and she will have all that she has been searching for."

Jonathan grabbed his son's hand and looked at it. "He put math magic on you? Are you working with a witch?" He let out a howl that was returned by a hundred similar voices. "Is that how you hope to save Miskatonic University? By joining with the witch and a Whatley? How lost are you to us, boy?"

Rage filled Ralph and he stared his father down before turning his gaze to their dead guest. "Are we done here?"

"Well," the corpse said, "I am, but it would seem your father and you have much to discuss." The fetid beast faded from existence and took his volcanic island with him.

Ralph turned back to his dad and stated clearly, "No, we're done."

"You will not get another chance to turn your back on us again," Jonathan said.

Then he hung up.

CHAPTER 16

"Hey," a voice said from beyond the darkness, "I think she's finally waking up."

Erin lifted her head and opened her eyes. A shift in vertigo caused her to vomit across the rough wooden floor she was laying on.

As she wiped her mouth, she looked around and tried to figure out what had happened.

The last thing that she remembered was sitting at the table in the Student Union with the Johnson girl and her friends. Then she was pushed...

Sunlight was threatening to blind her through a set of steel bars set into the nearest wall. While the floor was wood, the walls were stone.

Well, the one behind her and to her right were.

The other two walls were more steel bars.

"Where am I?" Erin asked as her kidnappers surrounded the cell.

Meredith stepped forward. "That isn't how any of this is going to work."

"Meredith," Erin hugged herself and stepped back from the bars. "I thought you were looking for a study partner, not whatever this is." Her voice took on a whimper as she spoke. "Please, let me go and I promise that I won't tell anyone."

"Cut the crap," Meredith was nervous, and it showed as she failed to control the volume of her voice. She repeated herself louder, "Cut the crap. What is the name of your cult?"

"Cult?" Erin looked to each of Meredith's friends and then back to her accuser. "Like that Haley's Comet thing?"

Meredith rose above her fear and put her face only inches

from the bars. "I'm Meredith Johannsen, and your people have been hunting my family for a century. What is the name of your—"

She was cut off as Erin lunged forward and grabbed Meredith by her shirt, pulling her into the bars.

Holding her like that, Erin looked to Meredith's friends.

"Let me out," she hissed, "or I will kill her."

"Go ahead," Stephanie, previously unnoticed by Erin, said. "You're in a jail cell in the middle of a pocket universe filled with trigger-happy cowboys. Kill her and see how your situation improves."

Erin took a moment to take in Stephanie's implied threat. She had given up her ruse when she had grabbed at Meredith, there was no point in holding onto it anymore.

"Which one of you is familiar with Euclidian Geometries?" she demanded.

Sheryl was about to open her mouth, but Stephanie was the faster thinker when math wasn't the primary subject.

"She is," Stephanie waved at Meredith. She wasn't sure if this world that Sheryl had created only existed as long as Sheryl was thinking about it, but she didn't want this cultist getting information that her group could use against them. For all they knew, Erin's people could be mounting a rescue mission that very moment.

"We could want her dead," Erin argued.

Stephanie nodded. "I can't imagine anyone here is going to be too willing to help the murderous prisoner when she starts killing." She held up her hands, indicating their odd surroundings. "At what point do you think you will wear out your welcome and this will all fade away into a hellish nightmare?" Stephanie held up her cell phone. "She wrote down some nasty geometries into an app on here. Are you ready to burn?"

Erin took another moment to decide if Stephanie was bluffing but, like most people, she couldn't get a read on the West girl's lack of emotion.

The cultist released Meredith and stepped back from the cell door.

"Much better," Stephanie said. "So, my friend was asking you who you were with."

Erin purposefully turned away from the group and walked back to the cot in the corner of the cell. Sitting down she took a deep breath and let it out slowly.

"Can we just shoot her?" Sheryl asked.

"Not yet," Meredith said. She turned her attention back to Erin. "Is Erin your real name?"

Erin laughed. "That's a great question coming from Meredith Johnson." She sighed. "We aren't some deep cover spy group. Of course that's my name."

"Chris's name wasn't real," Meredith countered.

Erin shrugged. "Men are childish. He wanted to play at being a spy, so he made up a name."

"She's lying," Carlos finally spoke up.

"See?" Erin smirked. "Childish men, making up spy stuff."

"Normally," Carlos returned her smirk, "I would agree with you. Unfortunately, I have had a lot of growing up to do lately." He crossed his arms as a dark look fell behind his eyes. "If I am lying, then who is Laura Hood?"

Their captive leaned forward on the cot. "Not me." She raised an eyebrow in appraisal of Carlos. "Well, aren't you the whole package? Cute and, what, are you a dreamer? You are, aren't you? I've never met a dreamer." She looked directly at Sheryl, ignoring her target and the undeniably terrifying Stephanie. "You can tell dreamers from the rest of folks, or so my mom told me, by the little bit of madness behind their eyes." She pointed at Carlos. "Can you see it? Has he started speaking in alien languages, yet?"

"Shut up," Sheryl spat. "Get the sheriff. Let's hang her and be done with it."

"Hang me?" Laura, formerly Erin, asked. "You're aware that the only law breakers here are you, right? You have me for catfishing, which is so not illegal that they make reality television out of it. At best, you can get me for assault, but that is, of course, after you kidnapped me and locked me in a cell." She leaned back and laughed. "And just wait until I tell them about my missing friend, Chris and how you were the last to see him."

"You misunderstand," Stephanie said. "We want to kill you as part of the interrogation."

Laura's smile faded in confusion. "What does that mean?"

"You seem to me," Stephanie said quietly, "like someone who has done her homework. You're aware of dreamers and you found Meredith, but do you know who I am?"

"Useless," Laura spat. "You are nothing and will be devoured by the coming storm."

"Not quite." Stephanie's voice grew quieter as she opened up her stained leather satchel and pulled out a glowing green syringe. "My name is Stephanie West, and I am wondering how many times you will have to die before you tell us what we want to know."

"West?" their captive's expression filled with both recognition and terror. "That isn't what I think it is, is it?"

Sheryl answered for Stephanie. "If you're thinking it's salvation from the fiery pits of Hell, then yes, it's exactly what you think it is." She lowered her voice before adding, "We haven't tested this new one out, so," she shrugged, "the fiery pits of Hell might be preferred."

"What the fuck is wrong with you people?" Laura, the cultist who was working with other cultists to kidnap and do who knows what to Meredith, asked.

"What do you want with me?" Meredith asked again.

"Forget it," Laura shook her head. "I'm not telling you anything."

"Kill her," Carlos said casually.

Laura shot to her feet. "Don't come anywhere near me."

Stephanie looked from the syringe to Sheryl. "We have yet to test the effects on living tissue. The results could be fascinating."

Sheryl nodded and held her hand out to her friend. "Do you mind?"

Stephanie shook her head and handed the needle over to her friend.

Meredith backed away from the cell door and handed Sheryl the key ring.

"This is your last chance," Meredith pleaded with her. "I just want to know why they are after me."

Laura let out a groan of frustration before yelling, "Fine."

Sheryl stopped moving but didn't back away from the door.

Laura returned to the cot and sat down.

"What your grandpa found in the Pacific has been hunted for thousands of years." Unlike earlier, her confidence and strength had fled her. She looked scared as she explained. "World leaders, crazy people, the desperate, the rich, creatures from other worlds, and worlds from other universes have hunted for what he found on accident while working as a hired hand on a boat."

Meredith slammed her hand against the cage. "We know that," she snapped. "What did he find?"

"Madness," Laura smirked. "His boat located the sunken city of R'lyeh."

The entire videogame-inspired world shuddered, only slightly, in response to Laura naming the sunken city.

"How does a boat find a sunken city?" Sheryl asked.

"Not easily," Laura answered. "What's better, and what really screwed you over," she pointed at Meredith, "was that finding it wasn't enough. They decided to explore this lost land." She took a deep breath, "We aren't just this," she pinched her arm. "People are so much more than that. These bodies are the vessels that our much-larger selves use to manipulate this reality. Our larger selves, our souls, are connected and press into this reality through multiple entry points that we, in our stupidity, call—"

"Family," Meredith finished for her.

"Exactly," Laura said. "Everyone has their opinions of what the city of R'lyeh actually is, but none of those theories matter because all of that city is an extension of his will." The world shook again. When the moment passed, she continued. "If you inject poison under your fingertip, it infects the entire body. He infected everyone who stepped on that island," she paused for dramatic effect that was entirely unnecessary, "and their families."

"And who are you? What are you?" Meredith asked.

"We worship the god that lives in that lost city. To raise the city and call forth our master, we need to find it. The old guard was made up of others infected by his touch and in their greed to keep the glory for themselves, they had everyone from that boat and their entire families removed." Laura crossed her arms. "Then they got old and died and we were all left with finding the one family that got away. Risky move, by the way," she added, "letting us know where you were. We don't need you, just one of you."

"And you won't find them," Meredith snapped. "I had to lead you to me, and they've been hiding for years. You're amateurs." Through gritted teeth she said, "Who are you?"

"We're a church that worships the sleeping god, Cthulhu," she spoke the word, but it seemed to trip over her tongue on the way out. Either way, Sheryl's world shook harder than before.

"The slumbering god is lost and we want to raise him. Many locks must be broken, but first we must find his prison."

"There," Stephanie stated in her flat tone, "we know who is after you. Can we end this now?"

"Kill me," Laura was shouting at the ceiling of her cell, "and I will only fuel the powers massing to waken him." She started chanting, "Cthulhu fthagn, ia! Ia!"

The fabric of the reality Sheryl had created wavered around them.

"You're going to have to get us out of here now," Meredith had to shout to be heard over the world shaking and Laura's rising chant.

"Wait," Carlos was shouting too. "What did she say about the locks? What locks is she talking about?"

Whether it was the noise or her math world crumbling around her, none of them knew, but Sheryl's head was filled with distraction and pain. Not everything Stephanie had said was a lie. Sheryl had created a few small applications based on the plan they had laid out.

The first application ran a string of math to create this world and drag each of them into it. The second would pull them all back to their world. Those were the only two they would need, but just in case, she had created a third.

She had put them on her friend's phone so that Stephanie could activate it if something happened to Sheryl.

"Plan C," Sheryl barked as she grabbed Stephanie's phone and hit the third application.

Laura blinked out of existence. No flash or pop or explosion or noise. One moment she was there and in the next moment she was clearly not. With her gone, the entire town of Easter stopped shaking.

Carlos's jaw dropped. "We didn't just kill her, did we?"

That was when each of them remembered how they had decided not to mention this part to Carlos until it was done. He had made the horrible mistake of leaving the three friends at the table to make their plans while he took a short bathroom break.

"No," Meredith said. "She isn't dead. We sent her to the Dream Lands."

"What?" Carlos wasn't sure how to receive that information and waited on more to be provided.

"She's a normal person that is kind of nuts," Stephanie explained. "We had intended to leave her here, but it was obvious that her magic words were having a negative effect." Even having seen a lot of this magical stuff herself, Stephanie couldn't keep the sound of annoyance out of her voice when she said the word 'magic.'

"So," Meredith picked up, "we asked ourselves what the safest place would be to send a normal person in case this didn't work out."

"And you thought you would send her into the Dream Lands? We don't know what she's capable of. She made this whole world shake by saying the name of some old god and you dropped her into the world of imagination?"

"I told you he wouldn't like it." Stephanie sighed.

"Do any of you know anything about this Cthulhu Cult?" Meredith asked.

Carlos shook his head. "I'm more concerned with these locks she said they're trying to break."

Sheryl turned to him. "You think she means Miskatonic?"

"Of course she meant the school," Stephanie said. "The more important thing is to determine if they are the ones causing the most recent unmoorings."

"The Dream Lands aren't safe," Carlos returned to the matter that was bothering him. "For all you know, her religion could have people waiting for her there."

"Other dreamers?" Sheryl asked. "I hadn't thought of that. Are there a lot of dreamers?"

Carlos shrugged. "I don't know, and that's the reason we should have discussed it before you banished her there."

Meredith let out a heavy sigh. "Fine, we'll just bring her back and then figure out what to do with her."

Sheryl shrugged and hit the button on the app that was meant to run the math that would retrieve what they sent to the Dream Lands.

Nothing happened.

"And that," Carlos said, "is the other reason we shouldn't have sent her anywhere. You have no idea what you're doing with your magic. No more than I know with dreams." He was visibly becoming upset.

"Perhaps math geometry capable of manipulating reality is also subject to the rules of the reality that it is in?" Stephanie suggested. "Maybe if we return to the reality in which the equation was written in, it will work as predicted."

Carlos nodded. "That's as good an idea as any."

Sheryl could have done all of the math to return home in her head, but it was easier to have it already done and just sitting in the application. As she hit the button, she determined she would need to prepare more equations for regular situations.

When they returned to the cafeteria, nothing was different. It turned out that leaving reality meant that you were not subject to the passing of that reality's time. The only difference was that "Erin" was no longer with them.

"Alright," Meredith said. "We're back. Bring her home and we'll grab her before she can do anything."

Sheryl nodded and hit the next button on Stephanie's phone.

At first, nothing happened. Sheryl began to panic and was prepared to hit the button again when Laura was suddenly there, in the same seat that she had been in when she had first introduced herself as Erin.

Except she was definitely not alright.

Her face was covered with blue dots on the right side. Each dot seemed as if it was alive, shifting and sliding across her face as they coalesced together under her right eyelid. Once each of the dots had met there, she opened her eyes wide. The left eye was entirely normal, but her right eye was a swirling blue abyss of alien stars. Laura began panting quicker and quicker.

They were all so entirely focused on Laura and whatever was going on with her that they didn't notice Ralph had joined them until he said hello.

"What's going on with her?" he pointed at Laura.

Laura turned toward him and her panting stopped. She slowly began taking in one deep breath.

Ralph couldn't take his eyes from the freaky cultist sitting at the table, but he also couldn't forget his odd phone call from earlier.

"Uh," he distractedly started, "Sheryl, I ran into a dead guy, and he gave me a message or something that I am supposed to give to you."

Stephanie and Sheryl both yanked their eyes from Laura and focused on Ralph.

"Dead guy?" Stephanie asked.

"Message?" Sheryl asked.

Laura vomited black all over Ralph.

CHAPTER 17

Vomit, by any description, is never pleasant. The vomit that spewed from Laura's mouth was even more so. Whatever had climbed inside of her, while she had been in the Dream Lands, had hitched some sort of ride back to her original reality. The resulting negative symptoms included this black vomit that smelled like burned rubber and rot.

The smell had soaked entirely through Ralph's clothes before he could take them off and shower. The students he shared a dorm with would be avoiding that shower for the next three weeks.

Stephanie had been about to call an ambulance out of concern for their previously-imprisoned victim, but Carlos had stopped her.

"We don't know what's inside her," he had pointed out.

"Then what do we do?" Meredith asked as Ralph left without telling Sheryl whatever it was he needed to tell her.

As the cafeteria cleared out, Carlos tried to think of what was needed when one of his intuitions told him.

"Call Carol."

Carol Berg had arrived with the nurse and several chain restraints that made handcuffs look like toys. Once she saw the mess, she used her phone to request cleanup assistance.

The last they saw of the cultist before Carol and her cleanup crew whisked her away she was catatonic, with a blue eye, and black vomit dribbling down her chin.

Carlos waved a finger at Sheryl, Meredith, and Stephanie.

"Stop thinking you know what you're doing," this was the first time they had seen him so angry. "Stop thinking that because you have started to discover something about yourself that suddenly you're a master of it." He let out a sigh to try and calm himself down. "I have barely scratched the surface of what being a dreamer means, and I only know that because," he pointed in the direction that the cleanup crew had taken Laura, "I don't have a clue what happened there."

All of them, even Stephanie, carried the guilt on their faces.

"Carlos," Stephanie started to apologize for them.

He shook his head. "Don't apologize, just do better." He rubbed his face before turning back to Stephanie. "You are not Herbert, as you keep reminding us. You're morally grounded and ethical, but the minute that you start cutting corners or trying to take shortcuts is the minute you start traveling down that same path as him." His attention shifted to Sheryl, "You are trying to understand math magic. I get that, but you can't go shoving people into other dimensions that you haven't even been to before." He shrugged. "You have seen some of those dimensions. The really bad ones. What would you have done if she had been sent to one of them by mistake? Or if we couldn't have brought her back?"

Meredith straightened her shoulders when he turned to her. She knew he was mad, but she also knew that he wasn't wrong.

"I'm glad you found some clues and your friends," he waved a hand at the two other women before waving it at himself, "were able to help. Now be a friend back and start encouraging them to be their best selves."

Carlos took a deep breath and sat down on a nearby chair. "We can't save anything if we keep leaving victims in our wake."

Meredith eyed Stephanie and received a nod in return. They had wondered if Carlos had known what had happened to "Chris," and it turned out that his intuition had told him about the cultist's death.

Unless Carlos was hiding murderous secrets of his own, but they both doubted that level of secret could have been held by the boy scout.

The group was a flood of mixed emotions with Meredith being happy yet desperate for more answers, Sheryl and Stephanie feeling admonished and questioning their moral compasses, Carlos contemplating something that none of them were sure about, and Ralph smelling worse than death.

They went their own ways once the Student Union was back in order.

"Am I boring you, Mr. Davies?" the voice snapped Carlos back to the conscious world and he flushed with embarrassment.

"Sorry," he muttered loud enough to be heard.

"Not enough sleep last night?" Professor Stice asked with a slight smirk.

"Plenty of sleep," Carlos countered, "just not enough rest."

Professor Stice raised his eyebrow at that but continued with the lecture.

Being still in his first year, Carlos was sitting through a museum studies class to complete an elective. Museum studies tended to fall into one of two categories. You were either looking to put art into a museum, or you were studying historical art. This was the latter.

When the lecture finished examining the different pieces said to be coming to campus on tour from the Chicago Field Museum, everyone began filing out.

Carlos tried to stay hidden, but he wasn't as good at it as he had hoped that he would be.

"Mr. Davies," Professor Stice's voice echoed across the large room. "Would you mind staying back a moment?"

Carlos sighed and dropped his bag back onto his seat. When the room had emptied, Professor Stice walked up the row between the seats and spun one around so that he could sit and face Carlos.

"Sleeping, but never resting," he said as he let out a breath. "A lot of things could cause that. Some of them are why many of your friends were absent today. Parties, drugs, drinking, and carnal urges are all excuses for falling asleep in class that most people won't tell me but are clear to see." He held up his hand as Carlos moved to defend his behavior, cutting the young man off before he could start. "That's not what is going on with you, though, is it?"

"No," was all Carlos said.

"Nobody likes to say it out loud because they think they'll

break some universal rule about talking about monsters and demons and alien worlds, but that's not the case." He took a deep breath and shouted, "You are a dreamer."

Carlos was confused. He fell asleep in class. Nothing about that should have given him away.

"How could you possibly know that?" Carlos asked.

Professor Stice shrugged and crossed his arms, leaning back on the seat.

"Mysteries, legends, monsters, and aliens fill the shadows of our world only because we choose not to shine any light on any of it. Things wouldn't be as scary and momentous if we just talked about them more."

Carlos returned a smirk of his own. "Monsters might say the same thing to cause their own kind of trouble."

"True," Stice nodded in agreement. "And if you took a closer look at me, you might see me as a monster as well."

Once encouraged, Carlos could not help but look at the man as he looked in the realm of dreams and other-sight.

Carlos closed his eyes and cast his mind into the direction of the sleep between worlds. That was where he saw Professor Stice in an entirely new way.

Instead of Stice, he saw a cone shaped creature of fungus and tentacles with a stalk protruding from the tip of the cone. Lobster claws were attached at the end of stick-like arms. At the top of the stalk were three close-together orbs that Carlos assumed had to be eyes.

He forced himself fully back into his home reality and opened his eyes.

"What are you?" Carlos felt like he should be terrified by the vision he had seen, but he only felt curiosity and peace.

"I'm..." Professor Stice hesitated in his answer, "complicated. I am Professor Ronald Stice, and I am also known by another name. It is difficult to pronounce in your tongue, but I will try." He took a deep breath and said, "Kr'nak'tkon." When he saw Carlos's face at the pronunciation, he laughed and added, "You can continue to call me Professor Stice, for now."

"Are you a monster?"

"That is a rather uninspired question, don't you think? Are

you asking because of how you saw me in my natural form, or because I am different?" Professor Stice was enjoying this questioning, and Carlos could tell.

"I am asking because you are different, and I don't know what you are yet." He paused before adding, "You are right, though. My question was rude. I should have asked, 'What are your intentions?'"

"Much better," Stice gave a small clap. "My intentions are for you to get a 4.0 in my class," he paused again, "and to document the happenings of this particular decade in Earth history."

"The first was the professor and the second was your true self?"

"Correct," the smirk finally dropped from Professor Stice's face. "I will answer the questions you want to ask now so that we can get to the meat of why I revealed myself to you." He took another deep breath. "I am of the Great Race, the Yith. Have you ever seen Quantum Leap? No, likely not, you are too young. Anyway, my species transfers our conscious minds into different vessels in different eras to record history as it unfolds. We see everything, everywhere, eventually. We were at the birth of humanity and at its final days. When we take over a human mind, or any mind for that matter, we send their consciousness back to our body. It is a full trade. It is quite traumatizing at first. By all reports from my people, the real Stice was startled, but he has adapted well and is enjoying his anthropological study of my people. It is unfortunate that he will not remember any of it when he finally returns home."

"You chose Miskatonic University in this year to observe what happens in history?" Carlos felt like this was an ominous portent that he was not happy about.

Professor Stice lifted a hand. "Fear not, young padawan, I have been here for eight years. It has nothing to do with the disabling of the Miskatonic anchor. It is in the Great Race's best interest to keep the anchor intact."

"Why?"

"We are of this reality as well. Your planet is not the only planet in this plane of existence and our great city of Pnakotus is, was, and will be on this planet. To lose the Miskatonic

University anchor would threaten the greatest historical database of the universe to ever exist." His smirk returned. "Or will exist, or maybe it did exist."

"You're very forthcoming," Carlos said. "What do you want with me?"

"I told you," Professor Stice said. "I want you to get a 4.0 in my class, and your poor sleeping isn't going to make that any easier. So, I want to help you be the better dreamer you are." He waved a hand at his body to indicate what he really was. "The quickest way to help you is to convince you to trust me. Truth generates trust, so I revealed myself."

"How do you plan to help me?"

"For all of your travels," Stice explained, "you're still human. And while you might be taking what you're learning in stride, they are still going to cause your human mind some traumatic scars. I want to help you process what you see. Perhaps as an alien therapist of a sorts." He crossed his arms again. "Randolph Carter isn't the best of mentors when it comes to processing and understanding what a young adult is going through."

Carlos started to open his mouth and Stice cut him off again.

"Much as you looked at me and could see what I was, I have, for lack of a better word, a similar gift. Besides, Carter can't see a dreamer without at least visiting them with cryptic promises about gates and keys."

"What's in it for you?" Carlos pressed. "I don't think that I'm buying this 'help me do better,' angle."

"Documentation," Stice said. "Complete transparency, I will be documenting everything about your life for the archives, and I would have been doing it anyway, but this way I can see it first-hand and give a more accurate account. Not removed and from a distance."

"Won't that threaten space and time, or something like that? Normally, that's the first question when you're talking about a time traveler and what they can and can't do. Won't documenting me change history?"

"I won't be altering anything," Stice shook his head. "I want to help you achieve a potential you were already going to reach, with less anxiety along the way."

"You can't document a culture without directly affecting the culture," Carlos countered.

"Ah," Stice was grinning ear to ear. "Someone has been paying attention in class." He shook his head. "Time isn't as fragile as popular fiction would have you believe. You will know when you've meddled with time too much." The professor shuddered. "It has defenses."

Carlos wanted to ask more about that and time travel in general, but was cut off before he could.

"I have been as forthcoming as I can be," Professor Stice said. "Probably more than I should have. Either way, I will not be telling you any more. I'm here for you, not the other way around."

"When will Professor Stice return to his body?" Carlos asked anyway.

"There are too many factors involved for me to answer that, even if I could." His eyes turned wistful. "When he does, he will need someone to ease him back into his life. That is the other thing you can help me with. I will teach you about dreamers and document you and your time for the archives, and you will use your skills as a kind human being to keep Professor Stice from going mad when he returns."

"Before I agree to anything, I should probably see what you have to offer," Carlos said.

Stice nodded. "Well, first off, let's talk about dreaming easier. I know Carter has been all about bringing your body with you, as a security precaution, and he's not wrong, but he's also not being entirely truthful."

"How do you know so much about things I don't even tell my friends?"

Stice wiggled his fingers. "I'm from the future," he said in a voice that was eerily reminiscent of old sci-fi shows. "We have either already had this conversation, or we have already had a ton of conversations. Either way, the only way I know anything is because I read it in our archive. The only way it ends up in the archive is if I documented it."

"This is predestination paradox stuff," Carlos said. "If I

suddenly decide not to tell you anything, then you won't know anything more than I've already told you."

Stice tipped his head to the side, reviewing what Carlos had said internally before answering.

"Yes and no," he finally answered. He put his finger to his lips and lowered his voice, "This is a trade secret, so tell no one, but you're assuming that the Great Race only has access to one reality. Even if you didn't tell me something in a conversation, there might be a reality where you did, and that would have entered the archives."

"Then what's the point of this?" Carlos asked.

"I told you," Stice seemed to be getting frustrated. "I want you to help you and whether or not someone helped you in another reality does not change the fact that I want to help you in this one."

"So," Carlos finally sat down, "bringing my body with me is a bad idea?"

Professor Stice's frustration evaporated.

"No," he replied, "it isn't a bad idea, it's just not always a good idea. You don't use a hammer when you need a screwdriver, and you don't bring your body and claim security as the reason when a severe lack of security is left in its wake."

"How is it not secure?"

"When you're dreaming and floating through the cosmos, you can get lost. You are fortunate that your guide has been readily available. He won't always be, in those moments, your being lost might be a permanent condition. That wouldn't be the case if you cast your mind out from your body and left your body here and somewhere safe. Then your body would act as an anchor. No matter where you traveled, you could always return home to your flesh."

Carlos shook his head. "Randy said that leaving my body alone could leave it open for possession from interdimensional beings."

Stice barked a laugh. "He isn't wrong, but, again, he isn't right." He leaned in as he said, "These interdimensional beings don't need your body empty to take it over and most of the time they would prefer you were still in it."

"Why?" Carlos was bewildered.

"Humans are delicious." Stice laughed.

"Alright," Carlos joined in on the laugh, but he wasn't entirely sure it was a joke. "What happens to my body if my spirit is attacked?"

"When you enter the lands of dream your spirit becomes your body."

"What does that mean?" Carlos didn't understand.

"It means maybe nothing, or maybe everything that happens to your dream body happens to your real body." Stice shrugged. "Results may vary, depending on where you are in Dream."

Carlos nodded. "What else you got?"

CHAPTER 18

Class was something that Stephanie found relieving most of the time. Lesson plans and scheduled projects fit well within her regimented mind of logic and science.

It didn't matter that she already knew most, if not all, of what she was learning. She enjoyed finding the smallest bit of peace in a world of chaos and silly things meant to distract from the growth of her knowledge base.

Which was entirely unfortunate, as she was not enjoying her time in class at all today.

They were discussing diseases, she thought, and she couldn't focus. There was nothing that would stick in Stephanie's head as long as she carried with her the two most conflicting thoughts she had ever experienced.

The first thought was that she needed a dead thing, anything, to test her new version of the reagent on. They had only ever tested the earlier versions on cells, and everything had looked promising, but now they needed to know how organisms with complex brains would react to the reagent. They also needed to start testing to what level of decay a body could still be reanimated, or potentially rejuvenated, by the new chemicals.

She needed to test it to continue her work.

This conflicted directly with the second thought warring for attention in her mind.

Carlos.

Her friend had made a very astute observation about her own hypocrisy. She felt a moral obligation not to harm anyone or cause pain. Yet, she already had two victims.

Whenever her mind circled back to that thought, she couldn't help but try and solve Laura's catatonic state.

If only she could test her reagent, she could see if it had any potential to repair the damage caused by foreign influences. She might even be able to save the cultist.

Except to test her great uncle's corrected formula would require her to try it on a dead thing. Dead things couldn't give consent after the fact. That was the first moral dilemma, while the second was certainly more horrific.

What if the formula didn't work? Or worse: what if it did not work the right way?

Stephanie had no doubts that Herbert had discovered some level of success with his formula the century before. Each account of his victims showed errant behavior crossing the border from animalistic to practically demonic. Herbert could not have been directly responsible, especially if his notes on the subjects were to be believed. Even in his journal, he cited the erratic and violent behavior of several of his earliest subjects. They went wild, killed many, and had to be put down before they tore apart all of Arkham.

If the formula could do that, what right did she have to test it on anyone?

Besides, animals going insane and being resistant to death would be just as bad, if not worse, than loosing deranged human cadavers on the city.

Carlos wasn't right, and she knew that. They might have gone too far with the Laura girl, but cultist Chris was going to hurt them, and their options had been limited.

All the while that these thoughts were burning away in her mind, Alicia Halsey was casting glares in her direction.

Today was the day they would go to the crematorium and assist, and Halsey had made it clear that she didn't like Stephanie anywhere near anything like practical medicine.

Halsey and her issues with Stephanie would have to wait. Her personal dilemmas were causing her enough issues and the moment was approaching. Would she just ask about how to get access to a corpse for her own experiments or would she just steal one? Or would she do nothing, since doing something might only prove Carlos was right all along?

The Lab assigned to the class mostly consisted of prepping

the bodies for the incinerator. By the time they were in front of the incinerator, there wasn't much work left to do aside from the operation of the machine.

Stephanie found that when it was her turn, her heart swelled with sympathy for the owners of these pets that had been donated to the school. The majority of them were strays that had been sick, but she didn't know which ones were which.

And her pain caused her some relief. She couldn't imagine that the man from her uncle's journals would have felt much of anything at the death of, what he would have considered, viable test subjects.

"Don't you dare," a wisp of a voice hissed at her.

Stephanie spun, with her hand still hovering over the button to pull the deceased cat into the oven.

"What?" She was more annoyed than surprised to see Alicia Halsey staring directly at her. "I'm about to destroy the body. Not any of those other ideas you seem so keen to remind everyone that my bloodline is capable of. Ashes to ashes and dust to dust. Literally. So, what could have you bothered this time?"

"That's Pepper," the dam holding back her emotions released and Alicia began sobbing. "My parents said she ran away."

The teacher's look went from an annoyance that mirrored Stephanie's to a look of utter horror.

"Ms. Halsey," Professor Finn walked over and touched the student's arm," all animals are received by donation. If this is your cat, it was received through the same channel. Are you certain that this is Pepper?"

Alicia's face contorted to anger as she stepped over to the shelf of tools and grabbed a scanner. She walked over and pressed it to the back of the cat's neck. When it beeped, she didn't even look at it. She just handed it directly to Stephanie.

Stephanie turned the device around to see the display and along with a list of other data, including the owner's address, the microchip also provided a name.

Pepper.

She nodded to Dr. Finn.

"Stephanie," Dr. Finn said, "finish the last two animals."

She held up her hand to halt any questions and said quickly, "Do not incinerate Pepper. I am going to go to our acquisitions office and find the paperwork. We need to make sure this is legal and not someone's horrible idea of a prank." She turned to Alicia. "If it is on the up-and-up, then I will leave it to you on the final decisions."

Finn practically ran from the basement room that housed the incinerator. The class saw this as a chance to escape and within a minute all that remained in the room were three dead animals, Stephanie, and Alicia.

Stephanie gave Alicia time to grieve over her cat while she continued with the last animals and emptying the incinerator.

It was not lost on Stephanie that she had only minutes ago been empathizing with the owner of that cat and suddenly the owner was the only person on campus who she actively avoided.

When Alicia seemed to have her emotions in check, Stephanie took a step closer.

"How old was she?"

Alicia started, as if she had forgotten that Stephanie was there.

"Only four," Alicia answered.

"That is incredibly young," Stephanie put the empathy that she had felt into her voice and took another step closer. "I am sorry for your loss."

Alicia tried to give Stephanie a look of disgust, but only half-succeeded.

"No, you're sorry that you can't play with the dead thing anymore."

"What my distant, disavowed, and disowned uncle did was inexcusable, but I will no longer stand with you assuming I am the same as he was. I didn't even know him." Alicia hadn't been rebuked before and was at a loss to respond. "Additionally, I also once had a cat. She was hit by a car." Stephanie had a momentary lapse in her emotional shield and quickly wiped it away. "It is why I do what I am doing now."

Alicia nodded, thinking that she understood. "Veterinary degree. Makes sense."

Stephanie revealed a tight smirk. "That, and more. Alicia, I think we can help each other out, but before I get to how and what I mean by that, I think I need you to let me explain some things to you first."

"Such as?" Alicia couldn't keep the derision from her voice, but she didn't add to it. Instead, she remained quiet and waited for Stephanie to continue.

"Such as what really happened to your great-grandfather. Also, what really happened to my great uncle."

Quickly, in hopes of beating Professor Finn back, Stephanie took the biggest chance of her life and told Alicia everything about Herbert's research, how the original Dr. Halsey had died, been resurrected, and the mess that followed. She told her everything up to when she found her uncle's journal.

"Why should I believe any of this?" Alicia asked. "And why would you tell me? I hate you."

Stephanie shook her head. "No, I think you hate being reminded of why your family is famous."

"Excuse me?" Alicia balked.

"Jesse James the eighteenth doesn't go around lamenting the horrible murder of his great-something-or-another. Neither do you. You see his name everywhere. You hear all the rumors and stories. Now you've heard another one. One that you, for some reason, did not immediately ignore or attack me over. You want to be a new Dr. Halsey, one without the stigma of the past, so you hate me because I am here. Another reminder of what might have happened to some man a century ago."

"So?"

"So," Stephanie walked over to her bag and pulled out a glowing green syringe, "Pepper doesn't have to be dead." Stephanie paused while Alicia allowed herself to connect the dots. When the light started to dawn in her eyes, Stephanie continued. "Her body is in surprisingly decent condition and the, um, parts that are not would be healed by the reagent within a matter of hours," she paused, "I believe."

"Even if I believed everything you told me about my great-grandfather, which I don't," Alicia said, "why would I let you do the same thing to my cat?"

"Multiple reasons," Stephanie said matter-of-factly. "The

first being that this is not the same chemical that my great-uncle used. This is a formula that I have spent months making better."

"But haven't tested," Alicia had connected more dots than Stephanie had given her credit for.

Stephanie shook her head. "That is exactly my problem. I need a test subject, but I don't want to resort to the methods of my uncle and steal corpses or do things that cross the ethical line. That is why I am asking you to not only give me permission to save Pepper, but also if you would be my assistant and moral compass as we try to develop a better formula. A formula that can save lives."

Alicia said nothing. She stood there, entirely motionless as she stared at her dead cat.

Stephanie was also motionless, but on the inside, she was a tornado of terror and emotions. She had given Alicia enough to confirm her suspicions of the West girl and enough to get her expelled from any sort of education in the medical fields. Or worse, she could be arrested under allegations of illegal animal experimentation. She had not done anything yet, but it would be Alicia's word against hers.

"Fine."

The word was so quiet, Stephanie was not even sure she had heard it.

Alicia looked at Stephanie with red-rimmed eyes. "Do it and if it works, I'll help you."

Stephanie's smile was uncontrollable. She handed Alicia the syringe.

"From the notes," she explained, "the best places for the best reactions were the base of the skull or directly into the heart."

Alicia stepped up to Pepper and stroked her hair slowly. Tears dripped down her cheeks.

"There you are," Carol Berg stormed into the room. Her eyes fell on the syringe, then to Alicia, before turning on Stephanie.

"Your actions have consequences," she said quietly. "Your cultist spy had friends. They are making their move." She nodded to Pepper. "When you are done here, meet me at the Dean's office." She paused again. "Don't take too long or there might not be a world left to save."

With that, she spun and left as quickly as she arrived.

"Why didn't she ask what we were doing?" Alicia asked.

"She doesn't have to ask questions that she already knows the answers to," Stephanie answered although she was wondering the same thing.

Alicia whimpered and slammed the needle into the back of her cat's skull. She pressed the plunger and retrieved the needle.

Stephanie touched her gently on the shoulder.

"You need to step back. Just in case."

Alicia nodded and did as she was told, never taking her eyes from Pepper.

The amount of tension and excitement building up inside of Stephanie was unlike anything she had ever experienced. Aside from the possible miracle they might bear witness to, Stephanie was about to do something that her disgraced and failure of an uncle had never been able to do.

Pepper twitched and both girls gasped.

The previously deceased cat stretched in a slow and clearly painful manner. Stephanie watched as the discoloration of death began to recede from Pepper's face and limbs. Pepper was slow to stand but when she did, she looked directly at Alicia.

Neither woman moved out of fear that the Halsey family was about to experience another tragedy like the rampage that was visited on Arkham only a century previously.

Then Pepper purred and began hacking.

Without even realizing what she was doing, Alicia ran to a nearby sink and cupped her hands before sprinting back to her revived cat. Pepper lapped up the water quickly. When Stephanie shook from her own surprise, she ran to the sink and did the same thing. Even if Pepper hadn't been at least a week dead, the revitalization process was going to require moisture and energy. Pepper was going to need food and water.

"Perhaps," Stephanie voiced out loud, "that was part of my great-uncle's problem. Maybe he did not realize that his subjects would need energy and his being ill-prepared led to their madness in search of meat and hydration."

Alicia's eyes lit up and she ran to her bag, resting by the door on the floor. She pulled out a zipped plastic bag and poured the contents on the slab where Pepper still sat.

It was a bag of cheese crackers. Pepper vacuumed them up. She was obviously still hungry when they were gone, but she seemed sated enough not to maul them all to death.

Pepper leaped to Alicia's shoulder and began nuzzling her owner.

Alicia was crying as she turned to Stephanie.

"Thank you. Thank you, so much." Her eyes went wide. "You just created the cure for death."

While Alicia wasn't wrong, there were a lot of variables they still needed to monitor for. "And you will assist me in monitoring this patient and in finding new, and ethically sourced, test subjects?"

Alicia gulped, wiped her eyes, and looked to Pepper before nodding.

"It works, do we need more?"

Stephanie stepped closer and looked directly into Pepper's seemingly normal and incredibly less cloudy eyes.

"It worked for Pepper," she said. "And it worked for now. We will need to run calculations and monitor before we can definitively say that we've cured death."

Inside, though, Stephanie was screaming with excitement.

CHAPTER 19

The stench of that otherworldly vomit took more than one shower to get rid of. When the scent was finally gone enough for Ralph to be seen in public, he wanted to go and find Sheryl to let her know the message he was tasked with giving her.

Then he saw Levi stalking across the campus and all thoughts of messages fled his mind. When Levi saw Ralph, he pulled back and threw, showing that he was carrying a football as he walked. Ralph caught it easily enough and tossed it back. They continued in this manner until they were close enough to talk and still play catch.

"Did that Berg lady find you?" Levi asked.

"The Dean's assistant?" Ralph shook his head. "I've been in the shower for hours."

"Hours?" Levi smirked. "You can take the fish out of the water, but you can't take the water out of the fish?"

"That is enough of that," Ralph laughed in spite of the joke at his genealogical expense. "What did she want?"

"That kid that puked on you," Levi's face twisted at the memory of the stench, "well, she had friends. She wants you and your pals to meet her at the Dean's office."

Ralph threw the ball. "I should probably do that then. You coming?"

Levi shook his head. "Your friends and you keep pulling me into some scary crap. This seems like it might be another of those things."

"Nothing too scary," Ralph replied. "Just cultists trying to destroy the world. You'll fit right in."

It was Ralph's turn to smirk and wait to see how his joke landed.

If anyone else had said it, Levi would have torn them apart. Much as Ralph had told Levi about his family and their odd mannerisms, Levi had filled Ralph in on the difficult history of the Whatleys and how they had tried to bring an Old God into this reality.

But it wasn't anyone else. It was Ralph, and much as Ralph rolled with the joke at his expense, this newer and attempting-to-be-more-human Levi rolled with it as well.

"Hey, we almost succeeded." He shrugged. "Anyway, I am sure I will be drawn into whatever happens. I can't let you fight all the monsters by yourself."

Ralph laughed, and they continued to throw the ball around for a while longer before the weight of whatever he had been beckoned for finally convinced Ralph to head toward the Dean's office.

Either way, he didn't understand the message that he had for Sheryl, and he had a feeling she would need it before whatever was going to happen next.

At the door to the Dean's office stood a lanky, balding man.

"You must be Ralph," the man who looked a little too much like the standard school professor said. "I am Professor Stice. I believe that the rest are inside waiting on you."

"Are you part of all this?" Ralph asked.

"The coming end of the world?" Stice smiled. "No, I am just an observer." He paused before adding, "I am aiding Carlos with his education into the power of dreams. It is likely that you will see more of me in the future."

"Great," Ralph said with less enthusiasm than he was feeling toward the end of the world.

Whoever this man was, Ralph got the distinct impression that he was not what he seemed. That was entirely par for the course for Miskatonic University, and Ralph saw no reason to dwell on this new addition.

He stepped past the tutor, or whatever he was, and walked into the room.

The similarity to the last time he was in this office wasn't lost on Ralph. His friends crowded the too few seats while Carol and the Dean stood on either side of the desk.

The difference, this time, was the map of the campus spread out on the desk and what looked like a sports roster sitting next to a large book that was definitely not the Doran journal from before. This was a newer book and looked much thinner.

Ralph saw Sheryl and went directly to her.

"Glad you could join us, Mr. Allen," Carol said before he could reach her. "If you'll give us a minute before you start the chatter back up, we have a lot to go over and a short time to do it."

Ralph frowned but nodded his understanding.

"Great," the dean said. "I would like to take this moment to point out that we are in no way upset with how you have handled yourselves. The," Dean Ward took a deep breath before continuing, "issue with the Laura girl was unfortunate and could have been handled better, but," he smiled at Meredith, "how does one handle cultists hell-bent on bringing about the end of the world? No, we are not upset by that result."

"What we are upset about," Carol picked up where the dean left off, obviously not in full agreement with the dean's assessment, "is that her removal from the field has triggered a series of contingencies put in place if anything were to happen to her."

"Contingencies?" Carlos was eyeing his friends, thinking thoughts very in line with those of the administrative assistant.

"The Cult of Cthulhu, that has existed for millennia, has decided to make their move on destabilizing the anchor." The dean shrugged. "Now that they know they have a spiritual compass to the sunken city of R'lyeh, they are preparing the way."

"Which means destroying the lock holding our world in place before sacrificing Meredith Johnson to their old god," Carol elaborated.

"How are they going to destroy the lock?" Ralph asked. "We haven't seen anyone smashing stones or burning buildings. For that matter, how have the other unmoorings even happened?"

Carol sighed. "Mostly through attacks aimed directly at the different protection spells, or locks, hidden around the campus. Every building has several that tie the campus together as one larger spell holding the lock of our universe in place. The previous unmoorings have happened as a result of someone trying to cast a spell to destroy one of those smaller locks. We believe that these were tests of our defenses. That is no longer the case. They have arrived in legion and are stationing themselves, quietly, around the campus. They plan to coordinate their attacks at once."

"How do you know any of this?" Meredith said.

Professor Stice stepped into the room then. "From me, mostly," he said. "And I would prefer it if you didn't mention my involvement to anyone, ever."

"Professor Stice volunteered this information, and has done so at a heavy cost to his personal well-being."

"And we believe him?" Ralph threw a glance at the professor, sizing him up for the first time.

The dean touched the book on the desk with one hand and the "sports roster" with the other hand. "He has provided us with enough detailed information that we can confirm."

"So, this is happening," Sheryl's palms were sweating. "This isn't some big, Scion Cycle spell. This is a war for the campus. What do we do? What can we do?"

"We currently have the advantage," Carol said. "They don't know that we know, and in one hour," she sighed and tossed an annoyed look at Ralph who had been the last to join them, "their spells will be in place, and we will have a very short window to stop them."

"You're wrong, though," the dean looked at Sheryl as he spoke. "This is part of the Scion Cycle spell. This is a big part. You are here to stop the unmooring of our universe. They are attempting to enact the final unmooring. Either the Scion Cycle stops them, or our reality descends into madness."

"You're laying it on a little—" a sound like an explosion interrupted Ralph.

"What the hell was that?" it was Stice who asked. "They are spellcasters, not terrorists."

Carol looked out the window behind the dean's desk. "It would seem that they are a little of both." She looked at the dean. "They blew up the botanical garden."

"The first lock," he muttered. "That is one way to do it, I suppose. Why change tactics, though?"

Professor Stice crossed his arms and let out a slow breath. "I am afraid that might be my fault. My people must have caught on to my assisting you. They are offering an equal level of assistance to the opposition."

"Why?" Carlos demanded. "They lose if we lose, too."

Stice nodded. "Yes, they do, but they lose more if you win and the timeline is altered."

"Leave," Carol said. "Before you unbalance the scales even more. Or before they return the owner of that body. The last thing we need is someone traumatized by the Great Race while our campus is under attack."

Stice bowed his head in agreement and left the room.

"Now what?" Sheryl stood up and began looking in her bag for her phone.

"They know that we're coming," Dean Ward said. "We should confront them head on."

"They have explosives and who knows what else," Stephanie countered. "We are not soldiers. We should call the police and you should dismiss the students, immediately."

"In any other case, that is exactly what we would do," Carol said in the calmest tone she had used that entire meeting. "This is not something that the Arkham police, who are notorious for failing to respond to the weirdness that happens in this city, are capable of handling. And while you might just be students, you are also scions of some of the most powerful bloodlines of the New England area. They have magic users, but we have a math witch, something that no one has dealt with in a hundred years. We have a man with the blood of a god in his veins and the strength to match. We have the reincarnated spirit of the most powerful dreamer to ever step foot on this planet. We have the genius of West and the best investigator to ever hide in our city." She took a deep breath. "And you are not our only plan. I'm not saying get out there and jump in front of bullets. I'm saying, help us protect this reality, because you all live in it."

"Ms. West," the dean picked up, "I would like you and Mr. Davies to investigate the botanical garden. Mr. Allen and Ms.

Mason to the football field. Stay hidden, gather intelligence, and try not to engage unless they engage you. If you see an opening to disrupt their work, please do it."

"What about me?" Meredith asked.

"They want you," Carlos answered for the dean. "It would be a dumb move to put you out in the open."

"But," the dean added, "we do have a task for you, Ms. Johnson." He pulled open a drawer and pulled out a pistol. "I believe that you put in your transcripts that you were an excellent sharpshooter. Was that part of your cover story or an honest assessment?"

Meredith glanced at the gun and then to her friends. "It was an honest assessment. I learned to protect myself." She looked the dean in the eye. "I don't want to kill anyone."

"You need to protect yourself, and no," Dean Ward shook his head, "I don't expect that you will have any people to shoot at."

"Then why would I need a gun?"

"For the not-people," Carlos said. His expression didn't change and everyone in the room knew that it was not an attempt at Carlos's brand of humor.

The universe shook.

"We are out of time. You need to go." Carol scooped up the pistol and handed it to Meredith. "Take care of this. It belonged to a friend of mine."

Merdith looked it over. Thanks to her father and his years of justifiable paranoia, she was familiar with the use and care of most weapons. This was a Webley .38, made famous as Dr. Watson's weapon of choice in Conan-Doyle's stories.

"Where's the ammunition?" Meredith asked as she checked the cylinder and found the six-shooter empty.

The administrative assistant grabbed the weapon back from Meredith and fired it into the air. The loud crack of the gun echoed in the room as plaster dust fell from the ceiling.

"This isn't just any revolver, Ms. Johnson," she explained. "This is a magical gun and while it might look otherwise, I assure you that it is fully loaded. In the unlikely event that you run out of bullets, come see me, and I will help you." Carol smirked. "The idea of you running out of ammunition is highly unlikely."

Meredith took the gun back and asked, "Where would you like me?"

"You will remain—" another explosion, close enough to destroy the windows in the office and send everyone, except the entirely unphased secretary, to the floor.

Carol grabbed Meredith by the arm and pointed out the now-empty window to the night sky. "It was daylight a minute ago. This isn't our universe, an unmooring is happening and I need you here with us."

Meredith looked around. "Here? Why here?"

Her friends touched her arm as they each left and ran to their assigned tasks.

"Here," the dean answered instead of Carol as he climbed back to his feet, "because I am the last lock."

"What?" Meredith was surprised.

"The title of Dean for Miskatonic University has always had more actual power to it than one would know. To completely detach the school from our reality, the dean must be destroyed." He dusted himself off and continued. "Of course, this was all designed by Dr. Doran, and I wouldn't put it past him to have done that as part of some last stand type of thing." He lifted his head and saw the glowering gaze of Carol. "Or perhaps, um, because he knew the importance of the role."

"Either way," Carol turned back to Meredith, "Charles and I have our own methods of fighting, and someone needs to handle the magic pistol. So, you stay here and assist us."

Meredith protested, "If they are coming here for him and me, they will be people, and I will have to shoot them. I won't do that."

Carol's skin took on a pale shade as she grunted. Her nails beginning to elongate.

"I will handle the people," she growled as her eyes became animalistic and her teeth grew bigger than her mouth. "You handle the rest."

"What … what are you?" Meredith was more afraid of

whatever Carol was turning into than whatever was coming after them.

The dean answered, as his secretary was no longer capable.

"Years ago, they would have called her, incorrectly, a Wendigo." He rolled up his sleeves and shrugged. "I don't know that they have a more accurate term."

"She looks like a werewolf," Meredith's voice was a whisper.

"She's practically naked, grey, and hairless," Dean Ward snickered. "Have you ever even seen a werewolf movie?"

Meredith tore her eyes away from Carol and finally noticed that the dean hadn't done anything other than roll up his sleeves and square his shoulders.

"And what are you?"

Dean Charles Dexter Ward had joined Miskatonic University in the early nineteen thirties when those after him had thought him dead and gone. He had found a passion teaching and decided that he needed to reevaluate his life choices. Miskatonic had proven itself to be a space where he could live out his odd form of immortality in relative peace and in exchange for that peace, he would impart his wisdom and protection where needed.

It was much more rewarding than being hunted for his occult practices had been.

"Me?" he smirked. "I'm resilient."

CHAPTER 20

Ralph and Sheryl ran toward the football field. The dean hadn't told them where the lock would be hidden, but they both knew that they would have a good idea when they arrived.

Once they were at the edge of the field, Ralph led the way up and into the bleachers where they could hide and see what was happening.

Just as they had predicted, a large number of people, obviously not on the team, were centered around the northernmost goal post.

"Now what do we do?" Ralph asked.

Sheryl shrugged. "Wait and see what they are going to do, and break it up before it is completed."

"We know what they are going to do," Ralph was getting impatient and frustrated. He didn't disagree with Stephanie. Destinies and he had always been at odds, and now there was this one looming over him. He hadn't thought about it much since the last unmooring event. He had been distracted by Levi and football. As good as those distractions had been at helping him pretend that he was just another kid, here he was with destiny staring him in the face again and telling him how and what he should be doing.

Sheryl could see that Ralph was uncomfortable sitting still, and hoped that maybe she could distract him.

"Didn't you say you had a message for me?"

He looked at his friend blankly for a moment longer than Sheryl assumed he would need before his eyes lit up with the memory.

"Oh yeah," Ralph held out his hand.

"What are you doing?" Sheryl asked.

"This isn't a normal message," Ralph explained. "My people can make, uh," he searched for the word, "psychic calls, I think, with each other. We use the Dream Lands to do it. Sometimes, we can get barged in on. And this ..." he searched for the word again and this time failed, "thing appeared and demanded that I give you this message."

"A thing?" Sheryl asked. "Like a monster?" She shivered thinking back on all the places she had accidentally manifested in her life and the type of thing that might try to hunt her down through her friends.

"Kind of," he answered. "This was more like a rotting corpse that I couldn't tell the gender of."

"I am only getting more and more excited at the idea of this message."

"Shut up and take my arm." Ralph thrust his arm out again.

Hesitantly, Sheryl took it.

They stood on what looked like the surface of the moon, except there was no Earth in the sky and the stars were non-existent.

And they could breathe.

Sheryl pulled her arm back, but they stayed there.

"This is a pretty useless message so far."

Ralph nodded. "I wonder if this is a memory."

"More like a direct link," a voice familiar to Ralph rasped out.

They spun and were surprised to see Ralph's rotting messenger behind them. It was impossible to find any defining features to this corpse-thing's identity.

Sheryl raised her phone in front of her with her finger over one of the apps she had pre-written.

"Don't move," she shouted.

"Or what?" the thing asked. "You know that different realities have different math. Your spell won't work."

Ralph stepped forward and raised his fists. "I don't need math. Tell her what you wanted to tell her so we can get out of here."

The thing nodded before spreading its arms and pronouncing, "Your search for Keziah Mason is over."

Sheryl looked from the rotted thing to Ralph and then back to the corpse person.

"What?" she finally asked. "Are you saying that you're Keziah Mason?"

"I am what is left of her," it said. "The piece that could escape before she was murdered."

"And you escaped into the Dream Lands?" Ralph asked.

"I found refuge in the Dream Lands."

"Can you teach me?" Sheryl asked what she had been dying to ask since she had first learned of Keziah. "Can you teach me math magic?"

"That is my message," Keziah said, "I can teach you, but I can't do it here. You have to get me out of the Dream Lands."

"How are we supposed to do that?" Sheryl asked.

Ralph held up a palm. "Sheryl, is that something that we really want to do?"

"What?" She had genuine confusion on her face. "Why wouldn't we? I can't use apps to stop all of reality from slipping away. Carlos can't dream us a path to victory. I need her to teach me, and we need her if we are going to win this."

"What if she isn't actually Keziah?" Ralph asked.

"Wh—" Sheryl started but couldn't finish. Ralph was right. She had no idea who this thing was and had no way to confirm that it was actually the witch that she had hoped for.

"Cautious," the thing claiming to be Keziah said. "That is smart. Here," it dropped to the rocky ground and started scratching into it. "I have been in the Dream Lands long enough to have learned some of its math. I will prove who I am through an example."

When she was done scrawling into the dirt, she stood up and chanted a word that neither of the students had ever heard before.

Instantly, the corpse was transformed into a beautiful woman in her middle years, no older than 45 with streaks of grey in her otherwise black hair.

"Is that her?" Ralph asked.

Sheryl studied the new face before shrugging.

"I think so," she squinted as she looked at the math witch.

"There weren't many pictures of her, and the ones we found were not great." She gave up and turned to Ralph. "I think that's her."

Ralph wasn't nearly as sure as Sheryl was, but he only had his friend's word to go on. He gave her a sharp nod before they both returned their attention to Keziah.

"What do we need to do?" Sheryl asked her.

Keziah grinned. "Absolutely nothing, but I will need the assistance of your friends."

Sheryl let go of Ralph's hand and was returned to the football field bleachers.

"That was different," Ralph mumbled.

Sheryl's eyes were wide with excitement.

"It isn't on just us anymore," Sheryl said, but both Ralph and Sheryl were aware that she was really meaning that the pressure was no longer on her. Since the beginning of this Sheryl had been worried that all of this unmooring and other reality stuff would fall to her to solve, seeing as her magic specifically altered the states of reality.

If they could bring Keziah back, then Sheryl could relax. She wouldn't be the one person that the fate of all reality was resting on.

Ralph touched her arm again and she flinched.

"It was never just on us," Ralph said. "We're a team. We do this together."

"And with a real witch."

"You were real enough for me," he smiled. "It will be nice to have a powerhouse backup though."

"Look," Sheryl pointed out onto the field.

Someone was walking around with the field paint sprayer, drawing out something that was clearly not yard lines.

"Is that a pentagram?" Sheryl asked.

Ralph's genetics gave him an advantage over humans in many ways and vision was one of them.

"No," he answered. "That is a Seal of Kssogtha, Cthulhu's sister."

"He has a sister?"

Ralph shook his head. "No, that's just what puny human minds decided to call another creature of Xoth that is lesser than Cthulhu." He sat back and rubbed his face. "Lesser or not, they are summoning her power to disrupt the lock. That's why there have been explosions."

"Some of us weren't raised by a cult. Explain it like I'm five," Sheryl said.

"They didn't bring explosives with them," Ralph explained. "They have just brought magics that are in direct opposition to the locks and cast them right on top of them." He could see that Sheryl wasn't getting it. "Doors keep people out, but if you kick a lock hard enough, it will burst open." He gestured at the cultist rolling the paint sprayer around. "They are about to kick in the door."

Sheryl turned her attention back to the field and stared for a moment.

"What do we do?"

Ralph stood from his place behind the bleachers. "We break this up and we do it fast."

Sheryl stayed crouched where she had been but pulled her phone back out and began to frantically tap away at the screen.

While she did, she said, "And then we go and find the others."

Ralph said nothing, as the entire idea of this undead Keziah showing up at such a convenient time without much in the way of evidence of her identity was sitting with him the wrong way.

The painted circle and its runes were finished. He had no time to discuss his concerns with Sheryl if they wanted to stop reality from falling into chaos.

He wasn't sure she would listen anyway.

Just as Ralph was about to step around the field seats, they saw movement at the goal post. One of the cultists was making his way toward the circle. Ralph stopped to watch what was happening.

"Geeze," Sheryl said in surprise as the cultist got to the circle and dropped his robe to show that he was wearing absolutely nothing underneath. "These cultists must have an excellent gym membership."

"Look at what he's holding," Ralph pointed.

In the cultist's hand was a large dagger with a slim blade.

"A knife?" Sheryl asked.

"Ceremonial dagger," Ralph clarified as the cultist raised the dagger up to his chest and began carving symbols into it. Blood streamed down his body. The man seemed to show no notice of the pain.

"We're out of time," Ralph stomped off toward the field. Instead of going around the bleachers, he decided there was no point in holding back and he would use his considerable strength to toss them aside.

Just as his hand was about to close on them, the bleachers burst apart into their disassembled components. The pieces of different sized metals all hung in the air in front of him for a moment before he spun around.

There sat Sheryl, holding her phone up like some sort of wand in the direction of the bleacher pieces.

"Neat, huh?" she smirked.

"Show-off," Ralph smiled and ran through where the bleachers had been and straight at the cultist.

The naked cultist's front was entirely drenched in blood when Ralph tackled him with his full force.

That was when Ralph realized that this wasn't going to be easy.

Sheryl hadn't been wrong. These cultists had the best gym membership, if the way this man took a hit from a native of Innsmouth was any indication. He didn't go down as Ralph plowed into him and tried to drive him to the ground.

Instead, infused with strength given to him by his alien god, the cultist stayed on his feet and was driven back without being pushed from the circle.

Realizing that a football tackle wasn't going to be enough to interrupt the naked cultist's spell, Ralph stood up and squared off against him.

A manic look filled the man's eyes as he raised the ceremonial dagger in a defensive stance.

Out by the bleachers, the spellcasters of the Cult of Cthulhu weren't oblivious to what was going on. As soon as they saw the large Innsmouthian rushing their summoning circle, they began chanting.

Lances of pink energy blasted from the palms of their hands and directly at Ralph like arrows.

Sheryl hadn't been idle either. She punched another button on her phone and the field itself raised from the ground to take the impact of those magical spears. Then she used her phone to direct all of the metal from the bleachers directly at the cultists. Her own magical spears caught the cultists off guard, scattering most of them and wounding a handful.

Ralph swung twice at the cultist before concluding that this man was no slouch in a fight. He avoided both of Ralph's lightning-fast attacks easily enough before returning his own attack with the knife. Ralph managed to step back and avoid the blade, but only barely, falling to one knee as he momentarily lost his balance.

The cultist stepped in to press his advantage, the blade dancing quickly through the air as it sought a home in Ralph's flesh.

Ralph took his time and watched the man's face and hands simultaneously. The cultist attacked and Ralph threw up his arm just in time to block the knife. His arm ached from the impact, but that didn't stop him from throwing his own punch at the middle of the cultist.

Ralph put all his strength into that punch, standing as he swung. The hit knocked the naked man back, causing him to almost stumble out of the circle, but he caught himself just in time.

Rage filled the cultist's face and his eyes shifted to something not entirely human. He let out a bestial roar and ran at Ralph.

To say the least, Ralph flinched at the roar, but he squared off just as the cultist collided with him.

Sheryl was using math magic to warp the football field and keep the other cultists from running to the aid of her friend. The goal post bent down and wrapped around three of them while the ground continued to rise and block other angles of attack that they could use on her or Ralph.

She passively couldn't help but wish she knew something of what Keziah, who hadn't had to type all her equations and spells into a phone application, knew. She consoled herself with the knowledge that she was closer to learning those skills than ever before.

Birthday suit wasn't slowing down at all as he swung the dagger and his fist relentlessly down on Ralph. No place on Ralph was safe from attack, and it took everything for him to keep from getting stabbed.

Everything wasn't enough.

The blade sunk into Ralph's side once. In surprise at finally getting in an attack, the cultist stopped and looked Ralph directly in his large eyes.

"Cthulhu fthagn," he grinned and retrieved the knife before plunging the blade in again and saying, "Ia! Ia!"

Ralph felt his energy drain with the attack, but he couldn't let up. He tried to block the blade and was having less luck than before. Finally, the cultist backhanded Ralph and sent him to the ground.

Defeated and weak, Ralph struggled to get up, but laying there seemed to be all that he could do.

Sheryl didn't notice that Ralph was down until she looked back and saw the naked cultist carving the last of the symbols into his chest.

With a loud and guttural scream, he plunged the blade into his chest and fell, dead, in the center of the circle.

The circle lit up, briefly, flashing with that odd pink light from before.

That was when she noticed Ralph on the ground. He was still moving, but he wasn't getting up.

"Ralph," Sheryl shouted before remembering she had made an app just for this.

"Save him," she shouted again, and this time she launched the app.

As the Cult of Cthulhu's spell forced open a gateway to Kassogtha that split the ground, so too did another fissure in this reality open, directly on the men's football team locker room.

Levi Whatley burst from the portal in his practice pads and ran straight for his boyfriend. He one-armed the fishman onto his shoulder and ran him back to Sheryl where she could protect him.

"Where do you need me?" He wasn't even winded.

Sheryl pointed at where the ground was heaving under where the field had been painted.

"I think it is about to be obvious."

Tentacles burst up from the ground and grabbed at anything they could.

"What is that?" Levi shouted over the roar of noise that seemed to explode with the earth.

"I don't know," Sheryl admitted. "Ralph called it Cassie-something."

"Kassogtha?" Levi's eyes went wide. "That's an Old One."

"Can you fight it?" Sheryl asked in complete seriousness.

Levi laughed anyway. "Is that a joke? There is no fighting the Old Ones."

Sheryl shook her head. "Then this is a lost cause."

Suddenly, Ralph was standing between them, the holes in his abdomen leaking slowly, but consistently.

"Get back down, before you die," Levi shouted at him over the noise as another tentacle burst from the ground and destroyed the mounds of dirt between them and goal post. The goal post that had previously been the focus of the cultists was gone now and so to, it seemed, were the cultists.

"I will be fine," Ralph grunted. "Fishboys heal faster than most."

Levi looked like he didn't believe Ralph, but said, "Well, we can't fight that thing. What do we do now?"

"I think the lock that we were protecting was the goal post or something near it," Sheryl said. "With it gone, we have no reason to stay here."

Another tentacle burst up and as it writhed across the sky, it seemed to tear the fabric of reality. Half of the sky remained the same dark day that they had started their battle on, but the night sky on the other side of the divide was the oddest collection of blue colors mixed with stars and a foreign night sky.

The ground underneath the divide was blue grasses that were somehow carnivorous. The small bits of flesh remaining from the summoner were getting gruesomely chopped up by the tall blue leaves.

"Xoth," Ralph and Levi said at the same time.

At Sheryl's confused look, Ralph clarified.

"This is the rumored home of Kassogtha and Cthulhu."

"Real Housewives of Xoth isn't my cup of tea," Sheryl quickly threw up a stone wall. "Let's get back to the others."

Before they could agree with her, Levi was knocked back and Ralph was thrown into the Xoth side of the reality shift.

"No!" Sheryl shouted as she chased after her friend.

When she got over to where he had landed, she saw that Ralph was fending off larger blades of the alien grass. It had turned into some sort of razor-sharp tentacles and was grabbing at him, incensed by the blood still leaking from his side.

Sheryl did the only thing that she could think to do and dug her hands into the Xoth dirt as blades of violent grass tried to slit her wrists.

"What are you doing?" Ralph shouted over his battle.

In the distance, they heard a roar that had to have come from Levi, but was entirely not human. Ralph shot a distressed look in that direction and renewed his efforts with the tentacle grass.

"I need to sense the math of this world," Sheryl grunted as she felt as much with her mind as her hands in the dirt.

"Like in the Matrix, right? Wiggly numbers?"

Sheryl didn't bother to shake her head. "More like I'm solving for X." She took a deep breath before saying, "There you are," and leaping to her feet.

Her hands were a bloody mess, but she managed to type a new equation into her phone and cast her spell. A bubble of energy formed around her, big enough for three earthlings.

"Get Levi," Sheryl shouted.

Ralph nodded at his bloodied body and the grass. In response, Sheryl sent out a wave of energy from Xoth's reality that instantly dissolved the grass.

Ralph fell to his knees and then took off in the direction of the roar.

He found Levi in the air, wrapped in a tentacle of Kassaogtha and using his massive strength to tear the limb to pieces.

When Levi fell to the ground, Ralph ran to him and almost received the same treatment as the tentacle before his boyfriend recognized him.

Together, they ran back to the Xoth side of the barrier and into Sheryl's bubble.

"What are we doing?" Levi rasped. His voice sounded like had had just gargled glass.

"Going home," she answered. When she closed the bubble, they were no longer in it.

CHAPTER 21

The night sky shifted to hues of blue and green and the grass shifted to swords of pain before Stephanie and Carlos reached the botanical garden.

What seemed the oddest to Stephanie was that the buildings didn't change or disappear entirely when they shifted into this reality.

She said as much to Carlos as they reached the greenhouses.

"They are all connected to the anchor," he shrugged by way of an answer. "I think that means they go where the anchor goes."

The greenhouses were attached to the main botanical garden. The botanical garden itself was more of a glorified lobby made to look like a jungle with a gift shop.

Both students at once regretted trying to shortcut through the first greenhouse they came to.

The plants were no longer of their native reality. Every potted anything had been replaced with more of the alien plant life and in most cases, they had burst from their relatively small containers and their roots writhed across tables and concrete flooring as they spread out in search of sustenance.

Two long leaves lashed out at Carlos, who dodged both without even noticing.

"How did you do that?" Stephanie was in awe.

Carlos shrugged. "Time works differently in the Dream Lands. I am listening to the whispers, and they are telling me what they have already experienced."

"That is an entirely ridiculous idea," Stephanie waved at the plants, "but in light of our situation, I am less reluctant to doubt you and mostly jealous."

"Stick close to me," Carlos grabbed a shovel and a hoe and handed the hoe back to Stephanie.

She handed it back to him and yanked the shovel from his hand.

"Let the man with precognition take the sillier weapon to wield, thank you very much." Her mouth angled, only slightly, toward a smile, but it was enough for Carlos to notice.

The concrete cracked as a tentacle, covered in spike-like protrusions and orbs that looked like some sort of sea-creature's eye, snaked around. It shattered the tables and furniture of the greenhouse with no regard for what it was doing. If those orbs were eyes, then it didn't care what it was hitting.

The two students jumped each time the ground cracked, and soon the biggest threat wasn't the plants, not directly, but the tentacles and the odd chance that they might get hit into the meat-eating plants.

A tentacle lashed out at Carlos from behind and only a quickly-swung shovel managed to sever the alien limb before it took his head off.

"You didn't see that one coming?" Stephanie asked.

"You stopped it from getting to me," Carlos explained. "I think my spidey-sense only tells me when you aren't going to smack it."

A cry for help came from the other side of the door to the botanical garden. The two of them continued to hack and slash at the vegetation and calamari until they finally reached the door.

Worried about what they might find on the other side, Stephanie stopped Carlos so that she could check her bag.

Her great-uncle's stained, leather bag.

Inside was only one vial of reagent left. It was the same chemical consistency of what had revived Pepper.

"Don't use that on me," Carlos's voice was barely above that of a whisper.

Stephanie didn't know what to say. She hadn't even considered that Carlos might die. The idea that she might need to use her serum on him seemed entirely foreign.

He held up a hand and softened his eyes when he saw her struggling for something to say.

"I was hurting earlier, and I said some hurtful things. I don't believe any of it. This has nothing to do with that."

"Then what does it have to do with?" she asked.

"It has to do with me not wanting to fight the natural order of things. The whispers tell me things, and while most people are closed off to the Dream Lands, I am not." He shrugged. "I don't want them closed off to me and that juice of yours might just do it."

Stephanie took this in stride and seemed to understand, but she didn't say anything.

Carlos took that as understanding and reached for the door.

"It isn't just juice," Stephanie muttered before Carlos could pull the door open. Vines and grass thrashed behind them. "It is a complex combination of reagents designed to revitalize and revive deceased tissue."

The dreamer rolled his eyes and pulled open the door.

Goblins were tearing apart the botanical garden.

The lobby looked mostly like it did any other time. A front desk with a card reader sat to one side and the walls were a mix of shelves and monitors displaying the various indigenous environments for the plants that were on display throughout the facility. All of it was decorated with wood paneling to look as natural as possible for a lobby.

Behind the small desk was Nate Peasley and a woman that neither of them knew.

The goblins were not actually goblins, but that was the first word that Stephanie could think of to describe them. Whatever this new reality was, these were the natural inhabitants. Each of the creatures was a three-foot tall, naked thing with dark green skin. They were humanoid in that they had the same general shape as humans, but that was about where the similarities ended.

The creatures each had chubby, cherubic bodies, with long, thin fingers that ended in talons. They had no bellybuttons or nipples which Stephanie used to catalogue them as not mammalian. Their feet were similar to their hands, but with a dewclaw on the back. Their knees were inverted when compared to a human.

The oddest part of them was their complete lack of eyes. They could somehow still "see" their environment as they fought to get to the two people trapped behind the desk, but how they did it was completely lost on the students. Their noses looked like tiny nipple on their faces. The goblins' mouths were oval maws that opened to hair-like strands and a tongue that flicked about like another appendage.

Each of these odd creatures was holding a long stick that Carlos and Stephanie would have called a spear except that ended in a large pink bulb instead of a spear point. Every time that they jabbed it at something, a powdery substance would remain where it touched.

"Don't let that touch you," Carlos said.

"Obviously," Stephanie agreed.

Together, they inched along the walls to try and get around the crowd of goblins and make their way toward Nate and the girl.

They didn't make it far before the creatures noticed them. The ones closest turned and aimed their bulb spears at the two. Carlos tried to think of what to do next, but Stephanie was already in motion.

With a roar that didn't sound like something the shorter West girl was capable of, Stephanie lunged forward with her shovel.

Her swing came down and cleaved the head of the goblin in half, burying itself deep in his torso before her momentum was halted. Green blood splattered onto Stephanie's face. She stood there in shock, looking at what she had done and not moving.

Carlos was just as shocked, but he could see that the rest of them were not happy with this development.

"Get them," Nate yelled to his fellow students.

This seemed to galvanize Carlos and snap Stephanie from whatever shock she had been feeling.

Nate's female colleague also seemed to snap out of being the helpless victim and began throwing things at the goblins.

Carlos stepped forward, swinging his hoe. He was not trying to clear a space so much as he was trying to impale these things. His moral compass was replaced by the voice of Randy shouting at him.

"You or them."

When they began to get too close to him, Carlos relied on Stephanie to cut them back while he dropped his hoe and reached out with his hands.

"Do you dream?" Stephanie heard him say in almost a whisper.

Carlos grabbed two of them, one in each hand, by the top of their heads. Before they could smack him with their pink bulb spear, they collapsed, unconscious.

Nate's friend was not as lucky.

She swung with a computer keyboard at the nearest goblins and the keyboard bounced off their faces, loosing keys with each hit. She was wild in her approach, hitting everything she could as quickly as she was capable, but not doing any damage to the monsters.

Before they could get to her to offer any assistance, the woman was hit by several of the soft ends of the bulb staffs. Each one left a pink trail of dust on her clothing and flesh.

Her reaction was immediate.

The keyboard fell from her hand as she convulsed. The clothing and flesh the pink dust had touched started writhing before it dissolved into nothing. Much like an acid, the flesh continued to melt underneath each place that had previously been covered in the pink dust, drilling multiple holes into her.

Stephanie chopped the head off the last goblin between them and Nate and grabbed the football player's hand, pulling him to his feet and away from his friend.

"What the hell is happening to Nora?" He was obviously terrified by what he was seeing, but much like Stephanie and Carlos, he was having a hard time looking away.

Carlos didn't have any option, as he ducked several blows of the odd spears the goblins were using. He tried to watch what was happening, but if he did, they all would die.

Stephanie didn't answer Nate, because she simply didn't know.

After what felt like far too long, Nora fell to her knees

and the onto her face. The holes that were driving themselves through her abdomen popped out of her back and blackened around the edges.

Then they started to seal themselves shut.

It wasn't flesh that filled the holes, though, it was a blue fibrous material, and it wasn't until they began growing and spreading out over and through Nora's body that Stephanie understood.

"Those bulbs are spore pods," she explained to whichever of the men was still capable of hearing her over their own terror and battle. "They hit people with the pods and the spores grow into the carnivorous grass."

Time froze.

At first, Carlos thought he had managed to finally get the upper hand on the goblins. Then he realized that he wasn't doing any damage and all sound had stopped.

Walking through the violent plants and insane aliens from the doorway they had just entered from was Randy.

"You are going to die here," he said, plainly.

"Thanks for the heads up."

"I do not trust the Great Race," Randy continued as if not hearing Carlos, "but Stice is alright."

"Are you going to do anything? Or are you just here to making passing commentary?"

"Watch your tone," Randy said.

"Oh? My tone?" Carlos let out a bark of laughter. "You are obviously from a different era but allow me to enlighten you. You are not my parent, and I did not choose you to be my mentor, therefore, you get the same level of respect as the asshole who failed me on my driving test."

Randy made no movement to indicate he understood or accepted this announcement.

"I just watched a girl get eaten by seeds," Carlos continued. "If I die, Stephanie and Nate will, too. Are you here to help? If not, then just leave."

"This lock hasn't broken yet," the century old dreamer said.

"Where is it?" Carlos asked. "What is it?"

Randy raised his hands and the battle in the botanical

garden began to reverse itself quickly. Within seconds the room looked as it had before the unmooring event.

"The cultists are nearby," Randy explained. "They know it's here, but those things with the spears are fighting them, too. When they get here, they will want to destroy that," he pointed at a symbol in the tiles on the floor. It was a circle with a series of curves ending in smaller circles inside of it. The angles and multiple curves made it look as if someone had transposed multiple signs all in the same space. It took up most of the floor space. "They are prepared with two ways to destroy it. The first is a spell that will take time. If you were not already here, they would do that. The second is a summoning of an Old One to destroy the lock. That is what happened at the football field."

"Sheryl and Ralph?" Carlos feared for his friends.

Randy nodded. "They are on their way here."

"What do we do?"

"You have entangled yourself with Stice," Randy took a seat on the desk. "This has caused complications that you cannot ignore. You must let this lock break."

"That is not going to happen."

"Then you and your friends will die." Ralph had no emotions in his voice. He was only stating a fact.

"I thought that you were a mentor," Carlos screamed at him. "I thought you wanted to help me."

"Dammit, boy," Randy stood up and rage filled his face. His eyes darkened in an inhuman way, reminding Carlos how far from humanity Randolph Carter had traveled. "I am helping you. If the lock breaks, if the unmooring happens, you can at least have a chance to save yourself and your friends. It is going to happen, whether you are here or not. So, you can choose to stay here and die with the West girl and that asshole football player, or you can save yourselves and fight another day."

"We are surrounded," Carlos deflated as he said it. "We came here without a plan and now we're stuck."

"You're a dreamer," Randy said. "You are never without options."

When time resumed, Carlos ducked a swing from another bulb spear and kicked the goblin in its gaping maw.

Nate was useless behind Stephanie as she chopped at the goblin horde.

"We need to get out of here," Carlos said over his shoulder to his friend.

"What about the lock?" Stephanie asked. She grunted as she blocked another pink bulb attack. "Also, how?"

"Knowledge," Carlos said. "I searched the Dream Lands for where we are and what else might be near us on this strange world."

"When?"

"Just now," Carlos backed away and kicked the desk over to push the goblins back. "Something is coming. The lock is lost. We need to leave."

Cultists burst in from the door opposite the one they had entered through. Tentacles with black orbs and spikes along their length tore at a handful of them while one of their magic wielders sent a wave of energy that pushed back the goblins.

"Well," Stephanie sighed as the goblins rolled past them and bunched up against the wall as the desk shielded the three humans, "we are completely screwed now."

Carlos shook his head. "Get on the floor." He crouched down and pulled the desk closer to them, using it to create a box around them with the wall. Nate was slower to join them, so Stephanie grabbed him by the belt and pulled him to the tile floor.

The cultist with the magic was someone who liked to give speeches. They knew this because she took a deep breath to say something as a smirk crossed her face.

She never got to say it, though, as a large foot crashed through the wall behind Stephanie, Carlos, and Nate.

The foot stomped down on goblins and cultists, smashing everything in sight. It was the same color as the goblins but with only two toes and large enough to use the room as a shoe.

Debris rained down around the three students and they wiggled as best they could toward the nearest hole in the wall that wasn't surrounded by goblins, tentacles, or carnivorous grass.

The foot crashed down again, and blood sprayed in every

direction. Before they left, Carlos saw that the symbol on the floor had been cracked. The lock was broken.

"What the hell was that?" Nate asked when they were almost back to the side of the barrier that included the dean's office and the last remaining piece of their reality. They had been running, and Carlos was still panting as he spoke.

"When I was in the Dream Lands," Carlos explained around gulps of air, "I learned that the planet this is," he waved at the ground and the weird tufts of violet vegetation, "I found a species of giants that thinks of the goblin-things like termites. An infestation."

"Dream Lands?" Nate's confusion was ignored.

"So," Stephanie understood, "you let them know there was an infestation here." She stopped and grabbed Carlos's arm to stop him as well. "What about the lock?"

"Randy told me that there are five locks in total," Carlos explained. "Dividing ourselves to protect them individually was never going to work. We either need to succeed at protecting the dean or try and stop the unmooring another way."

"There is no stopping the unmooring if the dean dies."

Carlos hated having to blindly trust Randy's word on this, but he had little choice. He would be dead, multiple times over, if he hadn't. "We can cross that bridge when we come to it."

"What the hell is going on?" Nate shouted. "What are you talking about?"

Stephanie rolled her eyes. "Aliens are attacking us. That's literally all that you need to know right now."

A bright blue bubble appeared in front of them. The dirt and weird grass sizzled where it touched the ground. The bubble popped and Sheryl, Levi, and a very bloody Ralph stood in the center of it.

"We can save reality and stop the unmoorings," Sheryl shouted at her friends, "but we have to go to the dean's office now."

CHAPTER 22

Cultists had stormed the administrative building. Spell casters were around every corner and trying to burn their way through the staff, students, and walls to get to the final lock.

The staff, mostly unaware about what was going on, were working admirably to slow their progression, but there was only so much that a geologist could do against wizards, witches, and alien monstrosities from different realities.

The first wave was turned back, but only with the assistance of Dean Ward, Carol Berg, and Meredith Johnson. During their small reprieve, they managed to move themselves and the remaining faculty within the building to the large conference room at the end of the hall.

For defensible positions, they couldn't ask for better. It was essentially a former lecture hall converted to be a place to address the faculty on large events or changes to administration. It had two doors at the back of the room with a projector at the front. The middle of the room was filled with chairs and tables that, originally, sat facing each other.

Now, those same chairs and tables had been pressed to the doors and turned on their sides for cover.

Reports from the other locks and the teams meant to protect them were not good. Ralph had already texted Meredith a lot and the bits she could understand through the alarmingly large number of typos were not good. She had texted back where they were and that they needed to hurry. If she understood what Ralph was saying, the two remaining locks had already been broken. With the two that had been broken at the start of this assault, that only left one.

The dean.

Through all of this, her concern for her friends, and her deep-seated fear that this was not going to end well for them all, one thought continued to surface to the top of her mind.

Carol had really undersold this gun.

During practice, she would have steadied herself, taken aim, and gently pulled the trigger. The current situation didn't allow for any of that preparation.

It also didn't require it.

The pistol that the administrative assistant had told her was more than just a gun connected with her.

It was a common cliche to say that a gun was an extension of someone when they used it regularly. This gun did the opposite.

It made Meredith part of it.

Her skills, the processing power of her brain, the sheer ability to aim, and more were all being driven by what seemed to be an inanimate piece of metal.

A tentacle burst through the wall. Meredith noticed it out of the corner of her eye and under normal circumstances would not have been capable of aiming at the writhing thing, but the gun took over. Her arm yanked to the right, steadied itself and fired three times into the terrifying limb.

Except, it wasn't controlling her. They were in perfect harmony. The gun knew her thoughts as she had them. She had wanted to shoot the tentacle until it stopped being a threat. The thought hadn't even formed as words in her head and the gun was already working on making her thoughts happen before the message could reach her hands.

At one point, she could have sworn that the bullets had gone around a table and struck a goblin in the head.

Carol, in her Wendigo form, was tearing through the cultists with the fervor of a rabid bear. Meredith did her best not to look. She hadn't been lying about not shooting people and had so far managed to avoid what was becoming unfortunately more likely. The cultists were quickly becoming the greater threat and it was only a matter of time before she would need to defend herself.

She was building herself to this point. It wasn't the thought of these people hunting her family or the life she could have had if they hadn't spent their entire lives on the run. It wasn't even that they were looking to destroy this reality so that their greedy god could come back and devour everyone and everything she had ever known.

It was Chris.

She thought she had found a decent friend in Chris. He was someone who had shared interests and seemed to care about helping her help her friend discover her heritage. Instead, he was a lie designed to trick her into outing herself and her family. Making her desperate need for friendship and something normal a weapon to threaten those she loves.

They had built him into something that she couldn't resist. They had made her a killer because of it.

It had really been Stephanie who had done the deed, but it didn't release Meredith of any of her guilt. Stephanie did it to protect Meredith from having to do it.

So, when the first cultist managed to break through the door with a burst of magic and their arms turned into spider legs, Meredith had a choice to make.

The spider-armed woman rose on her new limbs as they walked her into the room, her body dangling behind. Each arm had turned into a pair of two, hairy and long, spider legs. Her mouth moved constantly but Meredith couldn't make out the words. The floor rippled in front of the spider person, and several of the faculty helping with the fight fell to the ground.

The magical .38 sensed what Meredith intended and her arm moved to answer the call.

She fired the pistol the moment it was aimed between the witch's eyes.

She ducked it.

That was an entirely new feeling. Until that moment, the magic gun had never missed for Meredith. She was almost too shocked to react.

Almost.

She dove behind a table as the spider-cultist raised its ridiculous limb and launched a … thing at her.

The thing turned out to be a wriggling mass of worm-like creatures that the spider-cultist had summoned out of thin air.

Meredith got behind the table just in time for the mass of stuff to slam into the floor where she had been standing. They spread out on contact, but only about a foot in every direction from where they had landed. Meredith didn't know what they would do, but she didn't want to find out.

Unfortunately, that didn't mean that the spider-cultist didn't want to show her.

One of the staff from the coffee shop on the first floor of the administrative building came running over with a knife and tried to leap and shove the blade into the dangling human leg of the spider-cultist.

She almost made it. Somehow, her presence had been sensed and the spider-cultist aimed an arm in her direction, firing another snot-rocket laced with alien worms.

They did the same thing they had done to the floor and spread out when they smacked her in the stomach. Unlike last time, they began burrowing into the barista's flesh.

She unraveled. Flesh tore into ribbons and those ribbons molded into cubes all while the poor woman stood frozen in place. As her flesh finished cubing, the pieces started falling off before she collapsed into a heap of cubed meat on the floor of the conference room.

Meredith gasped in horror that only got worse as the cubes of flesh turned into more of those same worms that had started the transformation.

The dean was suddenly beside her behind the table. His appearance startled her from her shock.

"The walls just turned to water," he mumbled. Meredith looked toward the nearest wall and noticed he was right. "The world is almost entirely unmoored." He stood up and shot some sort of energy from his hands before dropping back down. He shoved a sheet of paper into Meredith's hand. "If they get me, use this. Just because the lock breaks, it doesn't mean we can't find a way to put it back."

Carol landed beside them on all fours. She had someone's forearm in her mouth. When she saw Meredith and the dean staring at her, she spit the limb out.

Then she winked at Meredith and leaped back into the fight.

Meredith looked down at the paper in her hand. It was covered in a lot of writing.

"Not now," Ward hissed. "Only if I die," he shrugged, "and you aren't sacrificed to Cthulhu."

The dean jumped over the table and launched a fireball.

"How was that a pep talk?" Meredith said out loud.

Carlos's voice filled her head.

"It wasn't. It was the truth. We are losing, but there might be a path back from the loss."

"How?" Meredith felt hopeless as she spun around and fired at the spider-cultist again. This time, she struck it, but it had grown larger, with her human legs and abdomen swelling and head growing to at least four times its original size. The bullets were useless against it.

Meredith sat back down.

"We're almost to you," he explained. "Once we are together, Sheryl has a plan."

A tentacle with legs came around the table. Before Meredith could register what it was, her pistol was shooting. The tentacle was faster than most of the shots, though. She grabbed at a table leg and started clubbing it. The archaeology student pinned the tentacle beast before unloading the pistol into it.

"I don't know if I'm going to last that long," Meredith said.

"How long?" Ralph's voice came from behind her.

Meredith spun and saw Ralph collapse against the table she was using for cover. He was covered in blood and paler than usual.

"Ralph," Meredith shouted before tackling him in a hug. He groaned in pain, but she didn't let go. All her shock and pain and trauma were wrapped in that hug.

"Now is not the time," Stephanie said as she walked through the water wall and into the conference room. "We have," she sighed, "magic to do."

"Magic?" Meredith asked as she released Ralph.

Sheryl and Carlos were next to her now.

"Long story made almost too short," Carlos explained, "Sheryl found that witch she was looking for, but we have to summon her from the Dream Lands."

"Quit dallying and do the damn thing already," Dean Ward was stepping back, a shield of energy blocking a torrent of fire from overwhelming them.

The leg of the spider-cultist pierced through the fire and then through Dean Ward.

"Dammit," he said, before the giant spider legs ripped him apart.

All five of the students screamed.

Sheryl was the first to calm them down.

"With a real witch, we can undo all this. Let's do the spell."

Levi roared from the far side of the water wall the others had come through. Then he burst through.

He was larger than Meredith had seen him. Whatever had happened to bring him this far, he had been forced to rely on his inhuman heritage.

Possibly too much.

Levi slammed into the spider-cultist, now filling most of the room. He grabbed her by her long legs and swung her around, pushing back most of the cultists and giving the students room.

Carol used the distraction to return to the students. She reverted back to her human form and used the back of her arm to try and wipe the blood from her face.

"The final lock is broken. Reality is unmoored." There was sadness in her voice. "They will call their god if they get Meredith."

"We have a plan," Carlos said.

"What plan?" Carol asked, her voice holding a hint of hope.

"We are going to summon Keziah Mason back from the dead and have her save us," Sheryl answered.

Carol started to ask what that meant, but Sheryl shook her head.

"There's no time."

Carlos grabbed Sheryl's hand and together they focused like they had previously. He took her spiritual self into the Dream Lands. The journey was easier than ever before. The walls between the realities had broken down.

Sheryl's message from Ralph had included an innate knowledge of where their target was found within the Dream

Lands. With no conscious effort on her part, Sheryl led Carlos directly to the rotting corpse that had visited with her earlier.

Keziah held back her excitement upon their approach. There was still much to do. Keziah needed to teach Sheryl enough of the Dream Lands magic so that she could reach out when she returned to her body. She needed to be able to connect to the Dream Lands with her own math magic and open a gateway so that Keziah could return to the real world.

Time moved chaotically in the Dream Lands and while Keziah taught Sheryl, the part of broken reality that held their friends was moving almost not at all.

When Sheryl was confident that she had committed it to her memory permanently, Keziah tore off her own finger. She gave it to Carlos. Sheryl let out a gasp as he put it in his mouth and swallowed.

"Part of her spirit," Carlos explained. "It will help bring her to us."

The corpse-thing tried to grin but, without much in the way of lips, it was a horrifying sight.

"An anchor, if you will." She let loose a rasping laugh. "The shattering of reality does not mean we cannot have some symmetry."

When Ralph and Sheryl had showed up and explained the plan, Carlos could see Sheryl's excitement. He could also see Ralph's thoughts. Through the pain on his roommate's face, Carlos saw that Ralph did not trust a single thing that this dead thing said.

Carlos silently agreed with Ralph when he heard the plan, but at that point they had already lost four of the anchors and their good ideas were all gone. This was the last shot in the dark they had. If the Scion Cycle spell brought them together, maybe this was the reason.

It was more difficult to return to their bodies than it had been to get to the Dream Lands. With their reality adrift among all the other realities, finding and reentering it required a considerable amount of effort from Carlos. He found himself wondering where Randy had gone this time and why his supposed mentor couldn't help him when he actually needed it.

When they finally landed back in what remained of their reality, it came with the spiritual equivalent of whiplash. Both Sheryl and Carlos let out gasps of pain that let their friends know they had returned.

Carol was by their side immediately.

"Did you say you wanted to summon Keziah Mason?" she demanded.

Carlos nodded. "Yes. Sheryl is going to use the math magic of there and here to create a bridge between the realities." He waved his hand around. "We are going to use the fact that the Miskatonic anchor is broken the same way that the cultists plan to and summon our own defender between the realities."

"But—" Carol started, but Carlos leaped back so that the portal Sheryl was already summoning would have room behind their table.

On the other side of the table, what was left of Levi was at least 10 feet tall and partially invisible. He was still fighting the spider-cultist, but at this point she was more spider than cultist.

The strain on Sheryl's face showed that this bit of reality magic wasn't easy, even with the walls between realities collapsing.

Carol Berg was yelling something as the winds picked up from wherever Sheryl had connected to and Stephanie watched on in fascination while one of the quests that she and her friend had spent so much time on was finally concluding. Meredith fired over the table while Ralph worked on keeping the Scion students protected from more of the goblin-things.

A figure stood on the other side of the jagged tear in their world. Carlos shoved his hand through the portal and grabbed at the gnarled hand of the rotted thing. With a pull of both physical and spiritual strength, Carlos heaved and pulled the corpse through the portal.

It hit the floor in a slopping wet mess of bodily fluids and began gasping and writhing in pain on the tiles.

Sheryl closed the portal and thrust a hand out at Stephanie.

"We need the reagent," she begged.

Stephanie was surprised by the request. Until that moment, she had not known that she had been part of their plan to resurrect the ancient witch.

"It is not ready," she explained. "We need to test it."

"Keziah will be the test," Sheryl explained. "Please, or we could all die very soon."

Stephanie pulled the syringe from her uncle's old bag and held it. The cap over the needle was still in place and the serum glowed a bright green.

A bellowing scream of pain shook what remained of the building. They all looked over the table to see Levi getting mauled by the pincers of the giant spider. He was losing.

"This is the only bit of the reagent I have on me," Stephanie explained. "Levi is going to need it to heal, if not survive this encounter."

"Steph," Sheryl pleaded, "look around you. If Keziah doesn't stop this madness and use our world's math to lock our reality back into place, then we will all die." She paused and threw a glance at Levi. "Even him."

Stephanie stared at the syringe, struggling with the decision. She couldn't deny that their best bet would be if Sheryl and Keziah could pull the world back together, but something felt wrong about doing this.

A twisted hand of bone, muscle, and blood grabbed the syringe from Stephanie's hand, pulled off the cap, and plunged it into its chest before Stephanie could react.

That was when she saw it.

The thread along the neck, holding the head in place. Why did that bother her?

"It can't be Keziah," Carol was screaming again.

"What?" Carlos asked. "Why not?"

"I saw Keziah Mason's spirit jump from her body to another," Carol explained. "The act robbed her of some of her cognitive abilities and she has since lost the ability to do any magic, let alone anything this large." She pulled Sheryl back from the spasming corpse as flesh began to grow and heal. "She is alive and well and not anywhere near the Dream Lands."

"Then who is this?" Sheryl demanded.

Stephanie finally realized what had happened. She had listened to Chris ramble on in the car for the duration of their journey to the old West home. She had heard each of the stories on what had happened to her great-uncle and in most of them the ending for him had been the same.

"His head had been pulled off," Stephanie muttered.

As flesh and hair sprouted all over the former corpse that had been biding its time in the Dream Lands, Stephanie knew that she was right.

Each of the old threads popped out of the thing's neck, leaving a soft red scar as his flesh solidified.

Naked, he stood up and rubbed his face.

"That's Herbert West," Stephanie said with complete shock and disgust.

CHAPTER 23

"**No.**" Sheryl said in a whisper, before shouting it.

Herbert West turned to face the math witch.

"Well, yes," he let out a slow sigh that sounded as if it should be filled with empathy, but no emotions reached his cold eyes, "unfortunately, I had to lie to you to get all of this to work."

"You were destroyed by your creations," Carol said. "How are you here?"

"I think that you have other problems," he hooked a thumb over his shoulder where Levi was not faring well against the spider-cultist. "If you must know, those very same creations wanted to play with me. My only escape was into the Dream Lands."

Ralph lunged at the resurrected West, his wounds entirely forgotten.

Herbert raised a hand and Ralph froze in place before falling to his knees.

"Not so fast, my gilled friend," Herbert said.

The naked man spun and grabbed his bag from his great-niece.

"Thank you for collecting my gear. When you're ready to learn from a real teacher, come and find me."

Then he turned and ran through the same reality-broken wall that Ralph and the others had come through.

Sheryl fell to her knees, sobbing.

"I know it sucks," Carlos knelt beside Sheryl and put his arm around her. "We don't have time for this. They are coming."

As if on cue, a contingent of Cthulhu cultists came filing through what was left of the front of the conference room. Levi's efforts to keep the spider-monster back were costing him as she jabbed pointed legs into his expanded mass. There was so much blood, his friends couldn't see where the injuries were. A final squeeze by both Levi and the spider-monster, and they both collapsed to the floor.

The cultists marched around the fallen combatants and directly at the Scion students.

Carol began to shift, but the nearest cultist raised a pistol directly at Sheryl's head. Carol stopped mid-transformation and slowly shifted back to her human self.

A blonde cultist with stubble on his chin stepped forward and raised a hand. His mouth was moving but none of them could hear what he was saying.

What the friends did notice was their inability to move. They could only watch as the cultist with the gun stepped forward and removed his hood.

It was "Chris."

"This might be a little bit of a surprise," he shrugged before getting close to Meredith. "Especially after you threw me to the proverbial wolves." He held up his hands and smiled. "I don't blame you of course. I might be wearing the robes and leading this bunch of fools around, but that doesn't make my empathy just disappear. What we have done to you and your family is horrible. Perhaps you can have some empathy toward our situation, but I can't imagine you will. As much as it has absolutely sucked to do to you what we've done for the last century, it doesn't change that we believe that a better and more natural world awaits us when we are done."

Ralph let out a grunt and found his mouth could move.

"Built on the rubble of the old," he said through gritted teeth.

Chris raised an eyebrow and looked from Ralph to the cultist weaving the spell. The cultist was sweating, but he continued his silent mouthing of the magic.

"That's rich coming from the chosen children of Y'ha-nthlei." He looked to the rest of the Scion Cycle. "Has he told you what his people's dreams are? Has he told you how their god, Dagon, regularly confused with our own, only rejects Cthulhu's design for the world because it won't be him?" He looked Ralph directly in the eyes. "You are no better than we are."

Chris, or whatever his real name was, snapped his fingers and stepped away.

"Collect the sacrifice. The ritual is upon us."

His people moved forward and picked up Meredith, carrying her out the way that they had come in.

The entire time chanting, "Cthulhu Fthagn," under their breaths.

When they had all filed out, the spell holding them in place finally broke and they all fell back to their knees.

"We have lost," Sheryl was still crying.

Stephanie stepped up to her friend.

"I am as disappointed as you are that we were fooled by my uncle, but now is not the time." She grabbed Sheryl's chin and turned her head so they were eye to eye. "We will get him for that. First, we need to save Meredith."

"And the world," Carlos added from behind her.

"How?" Carol asked. "The ritual will take time, but not much. We have a very short window to save her. That, combined with the fact that they have magic on their side slims our chances down even further."

Ralph was staring at where his downed and misshapen boyfriend was lying when he said, "I have part one of the plan." He tore his eyes away and to his friends. "I can resist their magic, probably because of my family. So, part one is simple. I'm going to go in there and disrupt the shit out of their ritual in the most violent way that I can."

Carol nodded. "A distraction is imperative. As we are likely to all die anyway, this seems like a good start. What is next?"

Sheryl wiped her eyes and stood up. "The plan hasn't changed. It will still need to be the reality witch who pulls this all together. The damage done to reality won't get fixed until I pull our reality back into place."

"Can you?" Stephanie asked.

Sheryl shook her head. "I've done it before, but it hadn't been this far gone. Also, we had the anchors. All that I needed to do was set things right and the anchors held the world in place.

With them gone, I can't hold the spell for any length of time."

Carlos's eyes glazed over, and Randy's voice came through his mouth. "Beyond the gate is the Whatley truth. The dream must be continued."

Carlos shook his head and was himself again. "I think that's all we're going to get from Randy."

"What the hell does that mean, though?" Ralph winced and looked down at his side. The pain was still there, but his Deep One genetics had already began stitching up his wounds.

"It means," Carlos paused as he thought about it, "it means that Levi might be able to save everything."

Ralph's eyes were wet, but not from the pain. He looked again at where Levi laid on the ground. Still, four times his original size, and lumpy masses of flesh bleeding out.

"If he isn't dead," the Innsmouth student said, "then he's in no shape to save us."

Carlos shook his head. "He might actually be in the best possible shape to save us." Reality shook around them all. A fish with the face of a man, but teeth the length of a finger, floated by, ignoring the group. "The Whatleys were trying to bring Yog—" he stopped himself, worried about summoning something he couldn't handle right now before realizing they were already well beyond that being a problem, "Yog-Sothoth. They failed and created a hybrid with the powers of the sleeping god and the morality of a man."

"Levi," Ralph said.

"Right," Carlos nodded. "Except, Yog-Sothoth is an extension, or a child of Azathoth."

Carol caught on. "The dreamer."

Sheryl was getting confused by all of this. "I thought Carlos was the dreamer."

Carol shook her head. "A different kind of dream. Have you heard of simulation theory?"

Stephanie nodded. "The idea that we are all living through a simulation created by an advanced civilization." She saw that Sheryl still wasn't following and explained further. "It is the idea that we are all characters in a very complicated video game."

"Except that it isn't a game," Carol continued. "Our reality, and all realities for that matter, are a product of Azathoth's dreams. If he ever woke up, we would be no more."

"What does any of this have to do with Levi?" Ralph was finally limping his way toward his boyfriend.

"Azathoth doesn't have to be the one who dreams us," Carlos explained. "Not if someone with that kind of power, or even a fraction of that power, took over. He wouldn't have to be as strong as Azathoth. Azathoth dreams all of the realities, we would just need someone with a fraction of that power."

"You want to use Levi." Ralph was already sounding like he was against the idea.

"I don't want to do anything," Carlos countered. "But right now, he's the only person who is on our side and can do what we need to survive."

"I'm in," Levi growled. His voice had morphed with the rest of his body and now sounded much deeper, resonating in all of their chests. "What do I need to do?"

"No," Ralph said. "You're the only thing in my life that makes sense. You can't do this."

Levi ignored him and waited for Carlos to explain.

"Uh," Carlos was as caught off guard as everyone that Levi was conscious. "Alright. First, Ralph runs in," he slapped his own bicep, "guns a-blazing, and saves Meredith."

"I will go with him," Stephanie said. "Not much else I can do, and someone will need to grab Meredith while Ralph is punching everyone."

Carlos nodded. "Be stealthy. The spells are going to be everywhere."

Carol Berg frowned. "I am more valuable in that fight as well."

"Then while they are fighting," Carlos continued, "Sheryl will try to pull our reality back into place." He faced Levi. "Then I will push your mind into a place of Dream. It will have to be someplace just for you. It will be very lonely. I'm sorry."

"You're going to put him into a coma?" Ralph's face reddened.

Carlos nodded. "He will have to stay like that until the locks or anchors or whatever are back in place. Maybe longer.

Once you're in that state, either me, or Sheryl, or maybe both of us will need to make this reality your dream state. Your, um, father, can't exist inside his dreams and I don't think you will be able to either."

"But," Levi's lumpy face was looking sad at the prospect, "can I still see everyone? I mean inside the dream?"

"It will be like any dream you ever had," Carlos said. "You can see what's happening, you might even be able to influence things, but if Azathoth hasn't been seen in our reality before, I'm guessing that you won't be able to make yourself visible to us."

Levi forced himself to his mismatched feet.

"Let's go."

The rest gathered themselves, but Ralph grabbed Levi's arm and made the monster-man face him.

"You don't have to do this. We can find another way."

Levi shook his head. "Not before they kill Meredith. If Cthulhu comes here, then we will all die. Not just us, but everyone." He smirked and it looked almost normal on his twisted and alien face. "It's fourth down and 10 seconds on the clock. We either make this pass or we don't get to play the game anymore." He lifted his still normal human hand and touched Ralph's cheek. "I'll still be here, and you will still be able to live your life. This is the only way."

When Levi brought back his hand, it was wet with Ralph's tears. Tears continued to roll down Ralph's face as he pulled Levi into an embrace.

The cultists were in the center of campus, near the post that said hello in thirty different languages.

Meredith was conscious but tied down to a folding table like what the guys would have had at a beer pong tournament. Unlike the beer pong tournament, this table's legs were still folded up and the unique qualities of their broken reality meant that the table was floating above the ground.

Chris was standing next to her, chanting at the top of his lungs.

Ralph and the rest of the Scions watched from about a hundred yards away. He looked at Levi one last time, and then back at the cultists.

"I'm not waiting for any of you," he said. "So, keep up."

Then he funneled all of his rage at how unfair his entire life had been, up to and including the finally finding peace with new friends and Levi, into his legs and ran.

Deep Ones are naturally faster under water, but that same strength that made their legs the most powerful swimming tools in the animal kingdom also made them powerful runners.

He crossed the entire hundred yards in eight seconds.

The tether between Meredith's connection to her family and Cthulhu had already started to stretch out and an ominous shadow of black fog had begun to encircle the entire congregation of cultists.

Ralph hit the table first, trying his best to spin it back toward the way he had come. Then he hit Chris and the next four cultists with the full strength of a Deep One enraged.

Carol, in full transformation, was right behind him, while Stephanie was still about ninety yards away.

"Now or never," Carlos said to Sheryl.

"I can't do this," Sheryl said. "I don't even know what I'm doing. Keziah could have, but not me. I don't even understand this stuff."

"When you didn't understand it before, you built an entire reality. If you can't do this, we're all dead, or worse."

"No pressure," Levi smirked.

Sheryl shook her head a few times before saying, "Fine. Fine."

She opened her phone and started editing the app that originally was set to take her into her Wicked West world. Suddenly the phone was floating in front of her, and the math started to bleed off of the screen, hovering as gold numbers floating in the air. Sheryl didn't seem to notice, and the numbers only kept climbing and growing as she mentally began adding her head math to it.

"That's new," Carlos mumbled before turning to Levi. "Your turn."

"What do I need to do?"

"Try not to burn up my soul when I enter your mind."

"Wait," Levi said. "That can happen?"

Carlos shrugged. "I hope not."

He placed his hands on the sides of Levi's misshapen skull and closed his eyes.

Levi's mind was a hurricane made of multicolored fires. They whipped around him, attempting to taste him and know what this invader was. Carlos was surprised by how close his assumption had been. These flames of alien power could affect him if he wasn't careful.

Floating through the gaps in the intense heat, he sought out Levi.

Levi, in the form that his friends knew him in normally, sat in the eye of the storm.

He was almost to Levi when a lick of the flame hit Carlos's leg. He screamed, both in Levi's mind and in physical reality.

Carlos spared a glance at his leg and saw a hole where the flames had touched. There was no blood or gore, just a hole directly through his astral self.

Silently, he thanked Professor Stice for convincing him to stick to astral projection instead of bringing his body with him. Although, he wondered what kind of damage he had just taken to his spirit.

In what remained of the real world, Ralph was shrugging off spells and diving between Carol and the spell casters to stop them from hitting her. He was bleeding from so many places, but his rage wasn't letting him slow.

Chris finally stood from where Ralph had first tackled him and drew a long sacrificial blade, the handle carved with intricate designs stylized to look like tentacles.

"The ceremony must be completed." He ran at where Meredith's body was struggling against the floating table. "Ia! Ia!" he shouted.

"Hold on," a voice shouted from the other side of the table. Chris couldn't see who or where it was coming from, and he didn't care. He lunged at the table with the knife extended.

Then the table spun end over end quickly, smacking Chris in the face and knocking him back.

Stephanie stopped the spinning by grabbing it, and started

working on the ties.

"Sorry about that," she said to Meredith.

Meredith was trying to keep her lunch down as she answered, "No worries. You stopped me from getting stabbed."

"Well," Stephanie shrugged, "I at least postponed it."

One of the binds came undone and Meredith was able to begin assisting with her freedom.

Chris touched his broken nose and flinched before standing up.

Carol Berg was suddenly in front of him with her claws extended.

"Spawn of Ithaqua? Wendigo?" He shrugged and raised his hand in front of him, curling his fingers and furrowing his brow. "I give you a gift."

He strained and screamed as Carol lunged at him with her claws at full extension.

A wave of energy burst from Chris and slammed into her, mid-air. When Carol hit the ground, she was a human again.

Blood trickled down Chris's nose and he lowered his hand.

Carol looked at her hands and then tried to shift again, but nothing happened.

Confusion filled her eyes.

"What have you done?" Her voice was barely audible.

Whether he heard her or not, Chris couldn't help but gloat and explained it anyway.

"I severed your connection to Hyperborea. You are free from your curse." He waved his hand and Carol careened out of his path and into the distance.

Meredith and Stephanie stood behind where Carol had been. Stephanie reached behind her back and pulled out the magic pistol from before.

"You dropped this." She handed it, handle first, to her friend.

Meredith didn't even look up as she checked the chamber, remembered that while it looked empty, it wasn't, and closed the chamber again.

"Thanks," she said. She raised the pistol and fired four shots into Chris's face.

He fell to the ground before jumping back to his feet. His jaw was completely gone. Gore and tentacles burst from the hole that was his face.

His voice resonated around them.

"You think I survived you murdering me before?" He stalked toward them. "No. I died, rotting in the reward of my kind at the foot of the dead god. My loyalty was rewarded with resurrection as his general." His arms burst apart, replaced with tentacles that ended in spiked tips.

"Shoot. Shoot now, please." Stephanie's voice was growing louder with each word.

Meredith didn't need any prompting and continued to fire the gun at the Cthulhu-thing that had been Chris.

What they didn't notice as they tried to force the monster back from stabbing Meredith and paving the path for Cthulhu to step into and devour their reality, was that the table had settled back to the now green and entirely normal grass.

Sheryl was sweating as she worked. It wasn't just a matter of asserting the math of her reality, she also had to separate out the realities and maths that had bled into and divided theirs.

The effort was momentous, but she was succeeding. The campus, and reality, was looking close to normal again.

"Carlos," she shouted. "If you can hear me, we need to do this soon."

Levi's mind was trying to tear Carlos apart, but he fought it as he drifted toward his friend. When he finally reached Levi, Carlos was exhausted. His spirit was peppered with holes, making him look like some sort of human cheese.

"I don't know that I can do this," he panted to Levi.

"You can," he said. "Where will you send me?"

"There's only one place where I know you can sleep and dream. One place where the pipes play to keep the great dreamer asleep."

"Wherever Azathoth is?"

Carlos nodded.

"You can't send him there," Randolph Carter was suddenly beside them. "That's beyond the gate. I will take him."

"I thought you said going beyond the gate ruined you. Won't returning shut you off from us? From humanity?"

"You have Stice now," Randy explained. He touched Carlos, and the holes filled themselves. "I will take him and keep him company."

The flames all started to dissipate. Randy turned and took Levi's hand.

"Perhaps, we can teach each other something."

A gate of ivory and gold bars, a symbolic representation for Levi's mind to comprehend, appeared before them. Randolph reached into his own chest and pulled out a shining key of silver.

And then they were gone.

Carlos woke up on the ground next to where Levi's body had been. It was gone. Levi was with his father now.

Carlos looked up at where Sheryl stood, numbers dancing around her in a way reminiscent of the flames that had only just been tearing at his own soul.

"Carlos," Sheryl shouted. "I can't hold this any longer."

Carlos looked around at everything. Reality was back to normal. Sheryl had done it.

"Let it go," Carlos said. "Levi has it now."

Sheryl collapsed to the grass and the numbers all vanished.

Carlos flinched, worried that he was wrong about what Levi could do.

Nothing happened.

Levi dreamed of home.

Carlos crawled to Sheryl and pulled her exhausted form to his. He let the grass hold them while they rested.

Ralph broke the final cultist of Chris's congregation before turning toward where he had seen Carlos and Sheryl with Levi.

His friends were huddled together, and Levi was gone.

He fell to his knees and let his grief wash over him.

In front of Meredith and Stephanie, Chris was on whatever served him as knees now, and was struggling to get up. Whatever this pistol was that Meredith was using, it had a special surprise in store for things touched by the magic of the veil between worlds. Black globs of flesh were falling off of

Chris as he gurgled.

"I, ugh, don't need," he let out a wet slopping noise, "the table. Just for you to die."

"Funny," Meredith stepped up to him and put the pistol to his head, "I was about to say the same thing."

She fired the gun until it emptied.

EPILOGUE

Needless to say, classes had been disrupted and it was two weeks before regular schedules resumed. The spells in place to keep the general populace more willing to fabricate excuses on behalf of the unacceptable worked in some instances and failed miserably in others. Carol had explained that the nature of a flexible reality had made all the campus spells misfire in unpredictable ways.

The students that the spell was effective on believed that Miskatonic University had suffered a major power outage that resulted in fires and casualties. The rest of the students were being treated for psychotic breaks due to the stresses caused by the "outage." After their trauma was dealt with or they were at least convinced to keep it to themselves, they could return to their semester schedules.

Carlos hated that idea and had said as much. He felt that gaslighting the campus population would come back to haunt them all.

They were already haunted, though, by the god holding their world together. Levi was gone and reality had reasserted itself, but the friends believed they could still feel him around them and in everything they did. Ralph more than the rest.

Ralph was the last person to enter the classroom. 'Classroom' was a generous term for the break room the Scion students had been shoved into for this little experiment.

When the idea was first suggested, it was implied that the room would be filled with only the Scion Cycle students. That idea was soon demolished by the painful logic that Stephanie provided.

"I cannot spend my time with an assistant who knows less than I do. Alicia Halsey must be part of this," she explained. "Additionally, would you have excluded Levi? There are people outside of this 'Cycle' that will be more of a hinderance to us than not if they are not kept in the know."

Carol had acquiesced, aware that Stephanie was correct, but not willing to admit that it was anything more than Stephanie's persistence that had made her cave.

Ralph had been an almost non-existent roommate since Levi's disappearance and no one in the group was sure he would even show up.

Sheryl had decided that if she couldn't get Keziah to teach her, then she would have to find her education elsewhere and this new class by one of the Great Race was her best bet.

Meredith was the first student who showed up. She was craving the knowledge and was struggling with whether or not it was her depth of curiosity or a desperate need to avenge the traumas that her family had gone through.

After Meredith had given the recipe for Dean Ward's resurrection to Carol, and witnessed it in action, she was eager to see more magic. Eager to use more magic.

In what was a pleasant surprise to Stephanie, Sheryl and Alicia were getting along surprisingly well. It turned out that Alicia enjoyed the mobile gaming world and had found a port for Wicked West.

The Dean walked in soon after Ralph, followed by Professor Stice and Carol.

"In light of our recent battle for all of reality," the dean said.

"And how close it came to ending," Ralph interrupted.

"Yes," the dean acknowledged. "In light of that, I would like to welcome you all to Elder Gods 101."

ABOUT THE AUTHORS

Matthew Davenport hails from Des Moines, Iowa where he lives with his wife, Ren, and daughter, Willow. When his scattered author brain isn't earning weird looks from the ladies of his life, he enjoys reading sci-fi and horror, tinkering with electronics, and doing escape rooms.

Matt is the author of the Andrew Doran series, the Broken Nights series (along with his brother, Michael), *The Trials of Obed Marsh*, and *Satan's Salesman* among other titles.

He's also a self-styled student of the Cthulhu Mythos and exercises that influence in his stories and as part-time editor at the blog Shoggoth.net.

You can keep track of Matthew through his Twitter account @spazenport or his blog authormatthewdavenport.wordpress. com.

Mikey Davenport lives in Iowa with his wife, Colette, and his fur-kids, Caboose and Binx. A transplant to Iowa, he has found his stride in creative works with his brother, Matthew. His currently available novels are the Broken Nights series. He enjoys toying with the mythos of heroes and monsters, with his first work in the worlds of Lovecraft being *Miskatonic University: Elder Gods 101*.

Curious about other Crossroad Press books?
Stop by our site:
http://store.crossroadpress.com
We offer quality writing
in digital, audio, and print formats.

Printed in Dunstable, United Kingdom